NIGHT OWL SOCIETY

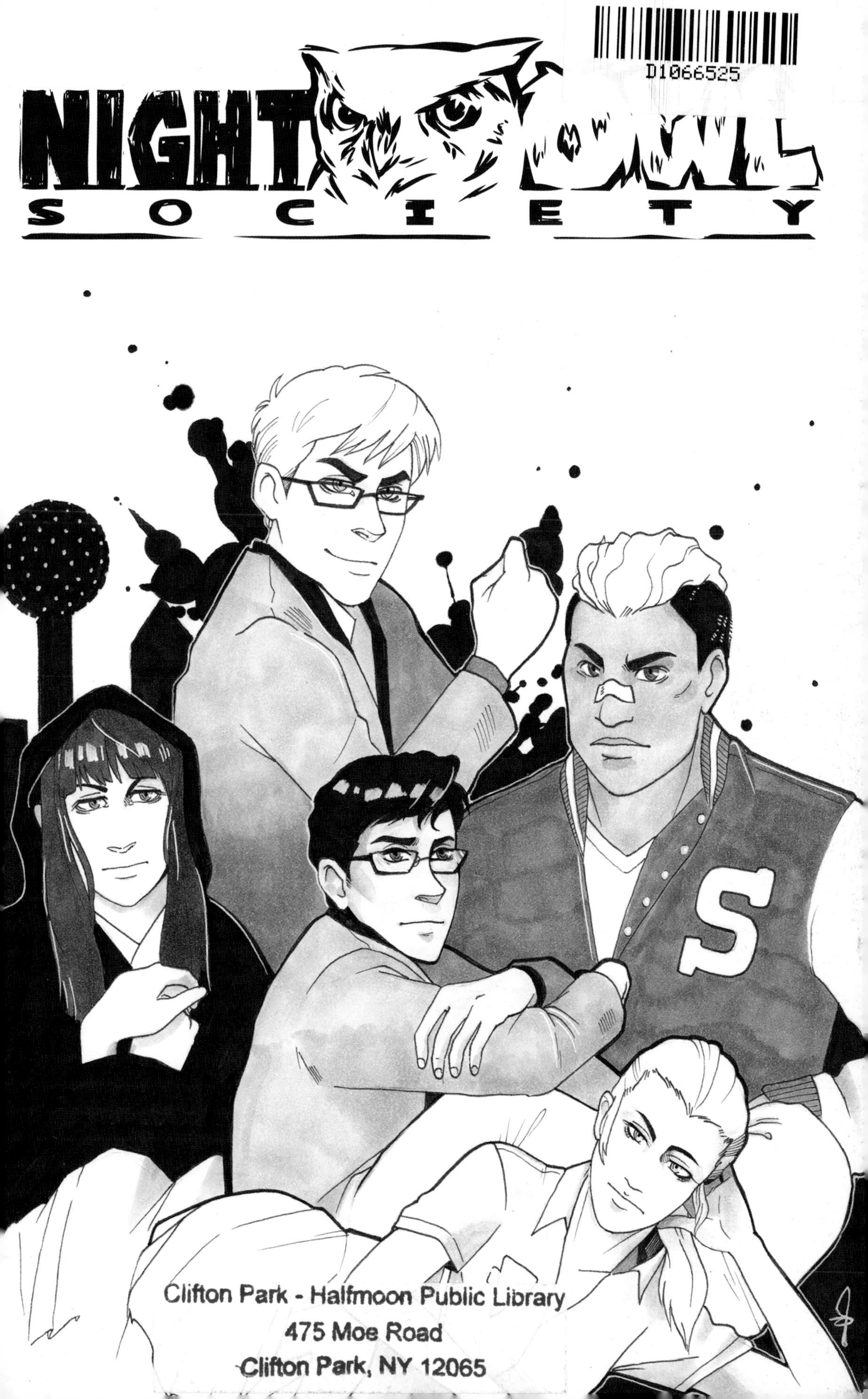

Written by **James Venhaus**

Art by **Pius Bak**

Lettering by **Marshall Dillon**

Series Edits by **Bobby Curnow**

Cover Art by **Pius Bak**

Collection Edits by **Justin Eisinger** and **Alonzo Simon**

Collection Design by **Ron Estevez**

Publisher: **Ted Adams**

  Become our fan on Facebook **facebook.com/idwpublishing**
Follow us on Twitter **@idwpublishing**
Subscribe to us on YouTube **youtube.com/idwpublishing**
See what's new on Tumblr **tumblr.idwpublishing.com**
Check us out on Instagram **instagram.com/idwpublishing**

ISBN: 978-1-63140-933-2   20 19 18 17   1 2 3 4

Originally published as NIGHT OWL SOCIETY issues #1–3.

Ted Adams, CEO & Publisher
Greg Goldstein, President & COO
Robbie Robbins, EVP/Sr. Graphic Artist
Chris Ryall, Chief Creative Officer
David Hedgecock, Editor-in-Chief
Laurie Windrow, Senior VP of Sales & Marketing
Matthew Ruzicka, CPA, Chief Financial Officer
Lorelei Bunjes, VP of Digital Services
Jerry Bennington, VP of New Product Development

For international rights, please
contact licensing@idwpublishing.com

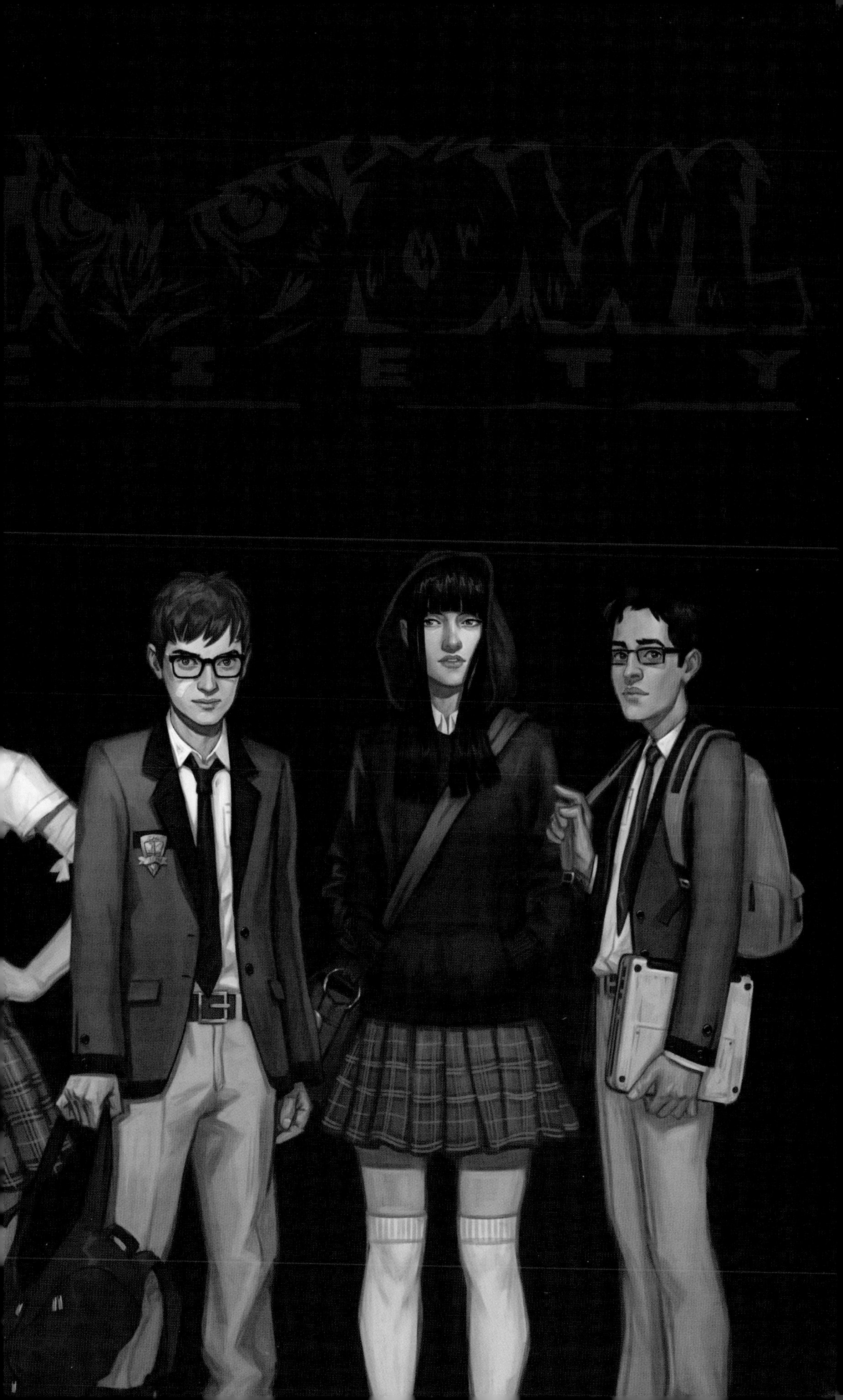

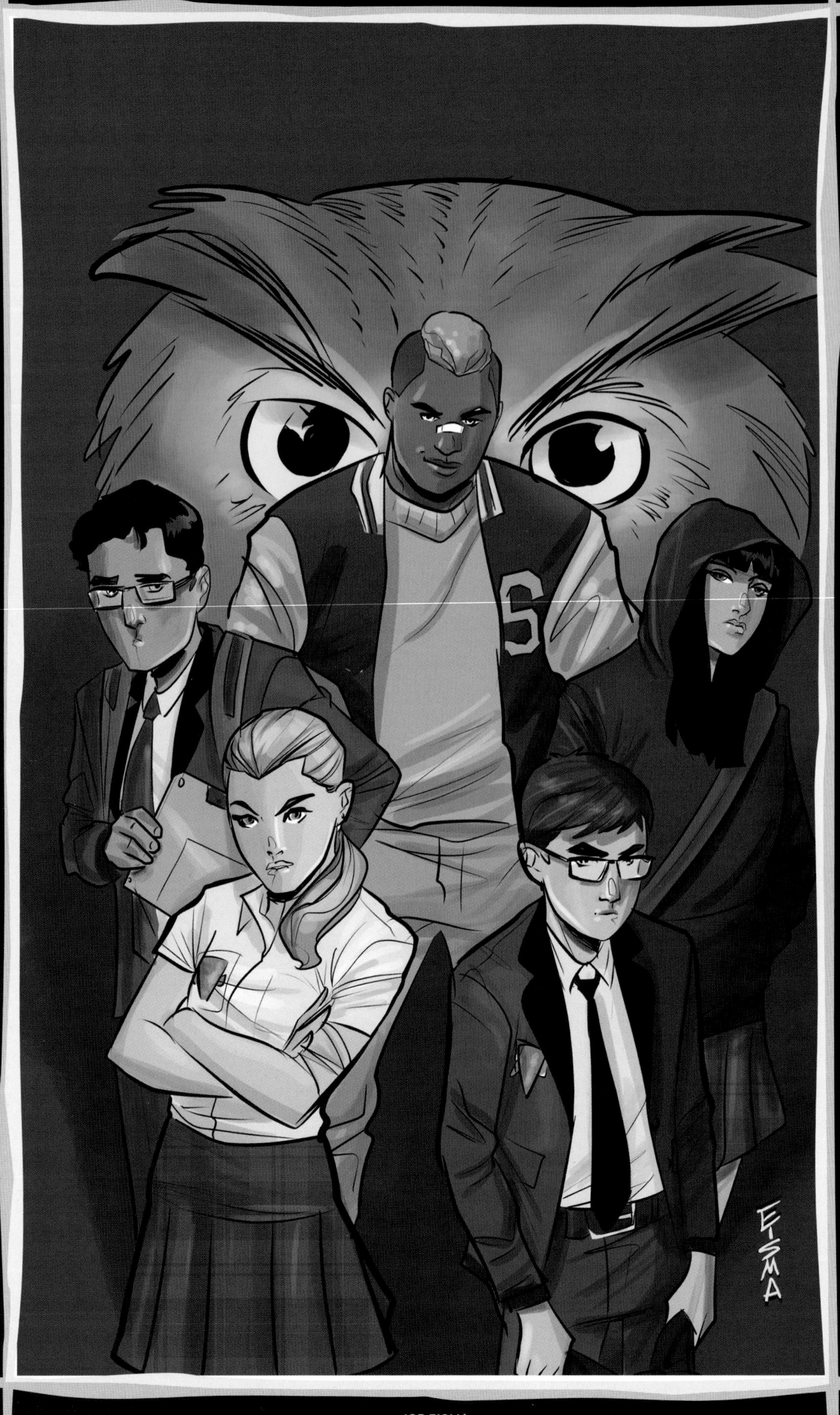
EISMA

ART BY JOE EISMA

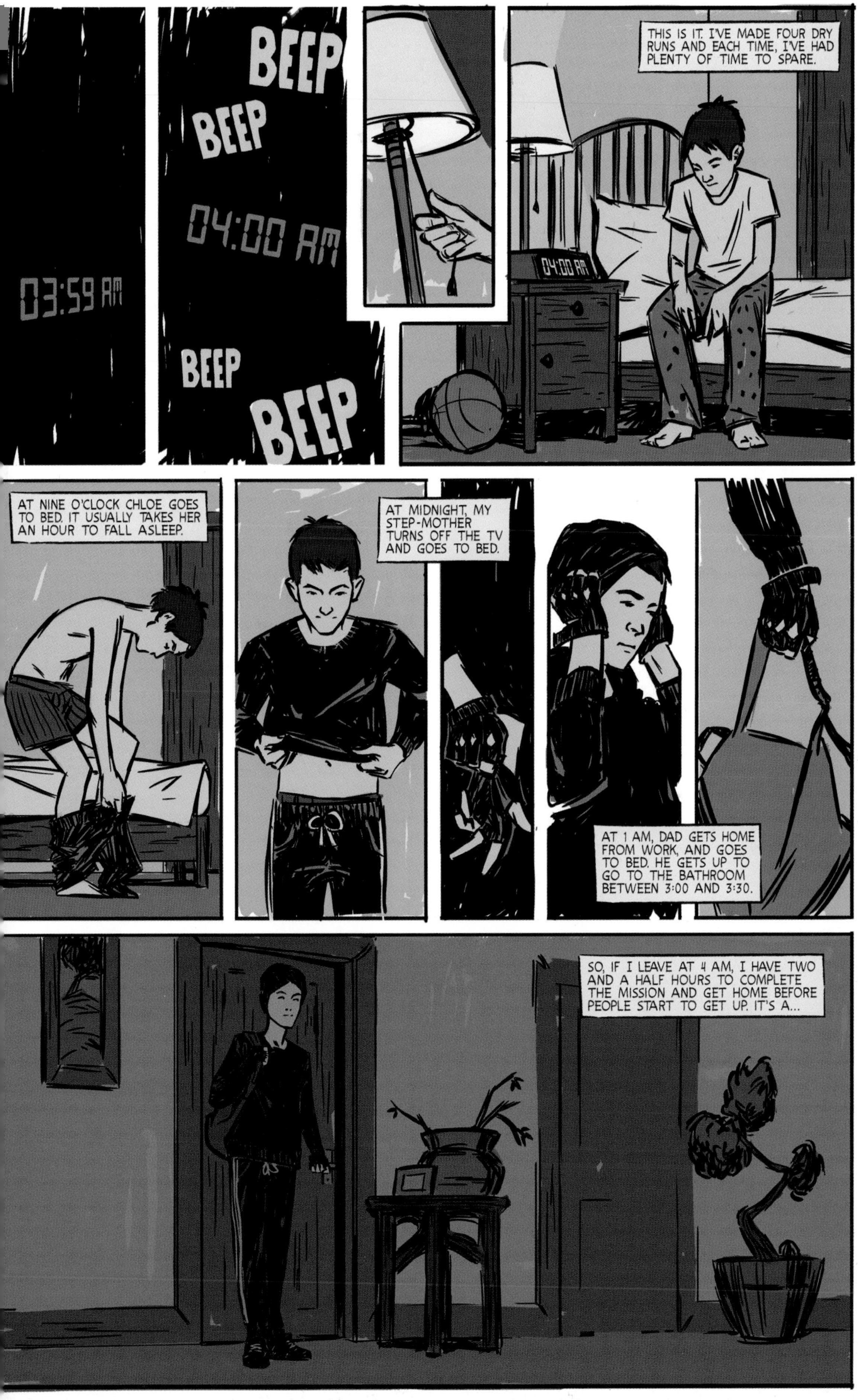
03:59 AM
BEEP
BEEP
04:00 AM
BEEP
BEEP
THIS IS IT. I'VE MADE FOUR DRY RUNS AND EACH TIME, I'VE HAD PLENTY OF TIME TO SPARE.
04:00 AM
AT NINE O'CLOCK CHLOE GOES TO BED. IT USUALLY TAKES HER AN HOUR TO FALL ASLEEP.
AT MIDNIGHT, MY STEP-MOTHER TURNS OFF THE TV AND GOES TO BED.
AT 1 AM, DAD GETS HOME FROM WORK, AND GOES TO BED. HE GETS UP TO GO TO THE BATHROOM BETWEEN 3:00 AND 3:30.
SO, IF I LEAVE AT 4 AM, I HAVE TWO AND A HALF HOURS TO COMPLETE THE MISSION AND GET HOME BEFORE PEOPLE START TO GET UP. IT'S A...

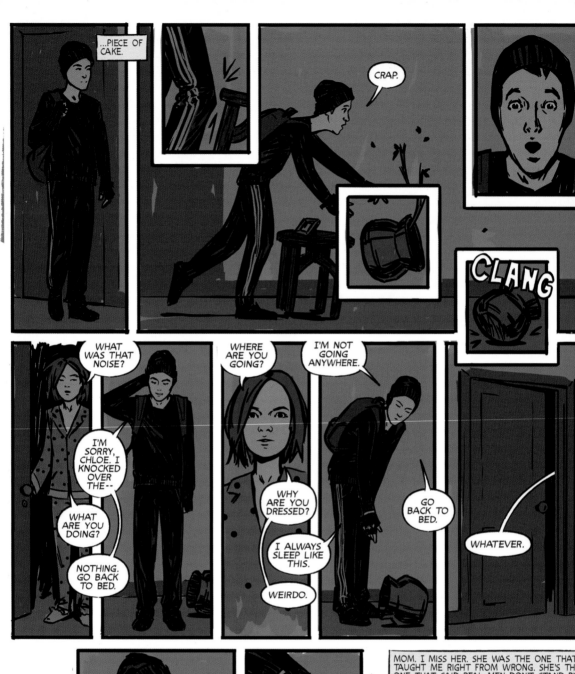

...PIECE OF CAKE.

CRAP.

CLANG

WHAT WAS THAT NOISE?

I'M SORRY, CHLOE. I KNOCKED OVER THE--

WHAT ARE YOU DOING?

NOTHING. GO BACK TO BED.

WHERE ARE YOU GOING?

I'M NOT GOING ANYWHERE.

WHY ARE YOU DRESSED?

I ALWAYS SLEEP LIKE THIS.

WEIRDO.

GO BACK TO BED.

WHATEVER.

MOM. I MISS HER. SHE WAS THE ONE THAT TAUGHT ME RIGHT FROM WRONG. SHE'S THE ONE THAT SAID REAL MEN DON'T STAND BY WHILE OTHERS ARE BEING HURT. SHE'S THE ONE THAT WOULD WANT ME TO TAKE ACTION. SHE'D WANT ME TO DO THIS. OKAY, MOM...

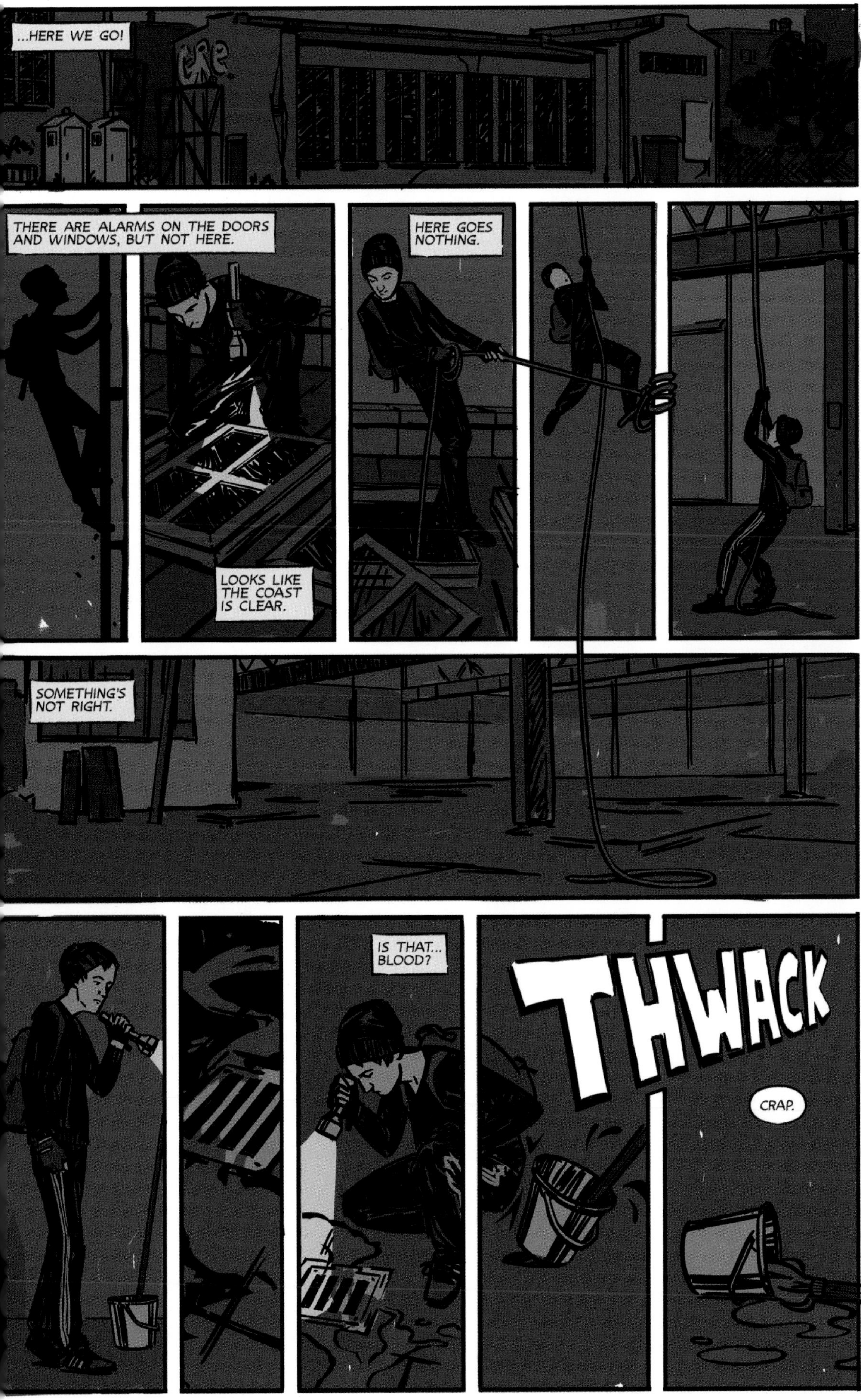
...HERE WE GO!
THERE ARE ALARMS ON THE DOORS AND WINDOWS, BUT NOT HERE.
LOOKS LIKE THE COAST IS CLEAR.
HERE GOES NOTHING.
SOMETHING'S NOT RIGHT.
IS THAT... BLOOD?
THWACK
CRAP.

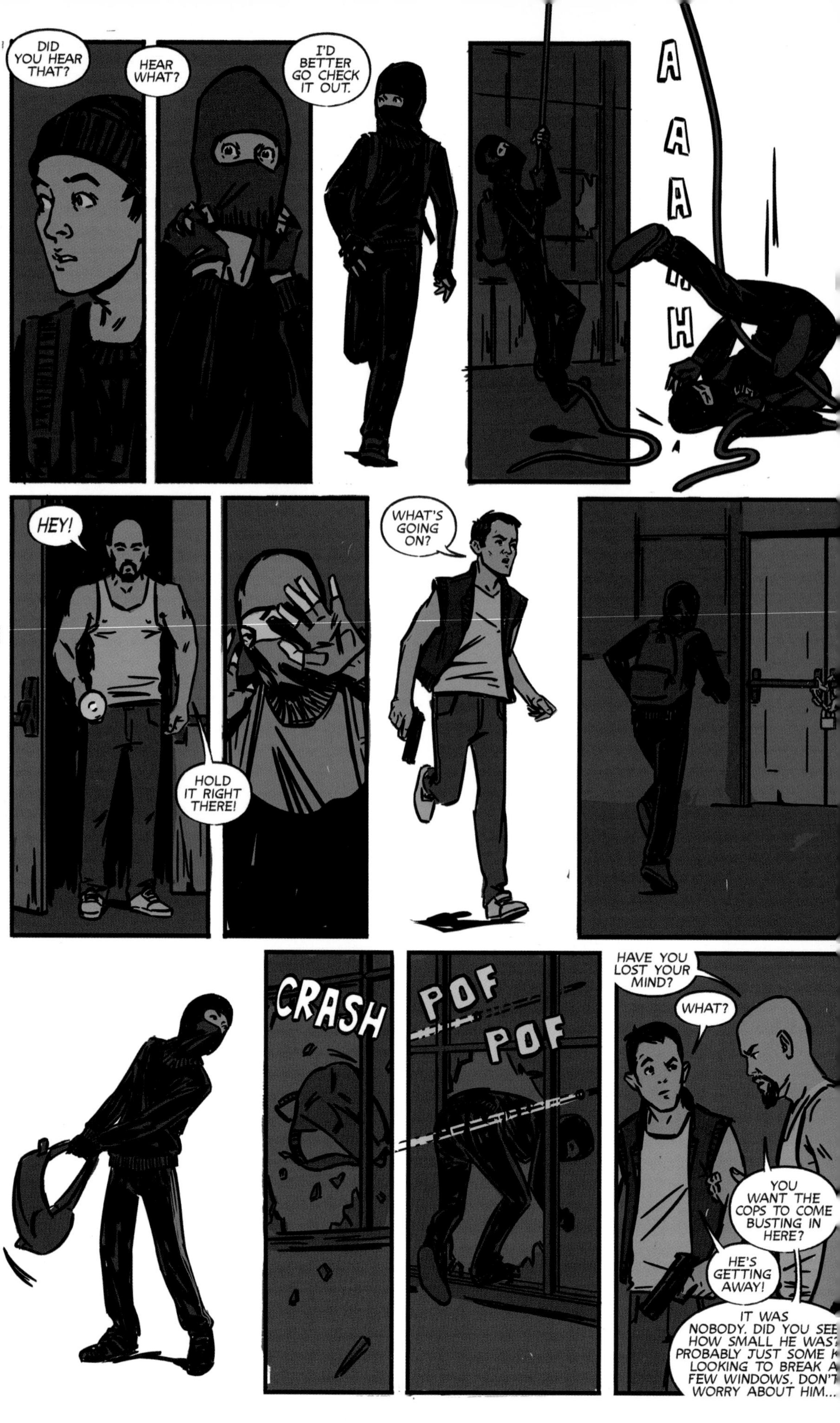
DID YOU HEAR THAT?
HEAR WHAT?
I'D BETTER GO CHECK IT OUT.
AAAHH
HEY!
HOLD IT RIGHT THERE!
WHAT'S GOING ON?
CRASH
POF
POF
HAVE YOU LOST YOUR MIND?
WHAT?
YOU WANT THE COPS TO COME BUSTING IN HERE?
HE'S GETTING AWAY!
IT WAS NOBODY. DID YOU SEE HOW SMALL HE WAS? PROBABLY JUST SOME K LOOKING TO BREAK A FEW WINDOWS. DON'T WORRY ABOUT HIM...

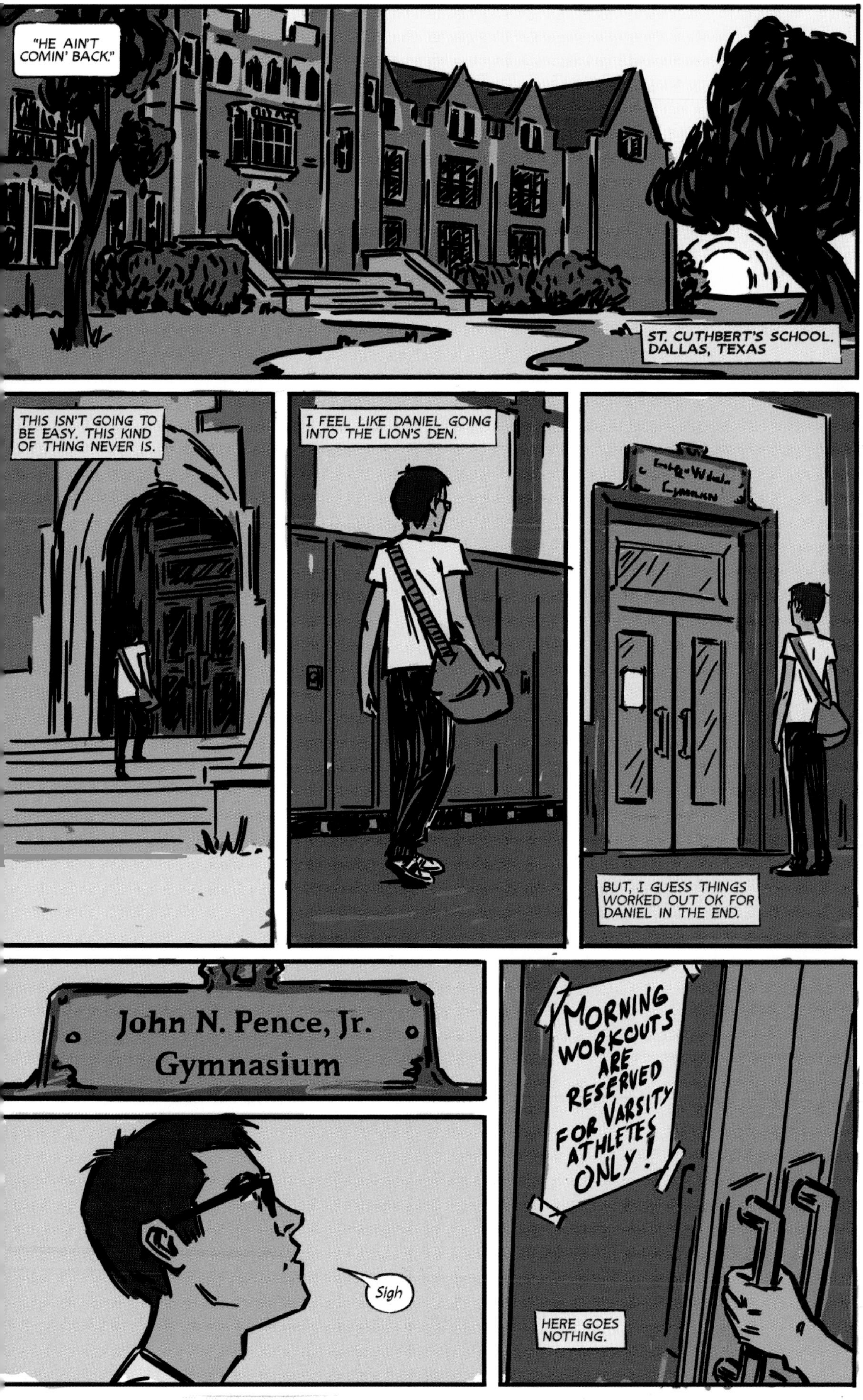

"HE AIN'T COMIN' BACK."
ST. CUTHBERT'S SCHOOL. DALLAS, TEXAS
THIS ISN'T GOING TO BE EASY. THIS KIND OF THING NEVER IS.
I FEEL LIKE DANIEL GOING INTO THE LION'S DEN.
BUT, I GUESS THINGS WORKED OUT OK FOR DANIEL IN THE END.
John N. Pence, Jr. Gymnasium
Sigh
MORNING WORKOUTS ARE RESERVED FOR VARSITY ATHLETES ONLY!
HERE GOES NOTHING.

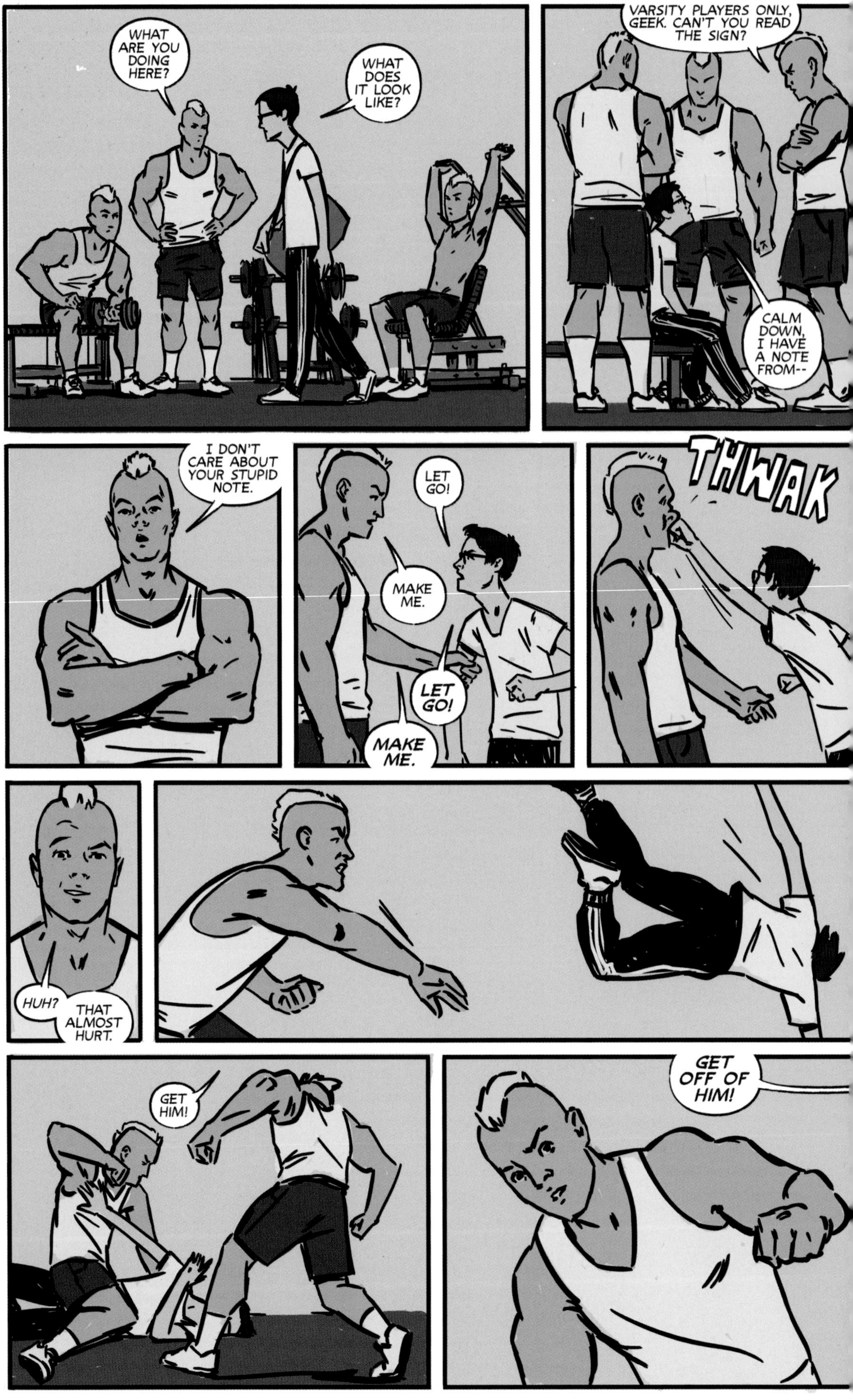
WHAT ARE YOU DOING HERE?
WHAT DOES IT LOOK LIKE?
VARSITY PLAYERS ONLY, GEEK. CAN'T YOU READ THE SIGN?
CALM DOWN, I HAVE A NOTE FROM--
I DON'T CARE ABOUT YOUR STUPID NOTE.
LET GO!
MAKE ME.
LET GO!
MAKE ME.
THWAK
HUH?
THAT ALMOST HURT.
GET HIM!
GET OFF OF HIM!

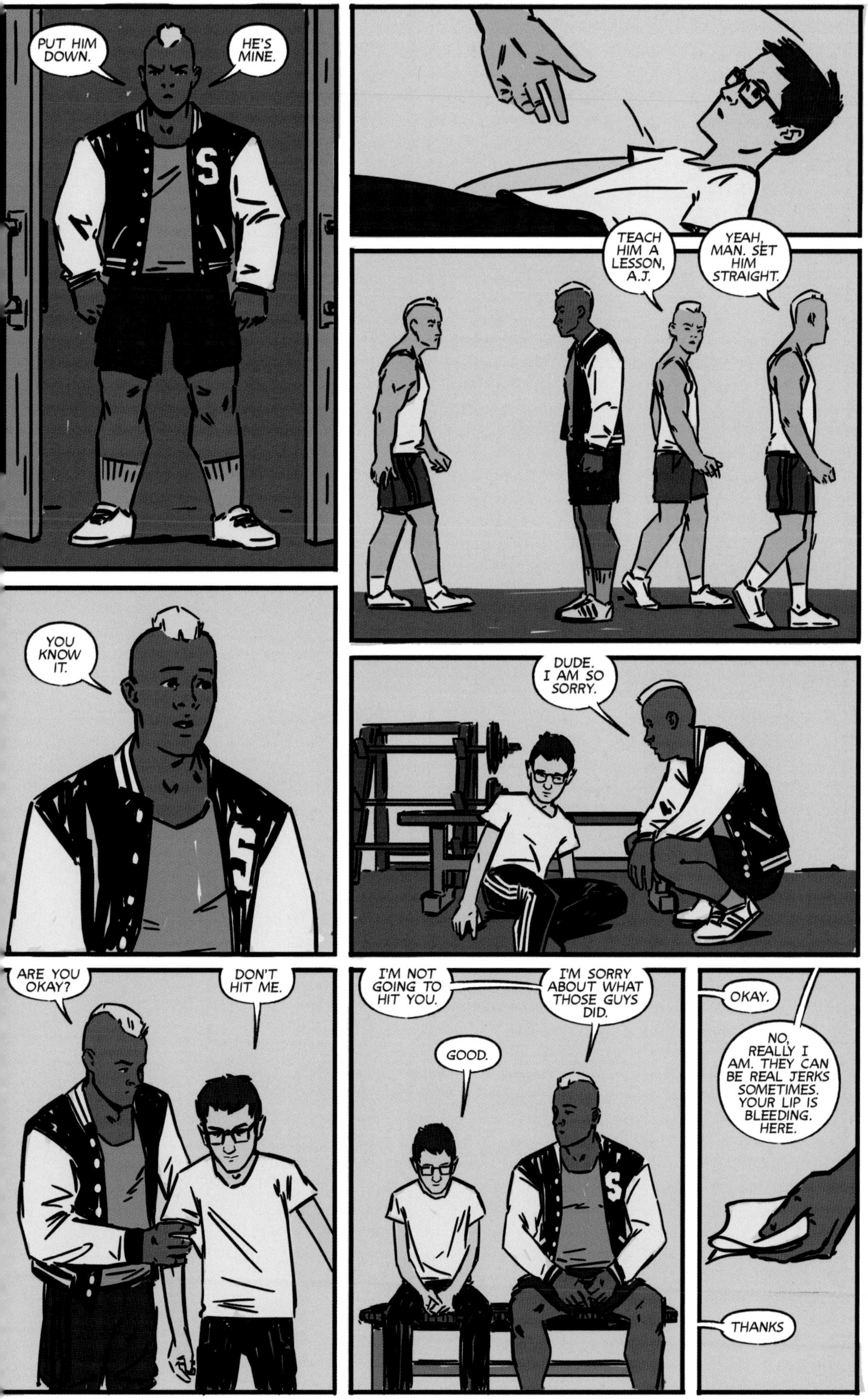
PUT HIM DOWN.
HE'S MINE.
TEACH HIM A LESSON, A.J.
YEAH, MAN. SET HIM STRAIGHT.
YOU KNOW IT.
DUDE. I AM SO SORRY.
ARE YOU OKAY?
DON'T HIT ME.
I'M NOT GOING TO HIT YOU.
I'M SORRY ABOUT WHAT THOSE GUYS DID.
GOOD.
OKAY.
NO, REALLY I AM. THEY CAN BE REAL JERKS SOMETIMES. YOUR LIP IS BLEEDING. HERE.
THANKS

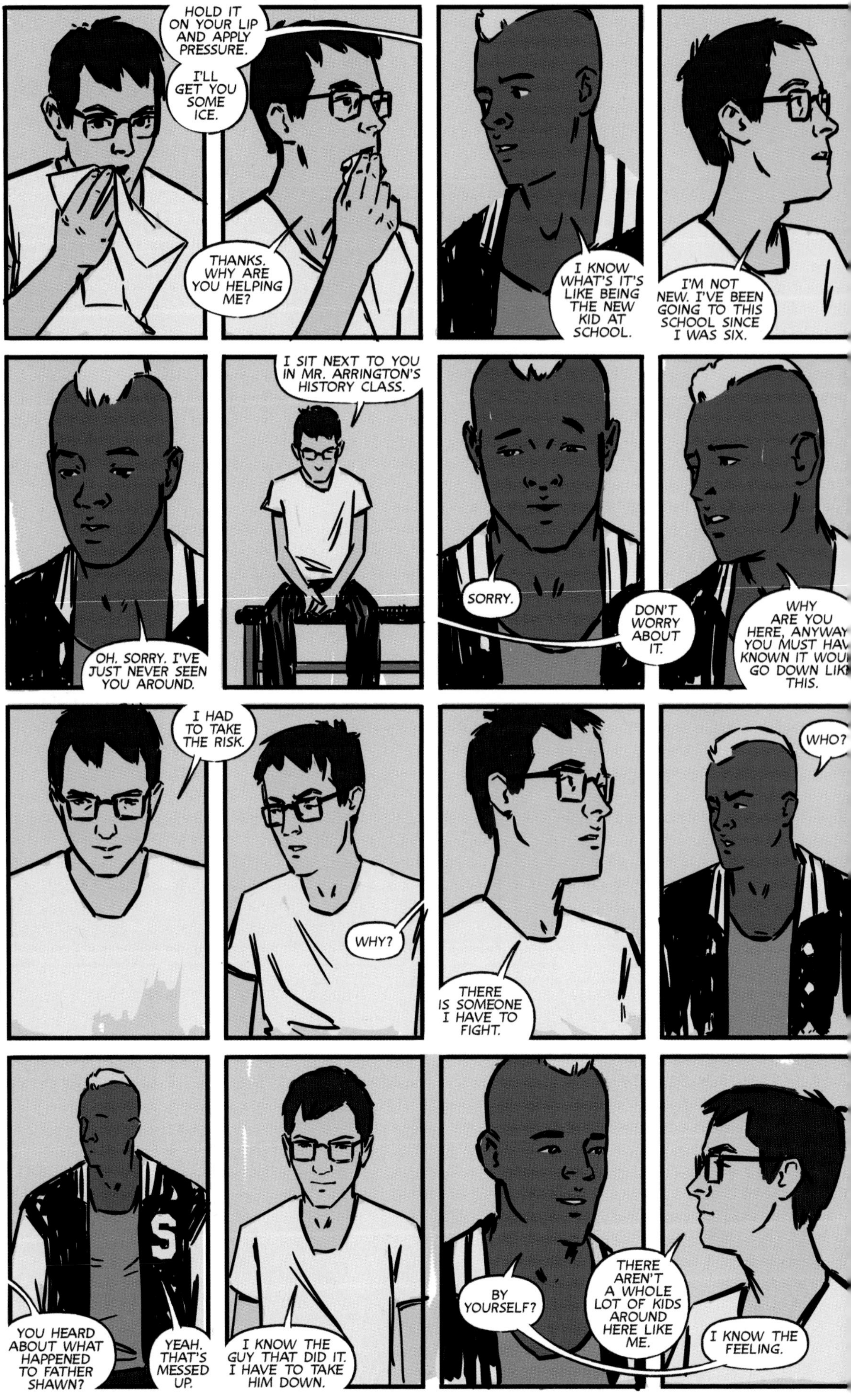

HOLD IT ON YOUR LIP AND APPLY PRESSURE.
I'LL GET YOU SOME ICE.
THANKS. WHY ARE YOU HELPING ME?
I KNOW WHAT'S IT'S LIKE BEING THE NEW KID AT SCHOOL.
I'M NOT NEW. I'VE BEEN GOING TO THIS SCHOOL SINCE I WAS SIX.
OH. SORRY. I'VE JUST NEVER SEEN YOU AROUND.
I SIT NEXT TO YOU IN MR. ARRINGTON'S HISTORY CLASS.
SORRY.
DON'T WORRY ABOUT IT.
WHY ARE YOU HERE, ANYWAY
YOU MUST HAV
KNOWN IT WOU
GO DOWN LIK
THIS.
I HAD TO TAKE THE RISK.
WHY?
THERE IS SOMEONE I HAVE TO FIGHT.
WHO?
YOU HEARD ABOUT WHAT HAPPENED TO FATHER SHAWN?
YEAH. THAT'S MESSED UP.
I KNOW THE GUY THAT DID IT. I HAVE TO TAKE HIM DOWN.
BY YOURSELF?
THERE AREN'T A WHOLE LOT OF KIDS AROUND HERE LIKE ME.
I KNOW THE FEELING.

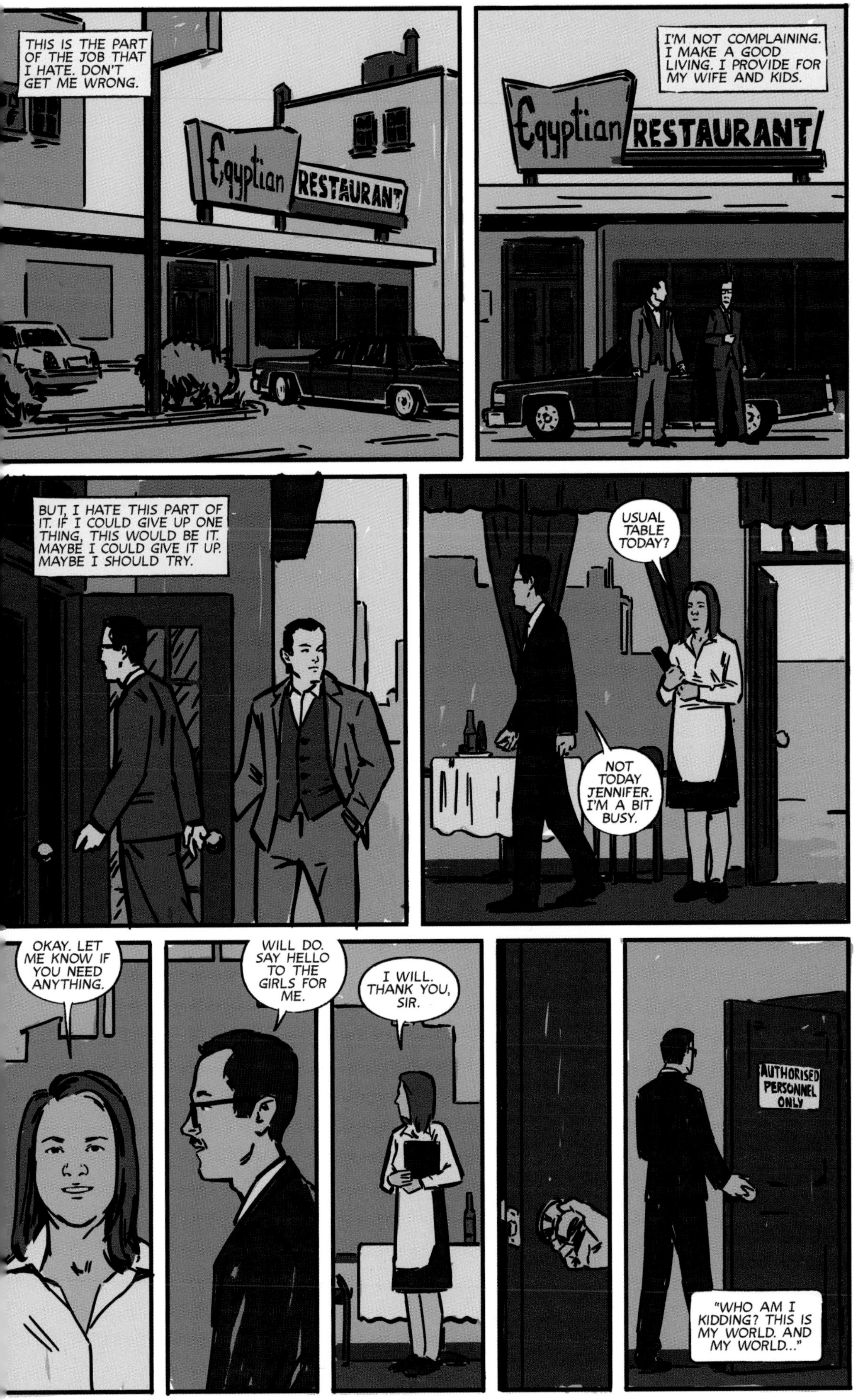

THIS IS THE PART OF THE JOB THAT I HATE. DON'T GET ME WRONG.
Egyptian RESTAURANT
I'M NOT COMPLAINING. I MAKE A GOOD LIVING. I PROVIDE FOR MY WIFE AND KIDS.
Egyptian RESTAURANT
BUT, I HATE THIS PART OF IT. IF I COULD GIVE UP ONE THING, THIS WOULD BE IT. MAYBE I COULD GIVE IT UP. MAYBE I SHOULD TRY.
USUAL TABLE TODAY?
NOT TODAY JENNIFER. I'M A BIT BUSY.
OKAY. LET ME KNOW IF YOU NEED ANYTHING.
WILL DO. SAY HELLO TO THE GIRLS FOR ME.
I WILL. THANK YOU, SIR.
AUTHORISED PERSONNEL ONLY
"WHO AM I KIDDING? THIS IS MY WORLD. AND MY WORLD..."

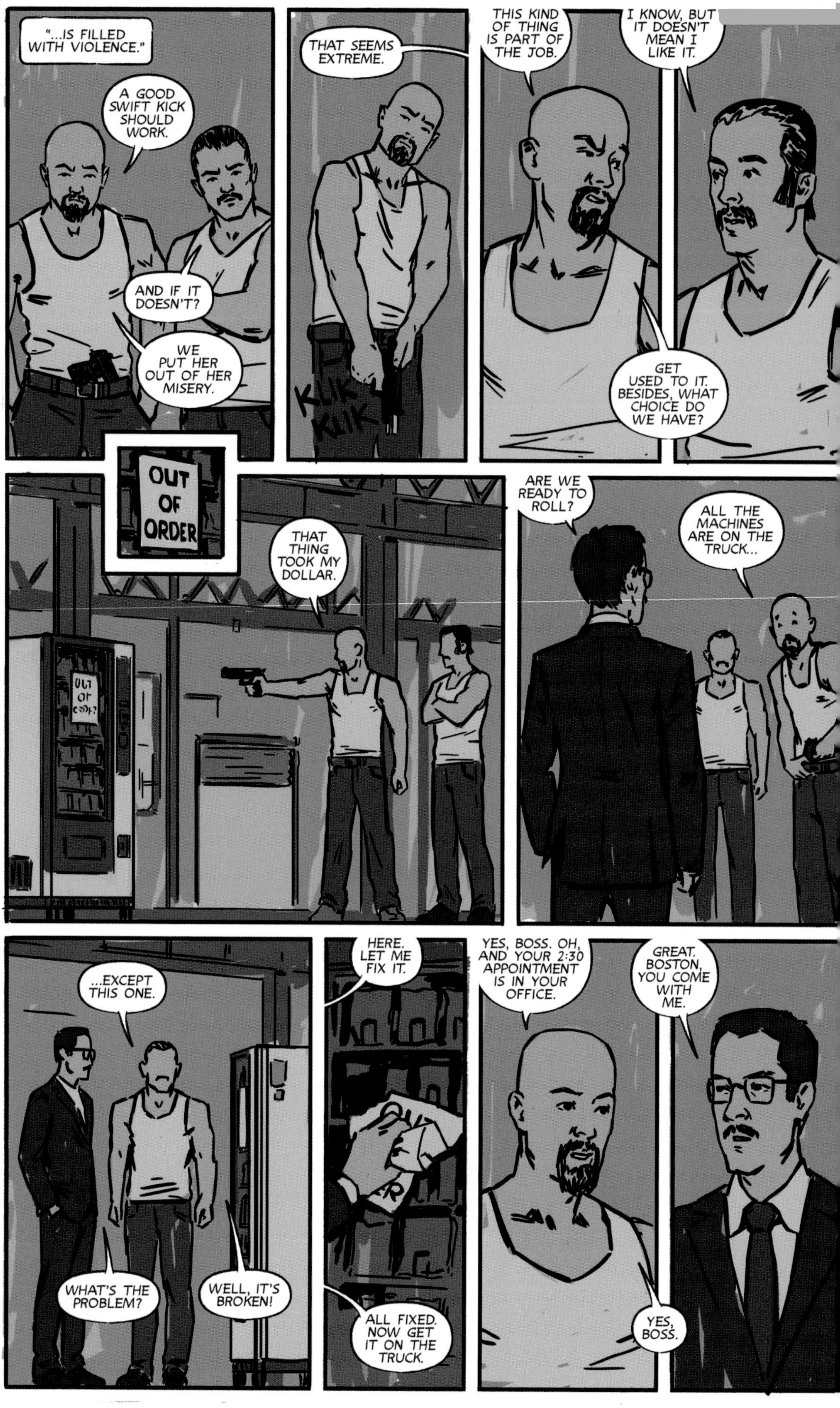
"...IS FILLED WITH VIOLENCE."
A GOOD SWIFT KICK SHOULD WORK.
AND IF IT DOESN'T?
WE PUT HER OUT OF HER MISERY.
THAT SEEMS EXTREME.
KLIK KLIK
THIS KIND OF THING IS PART OF THE JOB.
GET USED TO IT. BESIDES, WHAT CHOICE DO WE HAVE?
I KNOW, BUT IT DOESN'T MEAN I LIKE IT.
OUT OF ORDER
THAT THING TOOK MY DOLLAR.
ARE WE READY TO ROLL?
ALL THE MACHINES ARE ON THE TRUCK...
...EXCEPT THIS ONE.
WHAT'S THE PROBLEM?
WELL, IT'S BROKEN!
HERE. LET ME FIX IT.
ALL FIXED. NOW GET IT ON THE TRUCK.
YES, BOSS. OH, AND YOUR 2:30 APPOINTMENT IS IN YOUR OFFICE.
GREAT. BOSTON, YOU COME WITH ME.
YES, BOSS.

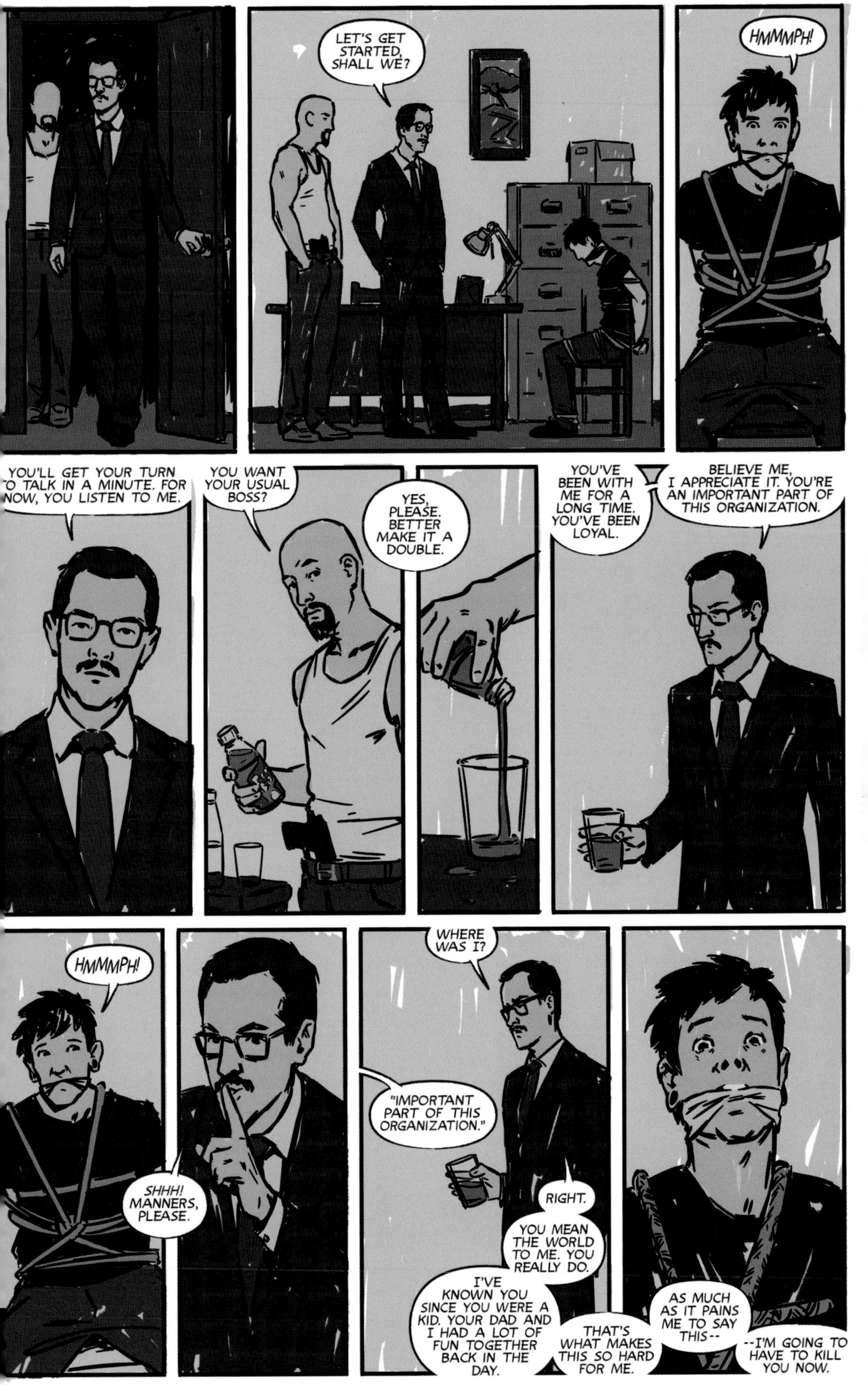
LET'S GET STARTED, SHALL WE?
HMMMPH!
YOU'LL GET YOUR TURN TO TALK IN A MINUTE. FOR NOW, YOU LISTEN TO ME.
YOU WANT YOUR USUAL BOSS?
YES, PLEASE. BETTER MAKE IT A DOUBLE.
YOU'VE BEEN WITH ME FOR A LONG TIME. YOU'VE BEEN LOYAL.
BELIEVE ME, I APPRECIATE IT. YOU'RE AN IMPORTANT PART OF THIS ORGANIZATION.
HMMMPH!
SHHH! MANNERS, PLEASE.
WHERE WAS I?
"IMPORTANT PART OF THIS ORGANIZATION."
RIGHT.
YOU MEAN THE WORLD TO ME. YOU REALLY DO.
I'VE KNOWN YOU SINCE YOU WERE A KID. YOUR DAD AND I HAD A LOT OF FUN TOGETHER BACK IN THE DAY.
THAT'S WHAT MAKES THIS SO HARD FOR ME.
AS MUCH AS IT PAINS ME TO SAY THIS--
--I'M GOING TO HAVE TO KILL YOU NOW.

SO, WE'RE GOING TO BE SUPER-HEROES?

NO.

WELL, WE'RE KINDA LIKE SUPER-HEROES, RIGHT?

NO.

BUT, WE FIGHT CRIME, RIGHT?

I SUPPOSE THAT'S ONE WAY TO LOOK AT IT.

YES!!

SHH! YOU WANT EVERYONE TO HEAR YOU?

I WANT A CODE NAME.

A WHAT?

A SUPERHE[RO] CODE NA[ME], YOU KNO[W] TO PROT[ECT] OUR SECR[ET] IDENTITI[ES]

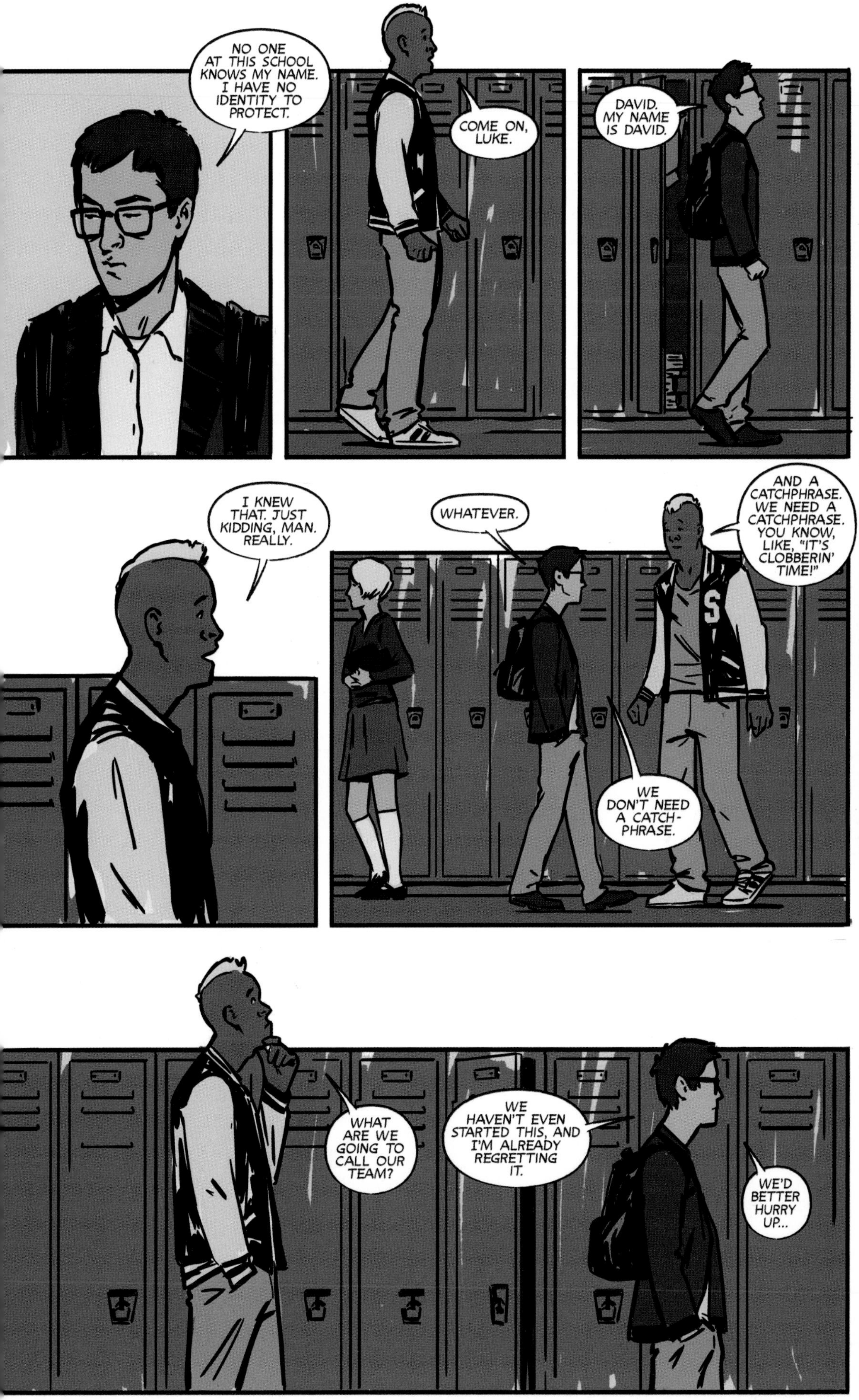
NO ONE AT THIS SCHOOL KNOWS MY NAME. I HAVE NO IDENTITY TO PROTECT.
COME ON, LUKE.
DAVID. MY NAME IS DAVID.
I KNEW THAT. JUST KIDDING, MAN. REALLY.
WHATEVER.
AND A CATCHPHRASE. WE NEED A CATCHPHRASE. YOU KNOW, LIKE, "IT'S CLOBBERIN' TIME!"
WE DON'T NEED A CATCH-PHRASE.
WHAT ARE WE GOING TO CALL OUR TEAM?
WE HAVEN'T EVEN STARTED THIS, AND I'M ALREADY REGRETTING IT.
WE'D BETTER HURRY UP...

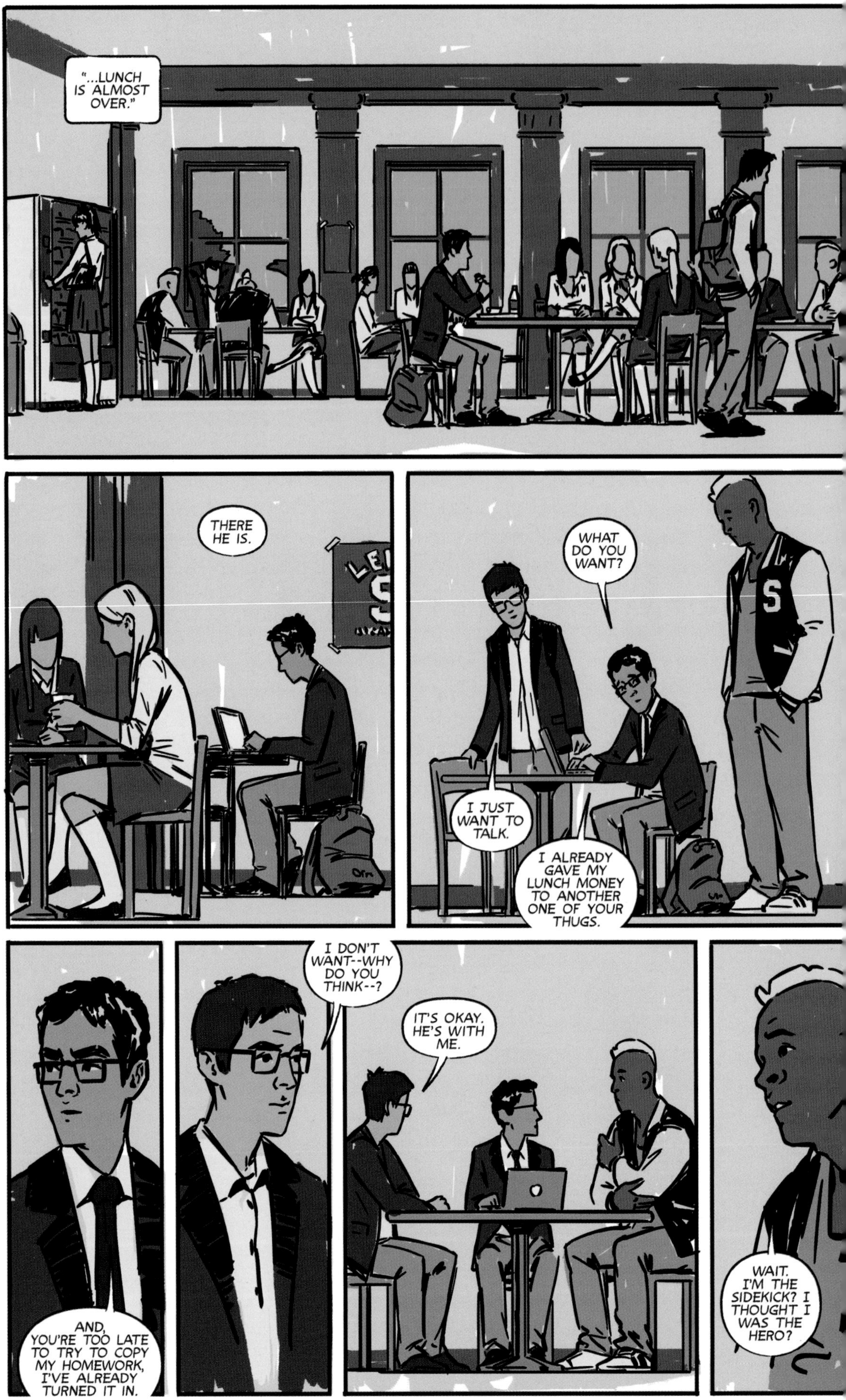
"...LUNCH IS ALMOST OVER."
THERE HE IS.
WHAT DO YOU WANT?
I JUST WANT TO TALK.
I ALREADY GAVE MY LUNCH MONEY TO ANOTHER ONE OF YOUR THUGS.
AND, YOU'RE TOO LATE TO TRY TO COPY MY HOMEWORK, I'VE ALREADY TURNED IT IN.
I DON'T WANT--WHY DO YOU THINK--?
IT'S OKAY. HE'S WITH ME.
WAIT. I'M THE SIDEKICK? I THOUGHT I WAS THE HERO?

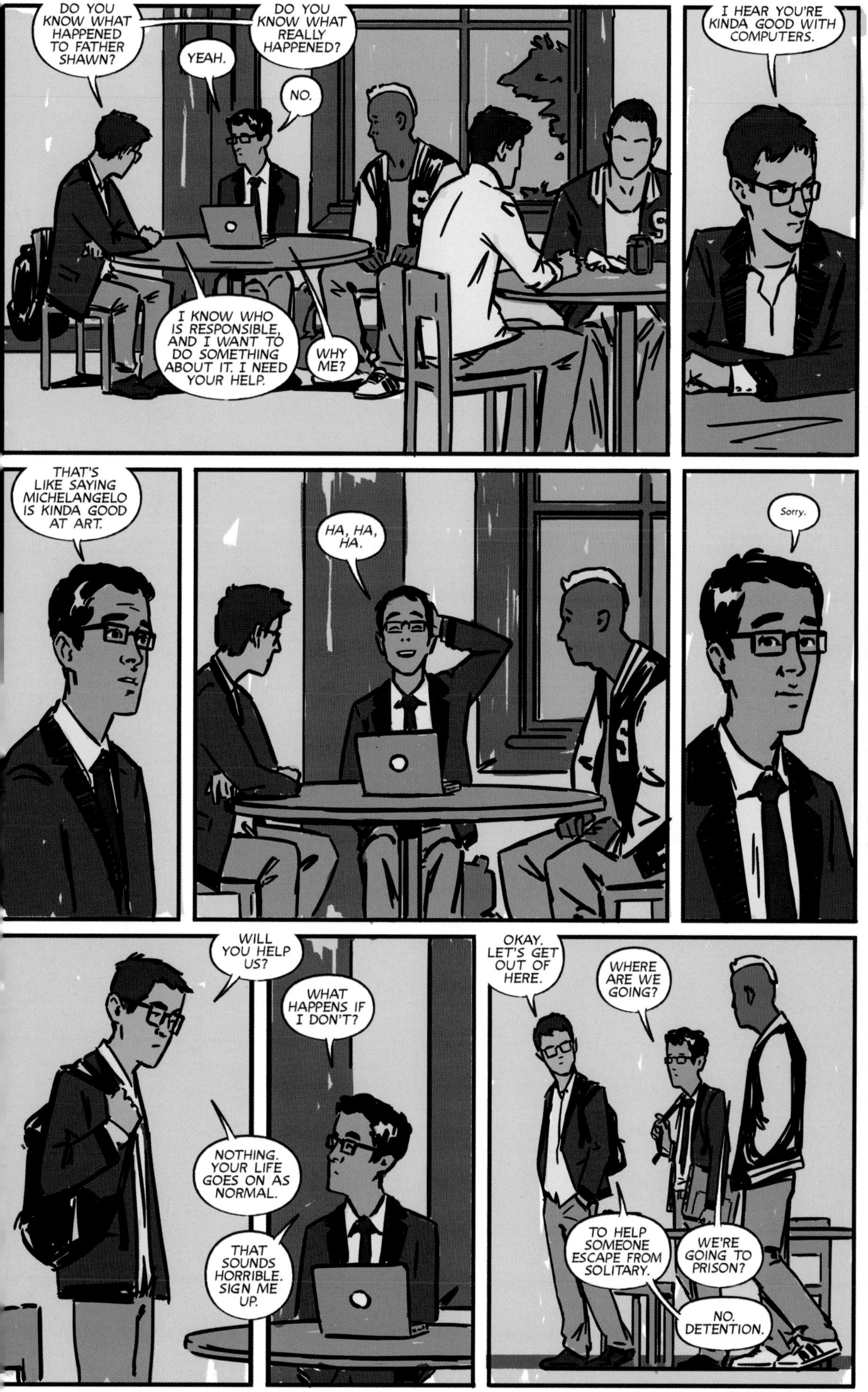
DO YOU KNOW WHAT HAPPENED TO FATHER SHAWN?
YEAH.
DO YOU KNOW WHAT REALLY HAPPENED?
NO.
I KNOW WHO IS RESPONSIBLE, AND I WANT TO DO SOMETHING ABOUT IT. I NEED YOUR HELP.
WHY ME?
I HEAR YOU'RE KINDA GOOD WITH COMPUTERS.
THAT'S LIKE SAYING MICHELANGELO IS KINDA GOOD AT ART.
HA, HA, HA.
Sorry.
WILL YOU HELP US?
WHAT HAPPENS IF I DON'T?
NOTHING. YOUR LIFE GOES ON AS NORMAL.
THAT SOUNDS HORRIBLE. SIGN ME UP.
OKAY. LET'S GET OUT OF HERE.
WHERE ARE WE GOING?
TO HELP SOMEONE ESCAPE FROM SOLITARY.
WE'RE GOING TO PRISON?
NO. DETENTION.

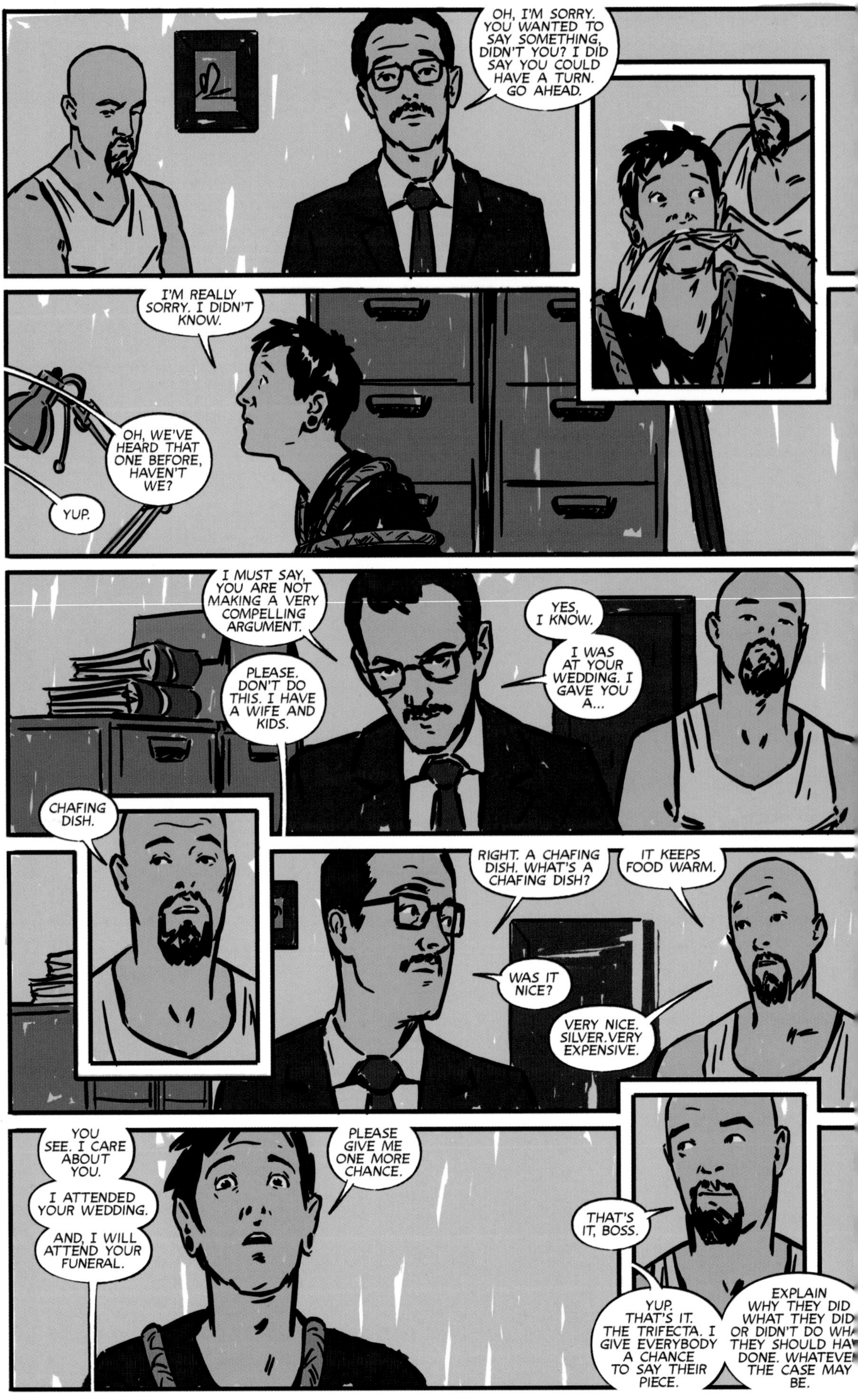
OH, I'M SORRY. YOU WANTED TO SAY SOMETHING, DIDN'T YOU? I DID SAY YOU COULD HAVE A TURN. GO AHEAD.
I'M REALLY SORRY. I DIDN'T KNOW.
OH, WE'VE HEARD THAT ONE BEFORE, HAVEN'T WE?
YUP.
I MUST SAY, YOU ARE NOT MAKING A VERY COMPELLING ARGUMENT.
PLEASE. DON'T DO THIS. I HAVE A WIFE AND KIDS.
YES, I KNOW.
I WAS AT YOUR WEDDING. I GAVE YOU A...
CHAFING DISH.
RIGHT. A CHAFING DISH. WHAT'S A CHAFING DISH?
IT KEEPS FOOD WARM.
WAS IT NICE?
VERY NICE. SILVER. VERY EXPENSIVE.
YOU SEE. I CARE ABOUT YOU.
I ATTENDED YOUR WEDDING.
AND, I WILL ATTEND YOUR FUNERAL.
PLEASE GIVE ME ONE MORE CHANCE.
THAT'S IT, BOSS.
YUP. THAT'S IT. THE TRIFECTA. I GIVE EVERYBODY A CHANCE TO SAY THEIR PIECE.
EXPLAIN WHY THEY DID WHAT THEY DID OR DIDN'T DO WHA THEY SHOULD HA DONE. WHATEVE THE CASE MAY BE.

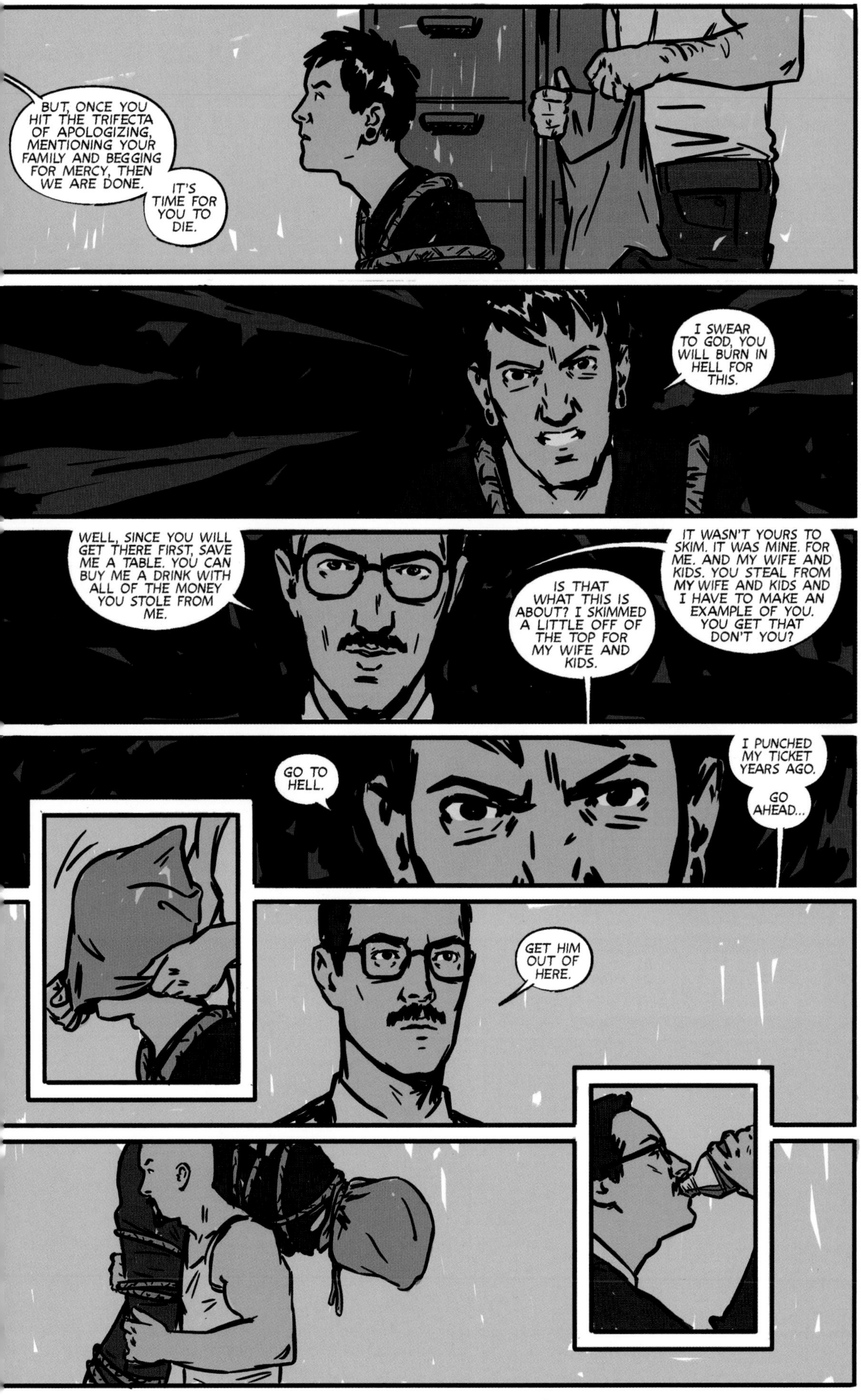
BUT, ONCE YOU HIT THE TRIFECTA OF APOLOGIZING, MENTIONING YOUR FAMILY AND BEGGING FOR MERCY, THEN WE ARE DONE.
IT'S TIME FOR YOU TO DIE.
I SWEAR TO GOD, YOU WILL BURN IN HELL FOR THIS.
WELL, SINCE YOU WILL GET THERE FIRST, SAVE ME A TABLE. YOU CAN BUY ME A DRINK WITH ALL OF THE MONEY YOU STOLE FROM ME.
IS THAT WHAT THIS IS ABOUT? I SKIMMED A LITTLE OFF OF THE TOP FOR MY WIFE AND KIDS.
IT WASN'T YOURS TO SKIM. IT WAS MINE. FOR ME. AND MY WIFE AND KIDS. YOU STEAL FROM MY WIFE AND KIDS AND I HAVE TO MAKE AN EXAMPLE OF YOU. YOU GET THAT DON'T YOU?
GO TO HELL.
I PUNCHED MY TICKET YEARS AGO.
GO AHEAD...
GET HIM OUT OF HERE.

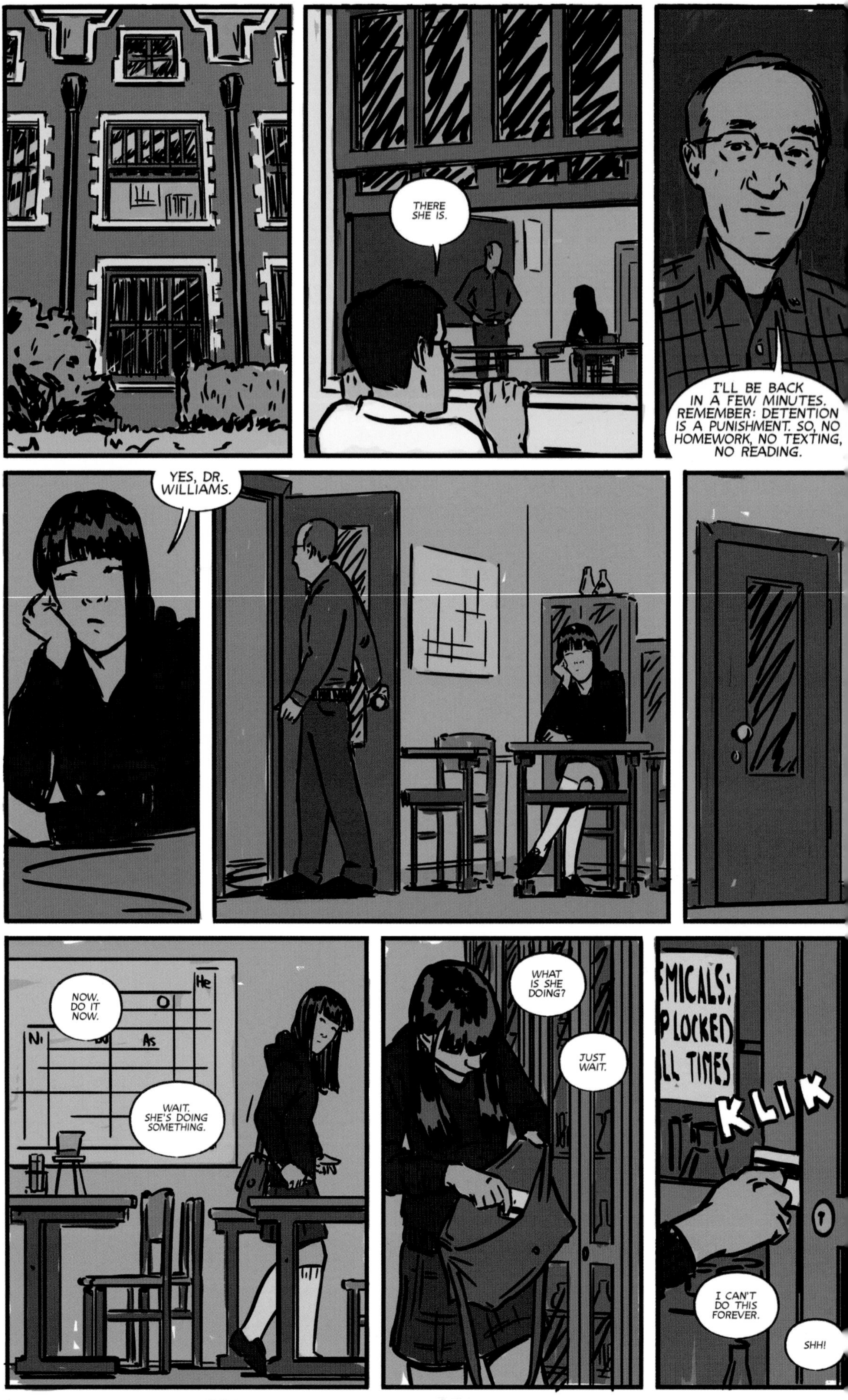
THERE SHE IS.
I'LL BE BACK IN A FEW MINUTES. REMEMBER: DETENTION IS A PUNISHMENT. SO, NO HOMEWORK, NO TEXTING, NO READING.
YES, DR. WILLIAMS.
NOW. DO IT NOW.
WAIT. SHE'S DOING SOMETHING.
WHAT IS SHE DOING?
JUST WAIT.
EMICALS:
P LOCKED
LL TIMES
KLIK
I CAN'T DO THIS FOREVER.
SHH!

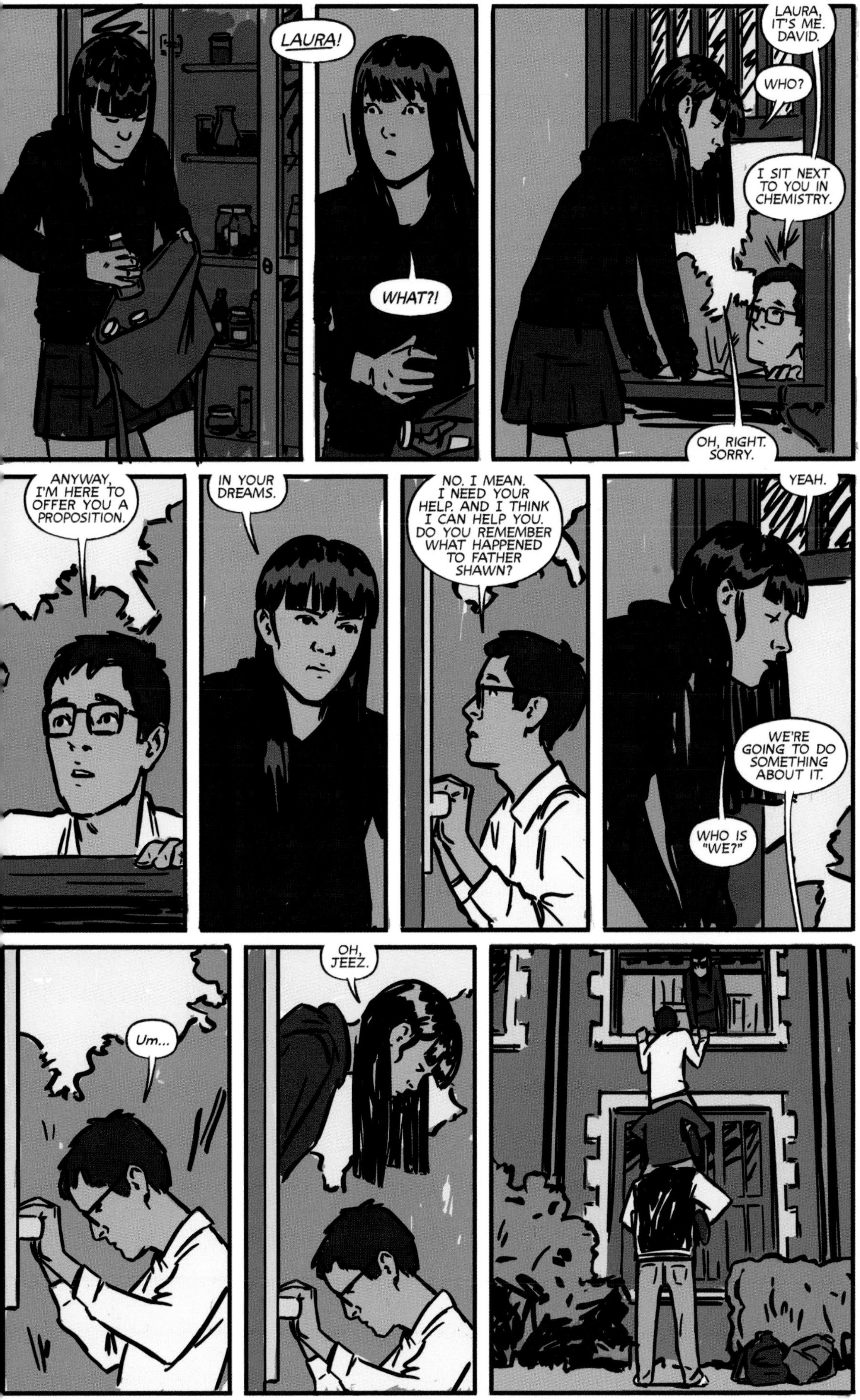
LAURA!
WHAT?!
LAURA, IT'S ME. DAVID.
WHO?
I SIT NEXT TO YOU IN CHEMISTRY.
OH, RIGHT. SORRY.
ANYWAY, I'M HERE TO OFFER YOU A PROPOSITION.
IN YOUR DREAMS.
NO. I MEAN. I NEED YOUR HELP. AND I THINK I CAN HELP YOU. DO YOU REMEMBER WHAT HAPPENED TO FATHER SHAWN?
YEAH.
WE'RE GOING TO DO SOMETHING ABOUT IT.
WHO IS "WE?"
Um...
OH, JEEZ.

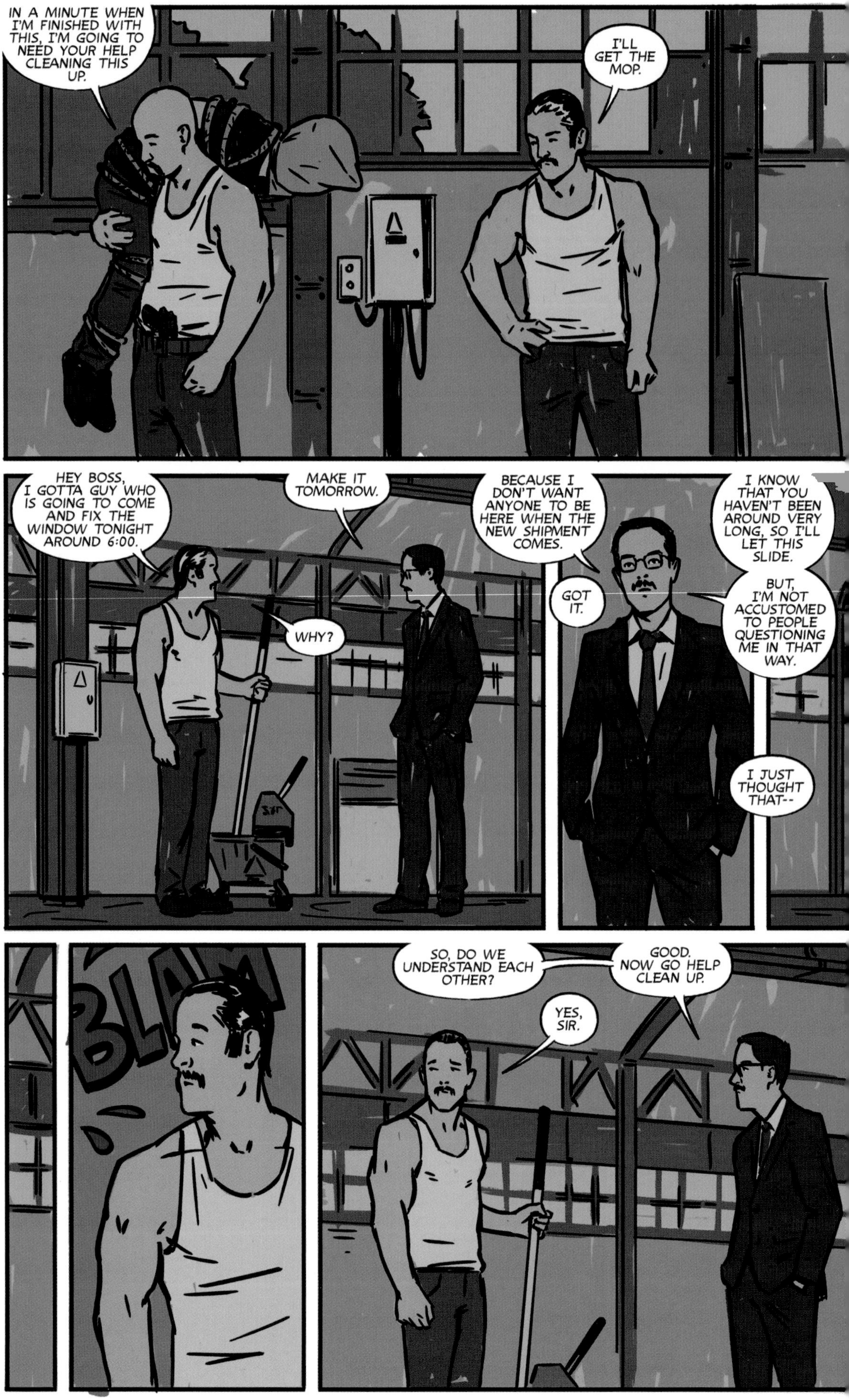
IN A MINUTE WHEN I'M FINISHED WITH THIS, I'M GOING TO NEED YOUR HELP CLEANING THIS UP.
I'LL GET THE MOP.
HEY BOSS, I GOTTA GUY WHO IS GOING TO COME AND FIX THE WINDOW TONIGHT AROUND 6:00.
MAKE IT TOMORROW.
WHY?
BECAUSE I DON'T WANT ANYONE TO BE HERE WHEN THE NEW SHIPMENT COMES.
GOT IT.
I KNOW THAT YOU HAVEN'T BEEN AROUND VERY LONG, SO I'LL LET THIS SLIDE.
BUT, I'M NOT ACCUSTOMED TO PEOPLE QUESTIONING ME IN THAT WAY.
I JUST THOUGHT THAT--
BLAM
SO, DO WE UNDERSTAND EACH OTHER?
YES, SIR.
GOOD. NOW GO HELP CLEAN UP.

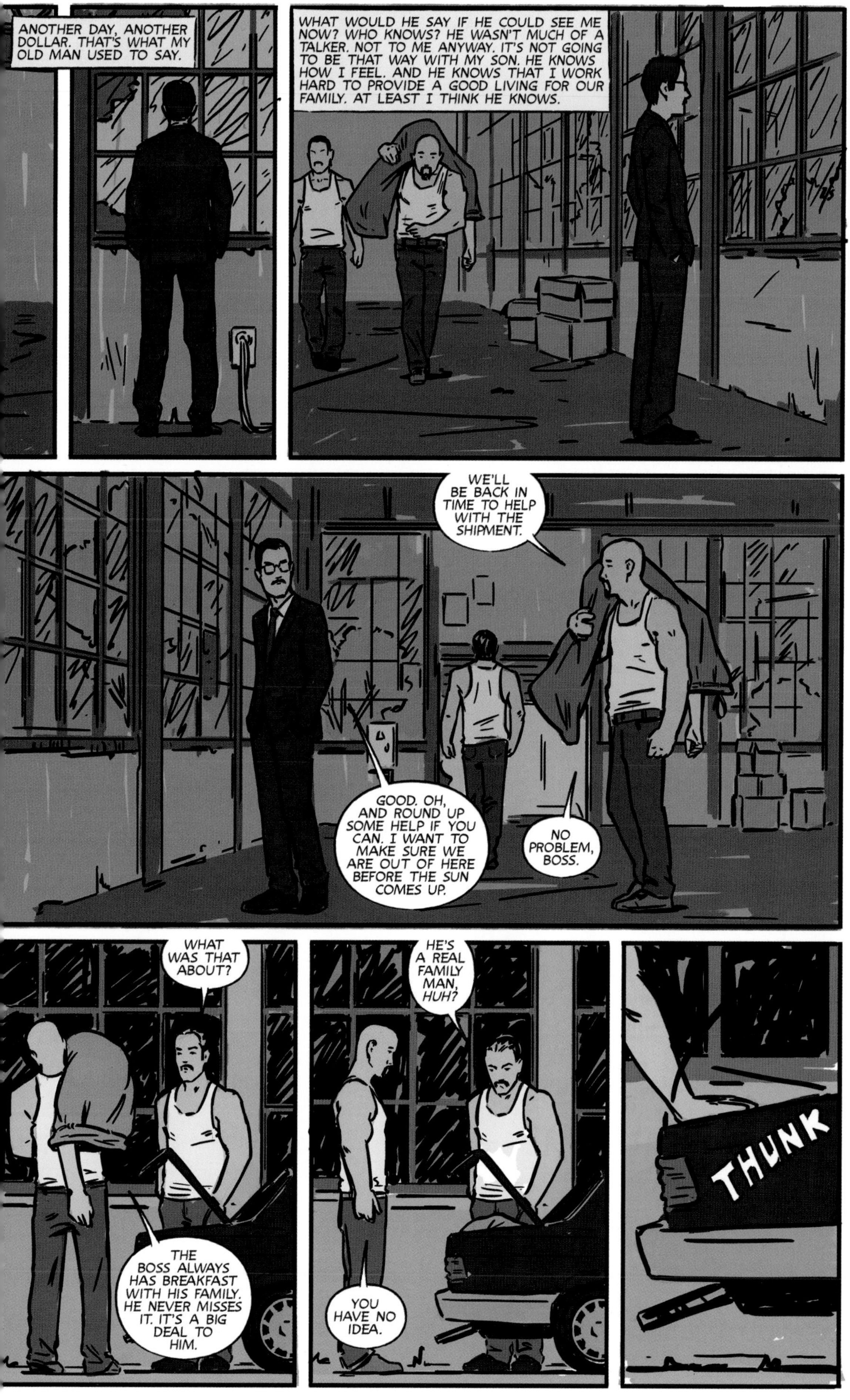
ANOTHER DAY, ANOTHER DOLLAR. THAT'S WHAT MY OLD MAN USED TO SAY.
WHAT WOULD HE SAY IF HE COULD SEE ME NOW? WHO KNOWS? HE WASN'T MUCH OF A TALKER. NOT TO ME ANYWAY. IT'S NOT GOING TO BE THAT WAY WITH MY SON. HE KNOWS HOW I FEEL. AND HE KNOWS THAT I WORK HARD TO PROVIDE A GOOD LIVING FOR OUR FAMILY. AT LEAST I THINK HE KNOWS.
WE'LL BE BACK IN TIME TO HELP WITH THE SHIPMENT.
GOOD. OH, AND ROUND UP SOME HELP IF YOU CAN. I WANT TO MAKE SURE WE ARE OUT OF HERE BEFORE THE SUN COMES UP.
NO PROBLEM, BOSS.
WHAT WAS THAT ABOUT?
THE BOSS ALWAYS HAS BREAKFAST WITH HIS FAMILY. HE NEVER MISSES IT. IT'S A BIG DEAL TO HIM.
HE'S A REAL FAMILY MAN, HUH?
YOU HAVE NO IDEA.
THUNK

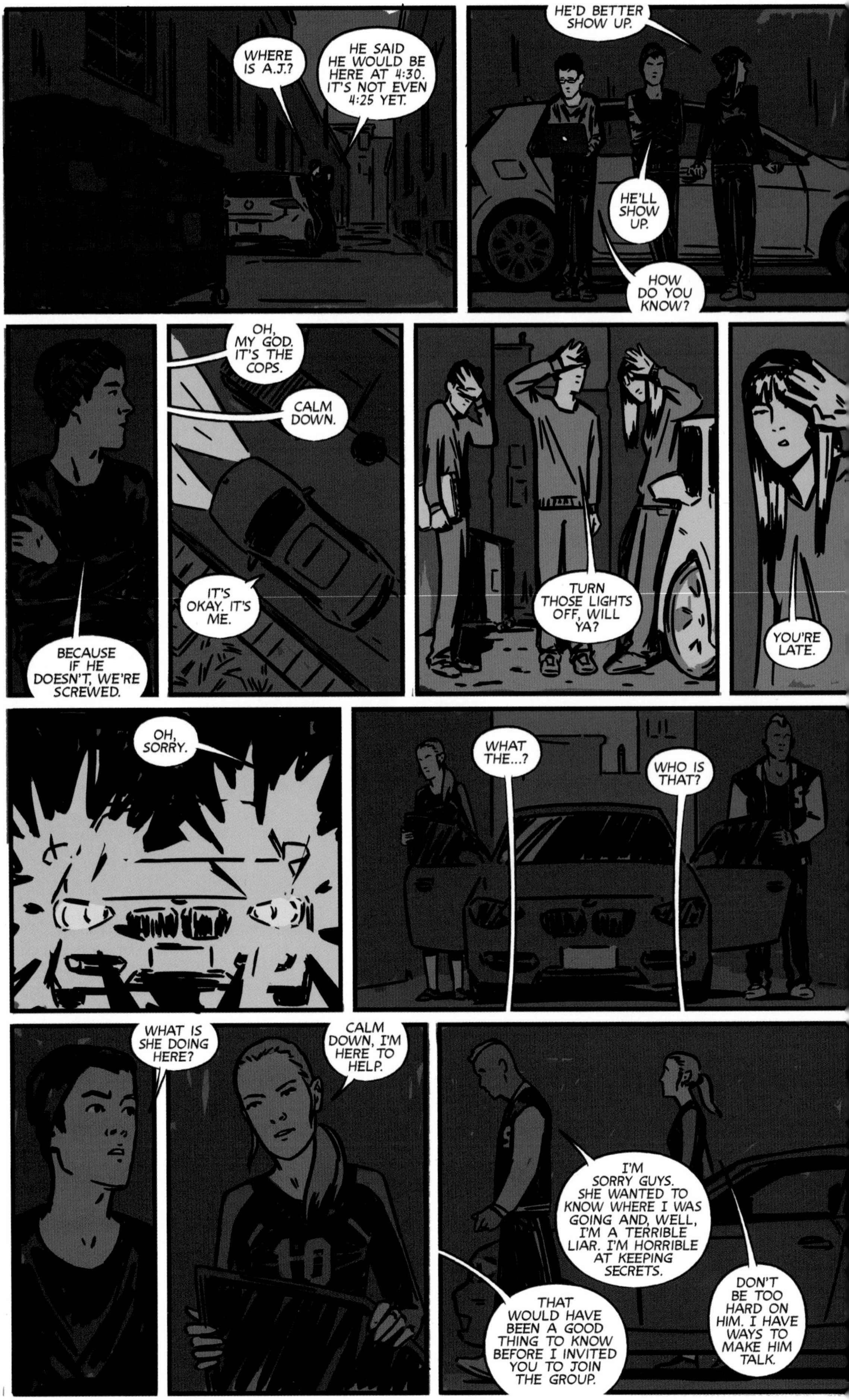
WHERE IS A.J.?
HE SAID HE WOULD BE HERE AT 4:30. IT'S NOT EVEN 4:25 YET.
HE'D BETTER SHOW UP.
HE'LL SHOW UP.
HOW DO YOU KNOW?
BECAUSE IF HE DOESN'T, WE'RE SCREWED.
OH, MY GOD. IT'S THE COPS.
CALM DOWN.
IT'S OKAY. IT'S ME.
TURN THOSE LIGHTS OFF, WILL YA?
YOU'RE LATE.
OH, SORRY.
WHAT THE...?
WHO IS THAT?
WHAT IS SHE DOING HERE?
CALM DOWN, I'M HERE TO HELP.
I'M SORRY GUYS. SHE WANTED TO KNOW WHERE I WAS GOING AND, WELL, I'M A TERRIBLE LIAR. I'M HORRIBLE AT KEEPING SECRETS.
THAT WOULD HAVE BEEN A GOOD THING TO KNOW BEFORE I INVITED YOU TO JOIN THE GROUP.
DON'T BE TOO HARD ON HIM. I HAVE WAYS TO MAKE HIM TALK.

I BET YOU DO.

SO, WHAT DO YOU KNOW?

JUST WHAT A.J. TOLD ME. THAT YOU KNOW WHO KILLED FATHER SHAWN, AND THAT YOU HAVE A PLAN TO GET BACK AT THE GUY. AND, THAT YOU NEED HELP.

WHY DO YOU WANT TO HELP?

THIS IS MY DAD.

HE GAVE HIS LIFE HELPING PEOPLE GET FREE FROM THE GRIP OF LOCAL WARLORDS IN AFGHANISTAN.

THIS "VICEROY" CHARACTER-- HE'S JUST A VILLAGE WARLORD IN A NICER SUIT. IF YOU ARE GOING TO TAKE HIM DOWN, I WANT IN.

OKAY. THANKS. I'M SORRY IF I WAS--

SO, THE VICEROY. HE'S IN THERE.

NO. NOT NOW. IT'S EMPTY.

EMPTY?

NOT EMPTY. BUT, THE VICEROY AND HIS GOONS ARE GONE. THEY WON'T BE BACK FOR HOURS.

SO, WHAT ARE WE DOING HERE?

I FOUND OUT THAT A MAJOR SHIPMENT ARRIVED TODAY. AND, THAT IT WON'T BE LEAVING UNTIL THE MORNING. USUALLY THESE SHIPMENTS DON'T STAY HERE OVERNIGHT.

"SHIPMENTS?" YOU MEAN DRUGS?

UNDERSTAND THAT'S HOW HE MAKES HIS MONEY.

AND YOU WANT TO...?

HE CAN'T GO TO JAIL. NOT YET.

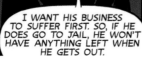

DESTROY THE DRUGS.

WHY NOT CALL THE COPS?

I WANT HIS BUSINESS TO SUFFER FIRST. SO, IF HE DOES GO TO JAIL, HE WON'T HAVE ANYTHING LEFT WHEN HE GETS OUT.

NICE.

COME ON. WE DON'T HAVE MUCH TIME.

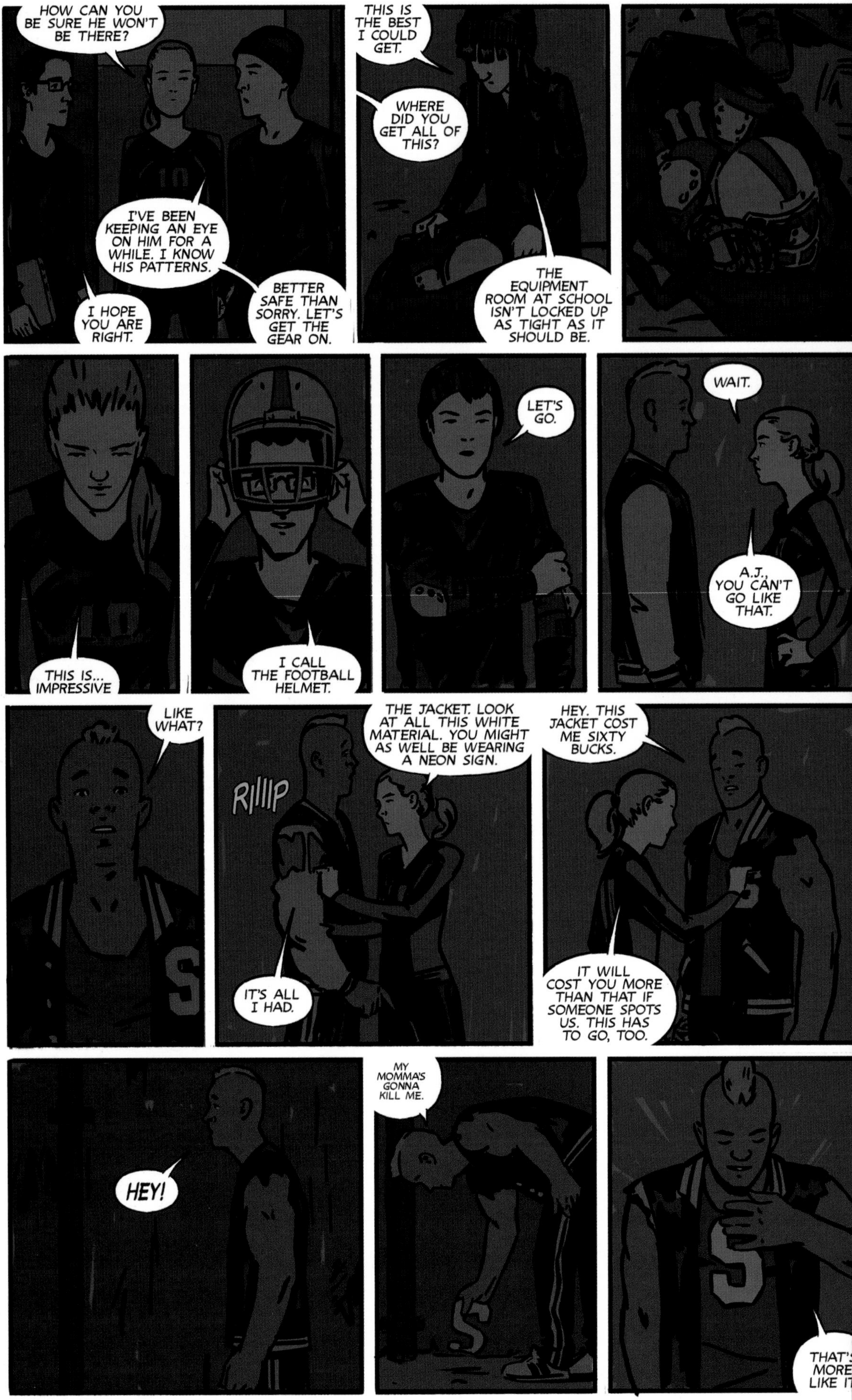
HOW CAN YOU BE SURE HE WON'T BE THERE?
I'VE BEEN KEEPING AN EYE ON HIM FOR A WHILE. I KNOW HIS PATTERNS.
I HOPE YOU ARE RIGHT.
BETTER SAFE THAN SORRY. LET'S GET THE GEAR ON.
THIS IS THE BEST I COULD GET.
WHERE DID YOU GET ALL OF THIS?
THE EQUIPMENT ROOM AT SCHOOL ISN'T LOCKED UP AS TIGHT AS IT SHOULD BE.
THIS IS... IMPRESSIVE
I CALL THE FOOTBALL HELMET.
LET'S GO.
WAIT.
A.J., YOU CAN'T GO LIKE THAT.
LIKE WHAT?
RIIIP
THE JACKET. LOOK AT ALL THIS WHITE MATERIAL. YOU MIGHT AS WELL BE WEARING A NEON SIGN.
IT'S ALL I HAD.
HEY. THIS JACKET COST ME SIXTY BUCKS.
IT WILL COST YOU MORE THAN THAT IF SOMEONE SPOTS US. THIS HAS TO GO, TOO.
HEY!
MY MOMMA'S GONNA KILL ME.
THAT'S MORE LIKE IT

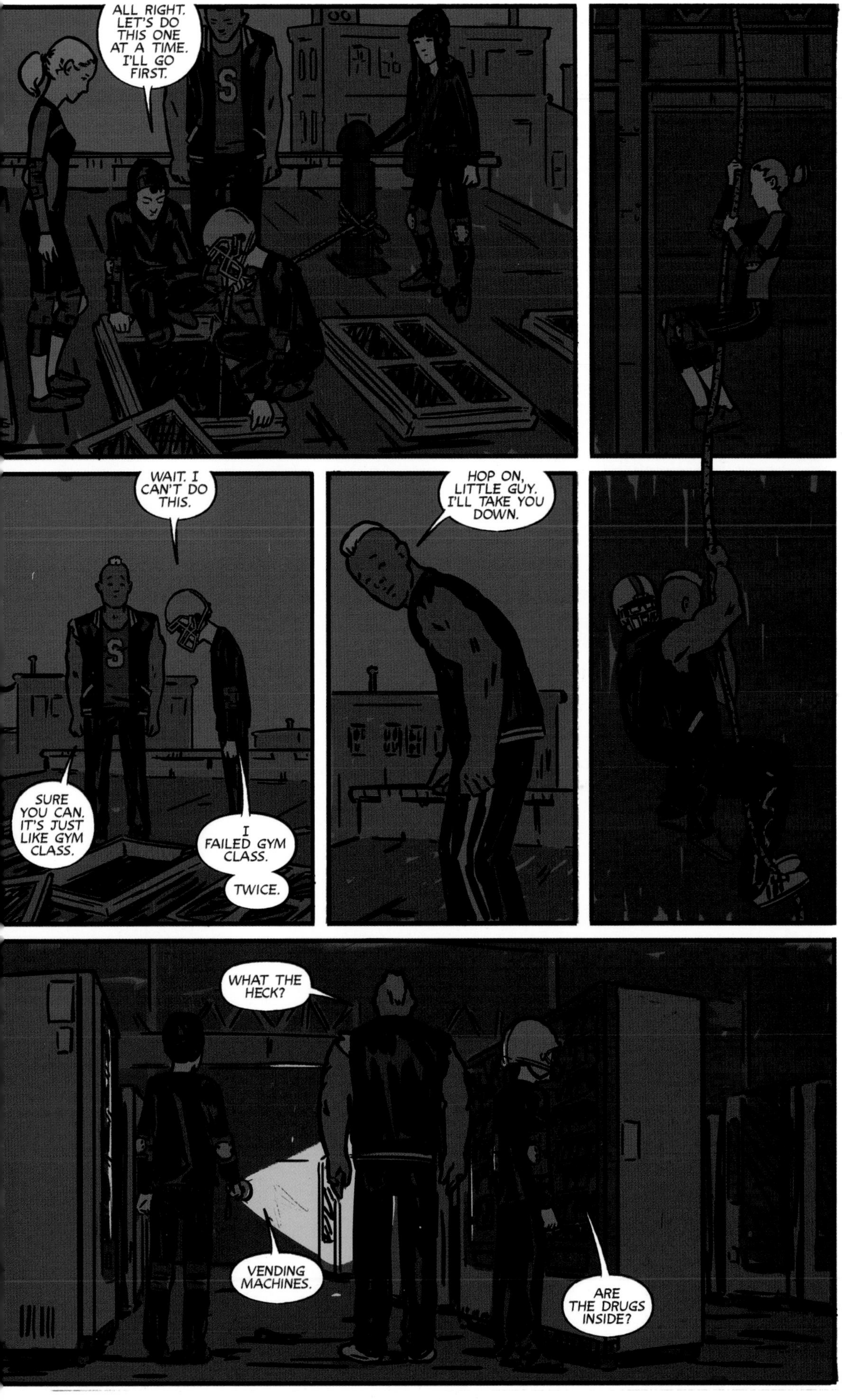
ALL RIGHT. LET'S DO THIS ONE AT A TIME. I'LL GO FIRST.
WAIT. I CAN'T DO THIS.
SURE YOU CAN. IT'S JUST LIKE GYM CLASS.
I FAILED GYM CLASS.
TWICE.
HOP ON, LITTLE GUY. I'LL TAKE YOU DOWN.
WHAT THE HECK?
VENDING MACHINES.
ARE THE DRUGS INSIDE?

NO, THIS IS THE SHIPMENT.

WHY WOULD HE WANT SO MANY VENDING MACHINES?

LOTS OF MOB GUYS ARE INTO VENDING MACHINES, LAUNDROMATS, CAR WASHES AND VIDEO GAME ARCADES. IT'S A CASH BUSINESS AND AN EASY WAY TO LAUNDER MONEY.

HOW DO YOU KNOW ALL OF THAT?

I KN LOTS STU

THESE LABELS SAY, "MOCKINGBIRD VENDING". ACCORDING TO THIS, IT IS THE BIGGEST VENDING COMPANY IN THE METROPLEX, AND THE THIRD BIGGEST IN TEXAS.

HOW DID I NOT KNOW THAT HE DID THIS?

I FOUND OUT ABOUT THE DRUGS, AND THE KILLINGS, BUT HOW COULD I NOT KNOW ABOUT THIS?

NOW WHAT WE D

WE COULD SMASH THEM UP.

TOO NOISY.

THIS IS HIS LEGIT BUSINESS.

HE PROBABLY HAS INSURANCE ON ALL OF THIS.

A.J., HELP ME MOVE THESE MACHINES TOGETHER.

LAURA, LET ME SEE YOUR BAG.

THIS WILL WORK.

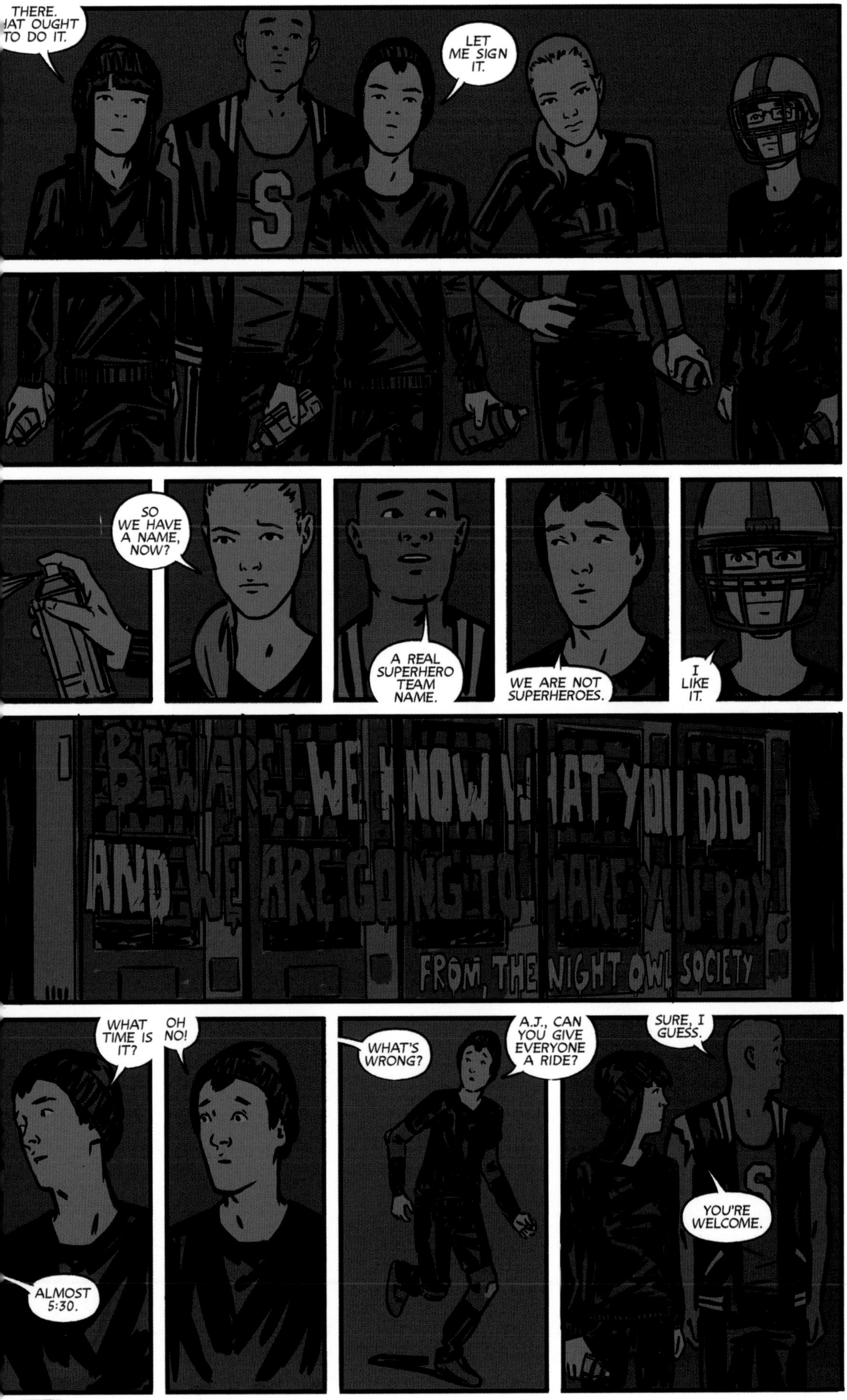
THERE. (T)HAT OUGHT TO DO IT.
LET ME SIGN IT.
SO WE HAVE A NAME, NOW?
A REAL SUPERHERO TEAM NAME.
WE ARE NOT SUPERHEROES.
I LIKE IT.
BEWARE! WE KNOW WHAT YOU DID AND WE ARE GOING TO MAKE YOU PAY!
FROM, THE NIGHT OWL SOCIETY
WHAT TIME IS IT?
ALMOST 5:30.
OH NO!
WHAT'S WRONG?
A.J., CAN YOU GIVE EVERYONE A RIDE?
SURE, I GUESS.
YOU'RE WELCOME.

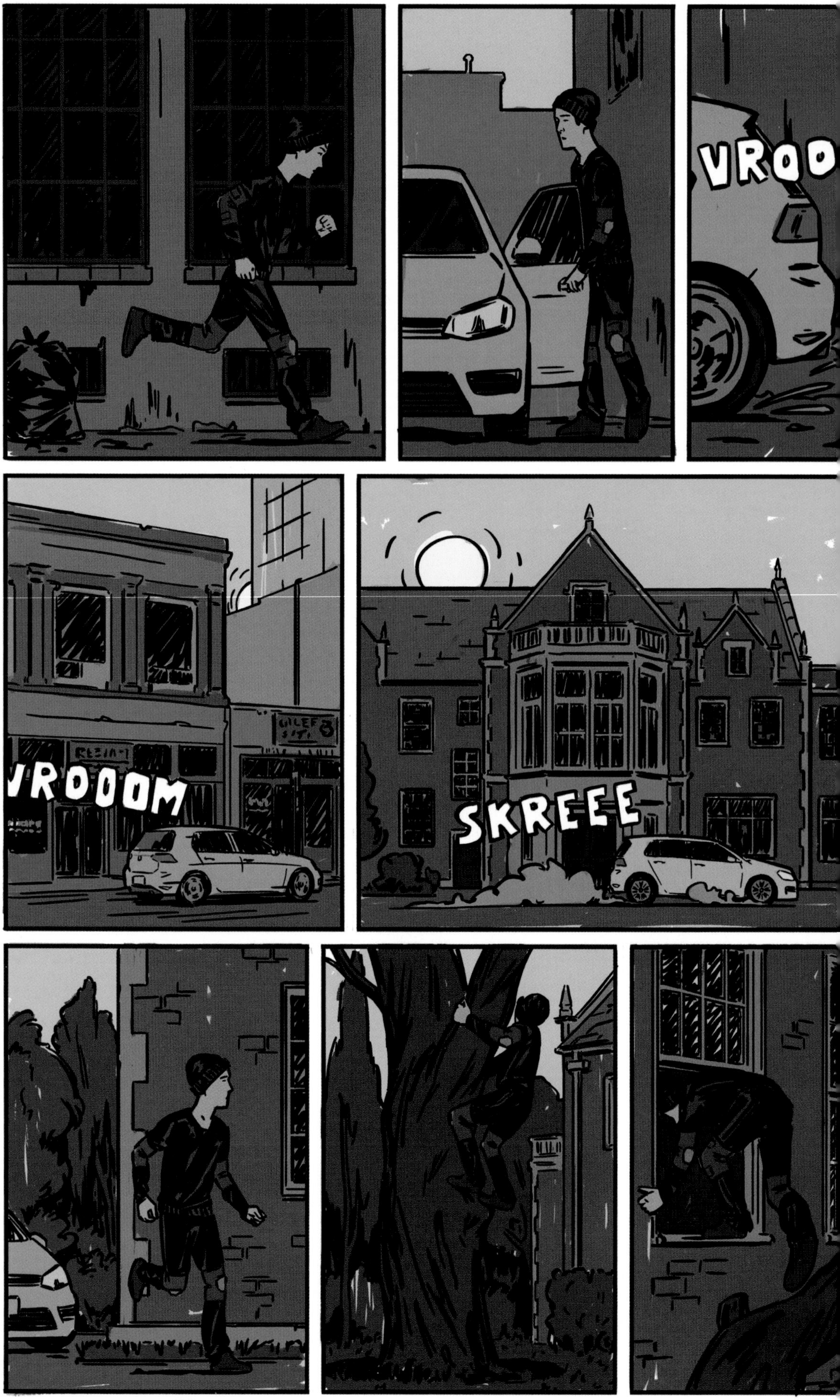
VROO
VROOOM
SKREEE

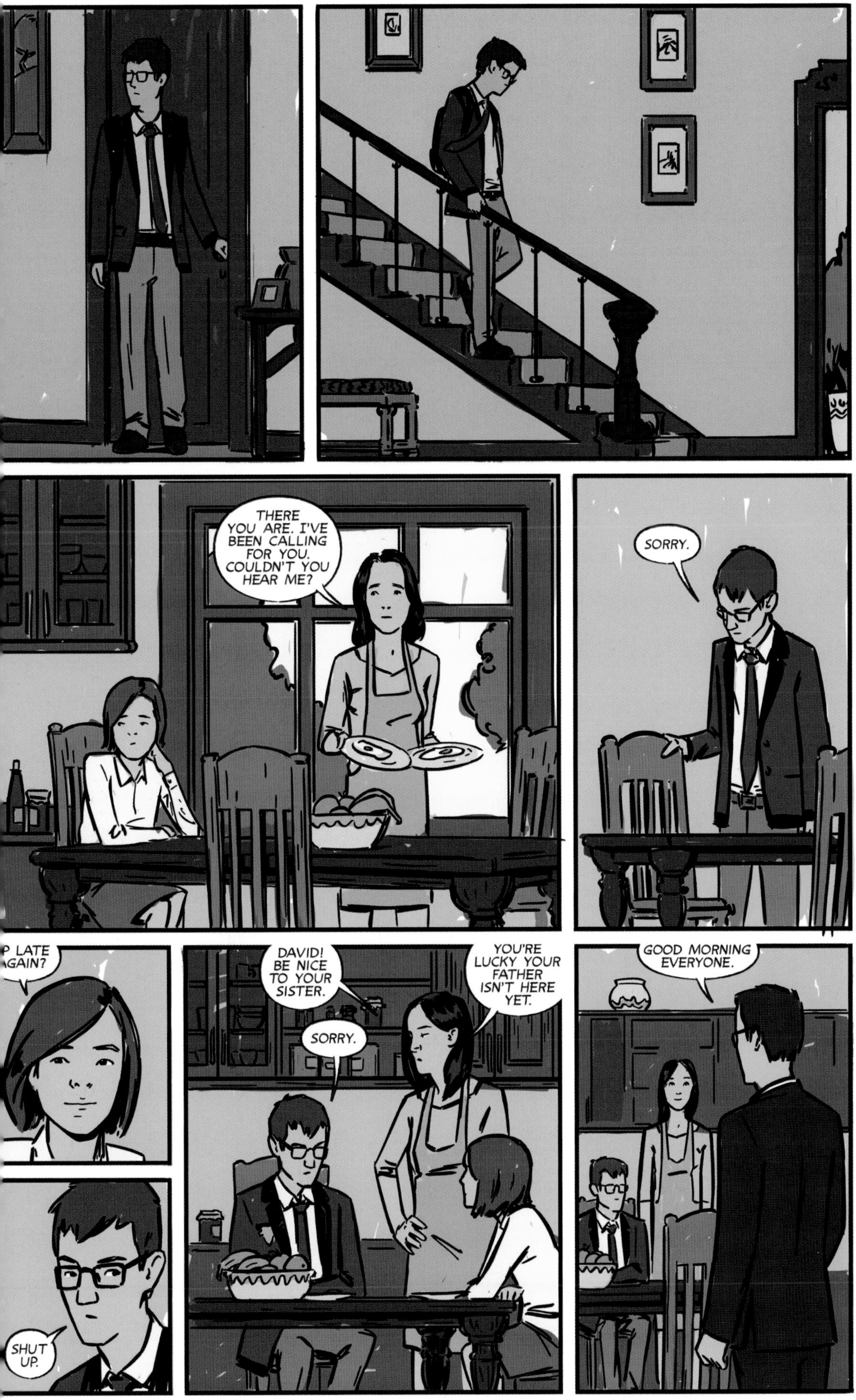
THERE YOU ARE. I'VE BEEN CALLING FOR YOU. COULDN'T YOU HEAR ME?
SORRY.
P LATE AGAIN?
SHUT UP.
DAVID! BE NICE TO YOUR SISTER.
SORRY.
YOU'RE LUCKY YOUR FATHER ISN'T HERE YET.
GOOD MORNING EVERYONE.

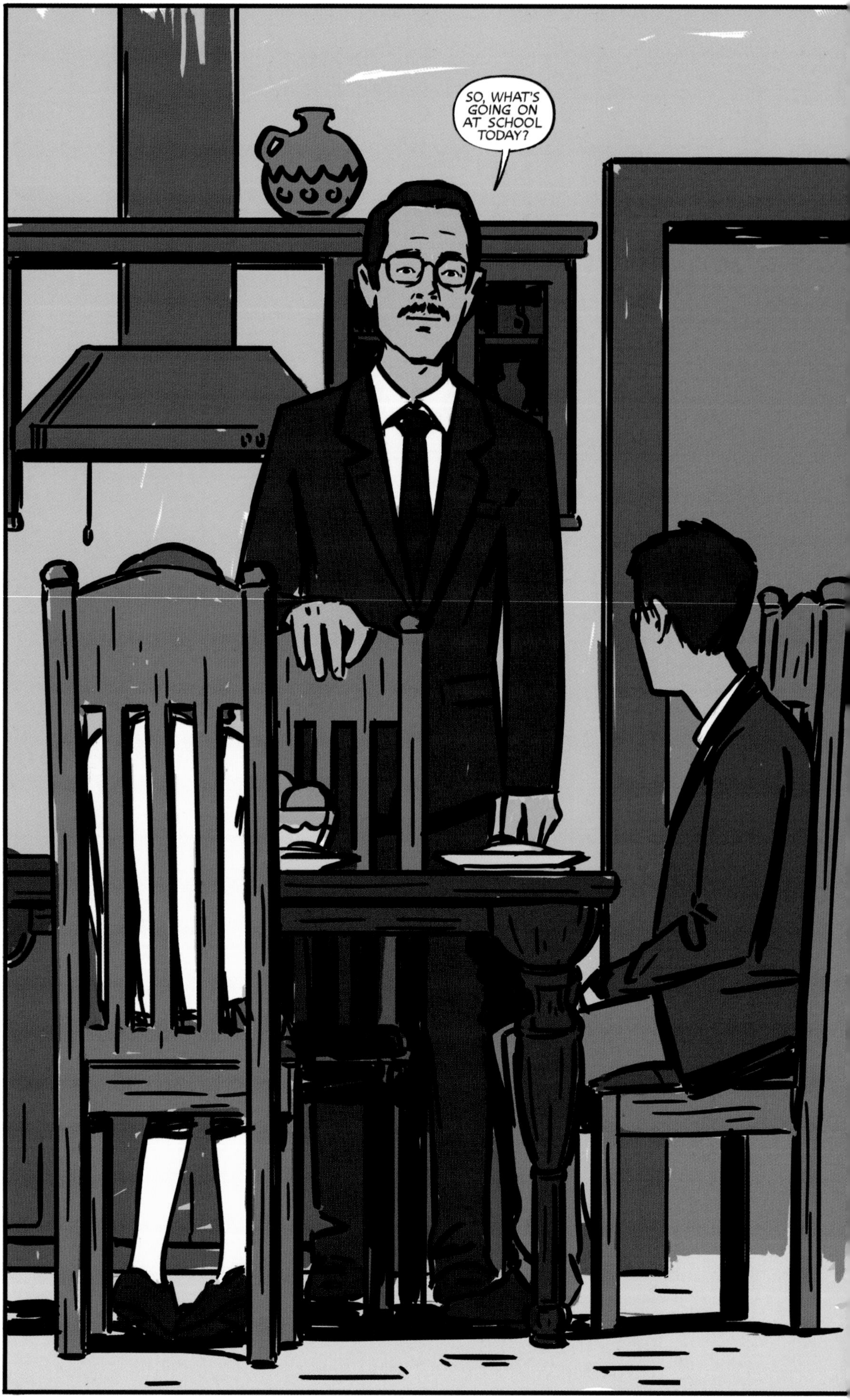
SO, WHAT'S GOING ON AT SCHOOL TODAY?

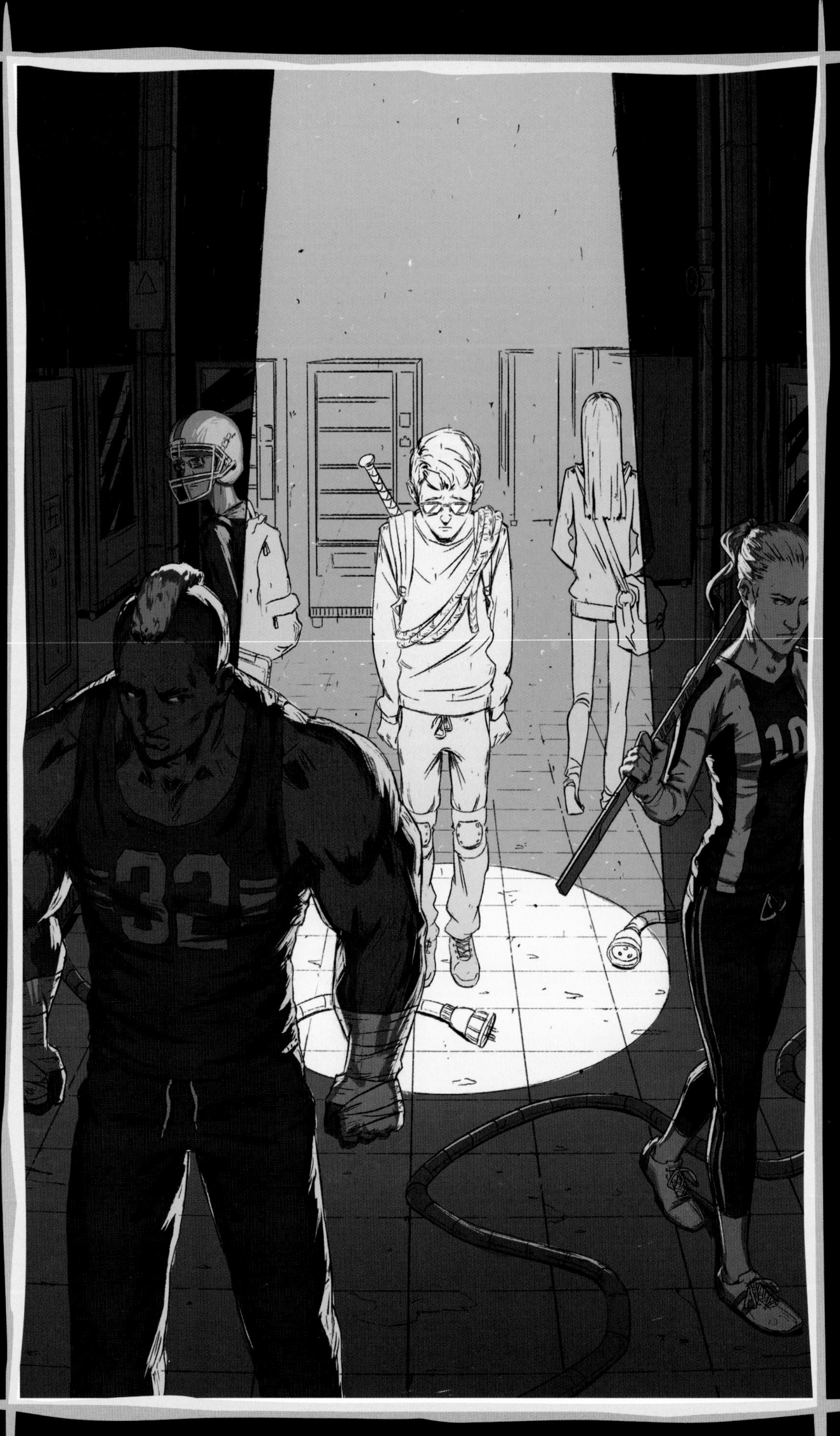

ART BY PIUS BAK

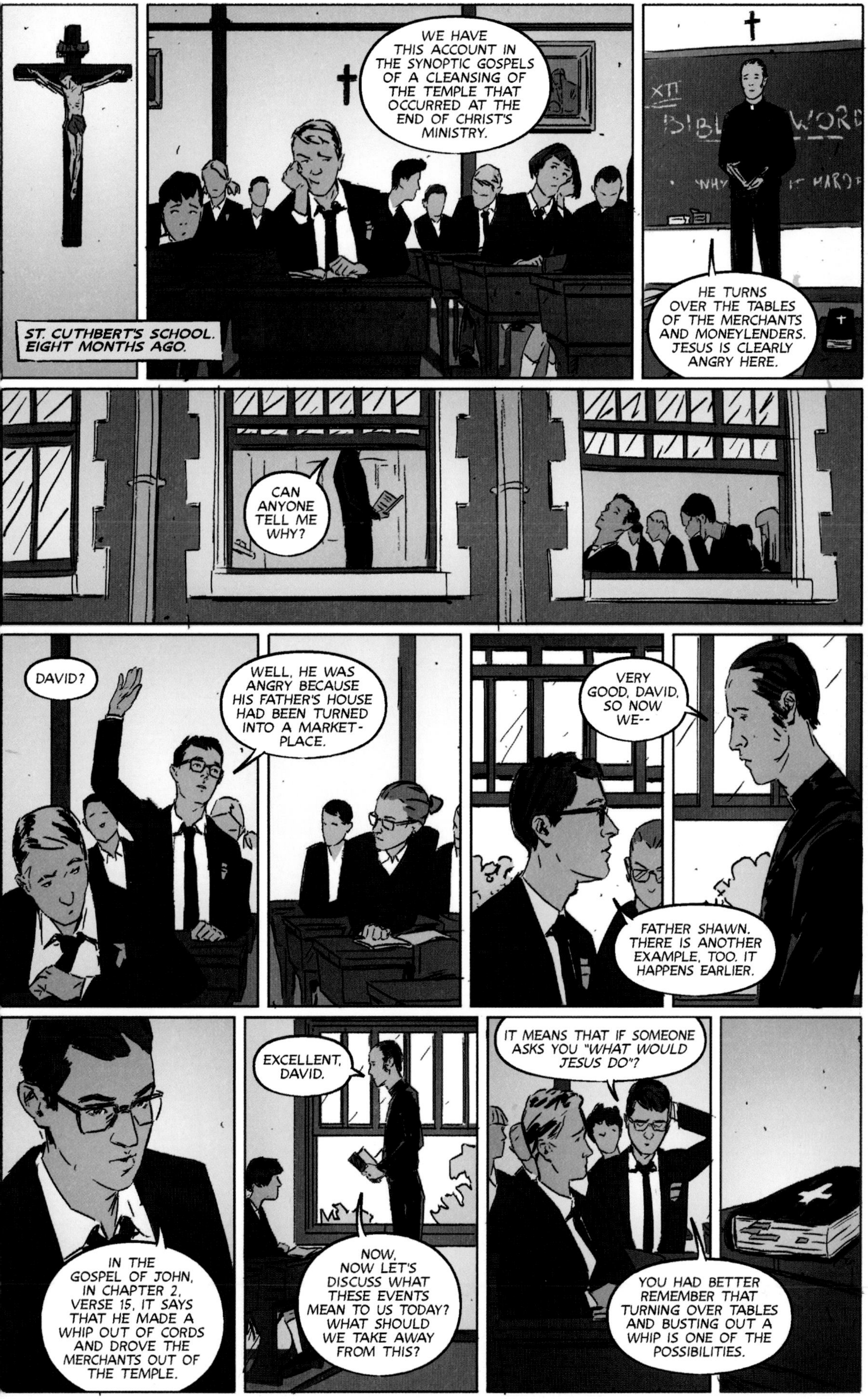
ST. CUTHBERT'S SCHOOL. EIGHT MONTHS AGO.
WE HAVE THIS ACCOUNT IN THE SYNOPTIC GOSPELS OF A CLEANSING OF THE TEMPLE THAT OCCURRED AT THE END OF CHRIST'S MINISTRY.
HE TURNS OVER THE TABLES OF THE MERCHANTS AND MONEYLENDERS. JESUS IS CLEARLY ANGRY HERE.
CAN ANYONE TELL ME WHY?
DAVID?
WELL, HE WAS ANGRY BECAUSE HIS FATHER'S HOUSE HAD BEEN TURNED INTO A MARKET-PLACE.
VERY GOOD, DAVID, SO NOW WE--
FATHER SHAWN. THERE IS ANOTHER EXAMPLE, TOO. IT HAPPENS EARLIER.
IN THE GOSPEL OF JOHN, IN CHAPTER 2, VERSE 15, IT SAYS THAT HE MADE A WHIP OUT OF CORDS AND DROVE THE MERCHANTS OUT OF THE TEMPLE.
EXCELLENT, DAVID.
NOW, NOW LET'S DISCUSS WHAT THESE EVENTS MEAN TO US TODAY? WHAT SHOULD WE TAKE AWAY FROM THIS?
IT MEANS THAT IF SOMEONE ASKS YOU "WHAT WOULD JESUS DO"?
YOU HAD BETTER REMEMBER THAT TURNING OVER TABLES AND BUSTING OUT A WHIP IS ONE OF THE POSSIBILITIES.

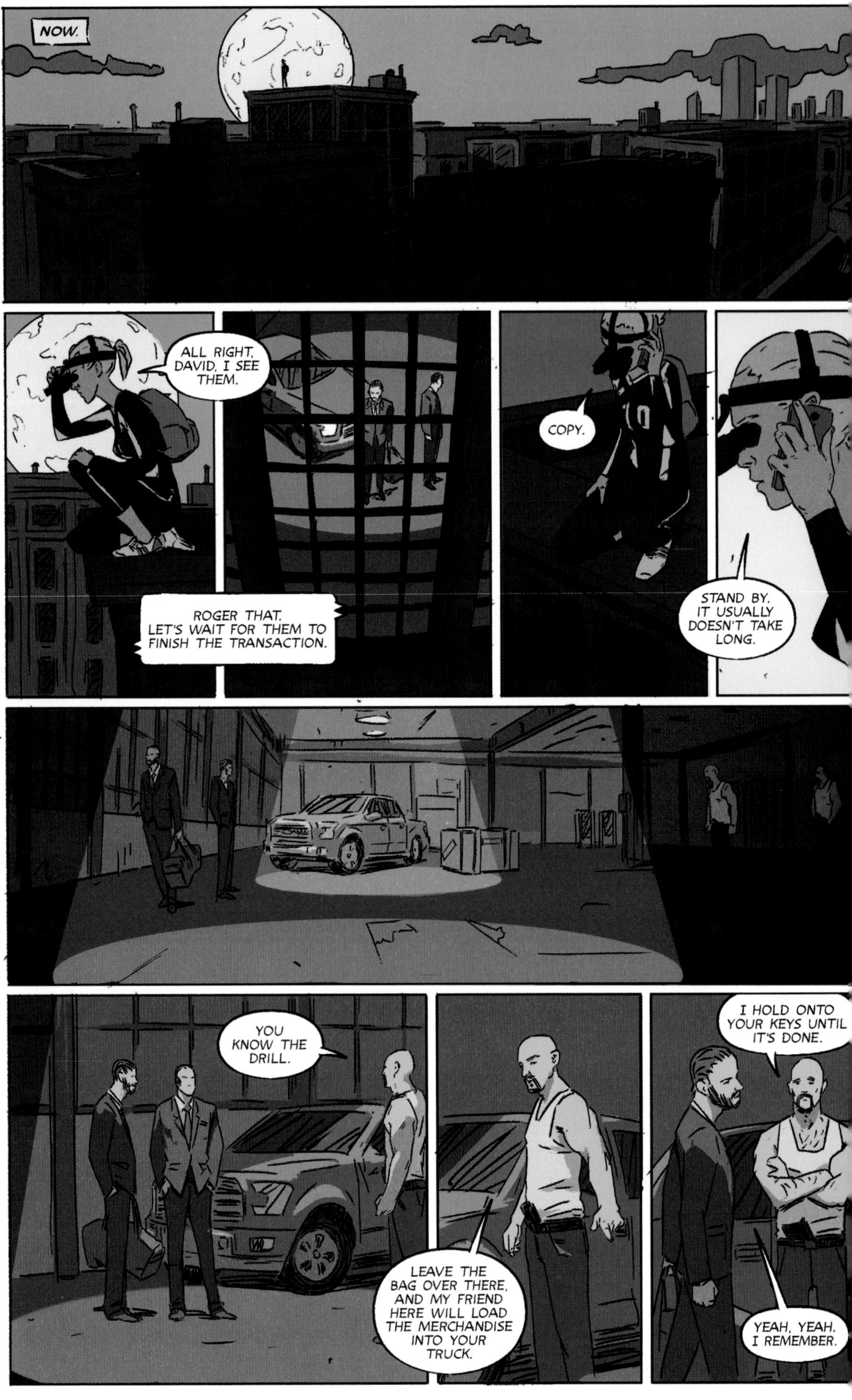
NOW.
ALL RIGHT, DAVID, I SEE THEM.
ROGER THAT. LET'S WAIT FOR THEM TO FINISH THE TRANSACTION.
COPY.
STAND BY. IT USUALLY DOESN'T TAKE LONG.
YOU KNOW THE DRILL.
LEAVE THE BAG OVER THERE, AND MY FRIEND HERE WILL LOAD THE MERCHANDISE INTO YOUR TRUCK.
I HOLD ONTO YOUR KEYS UNTIL IT'S DONE.
YEAH, YEAH. I REMEMBER.

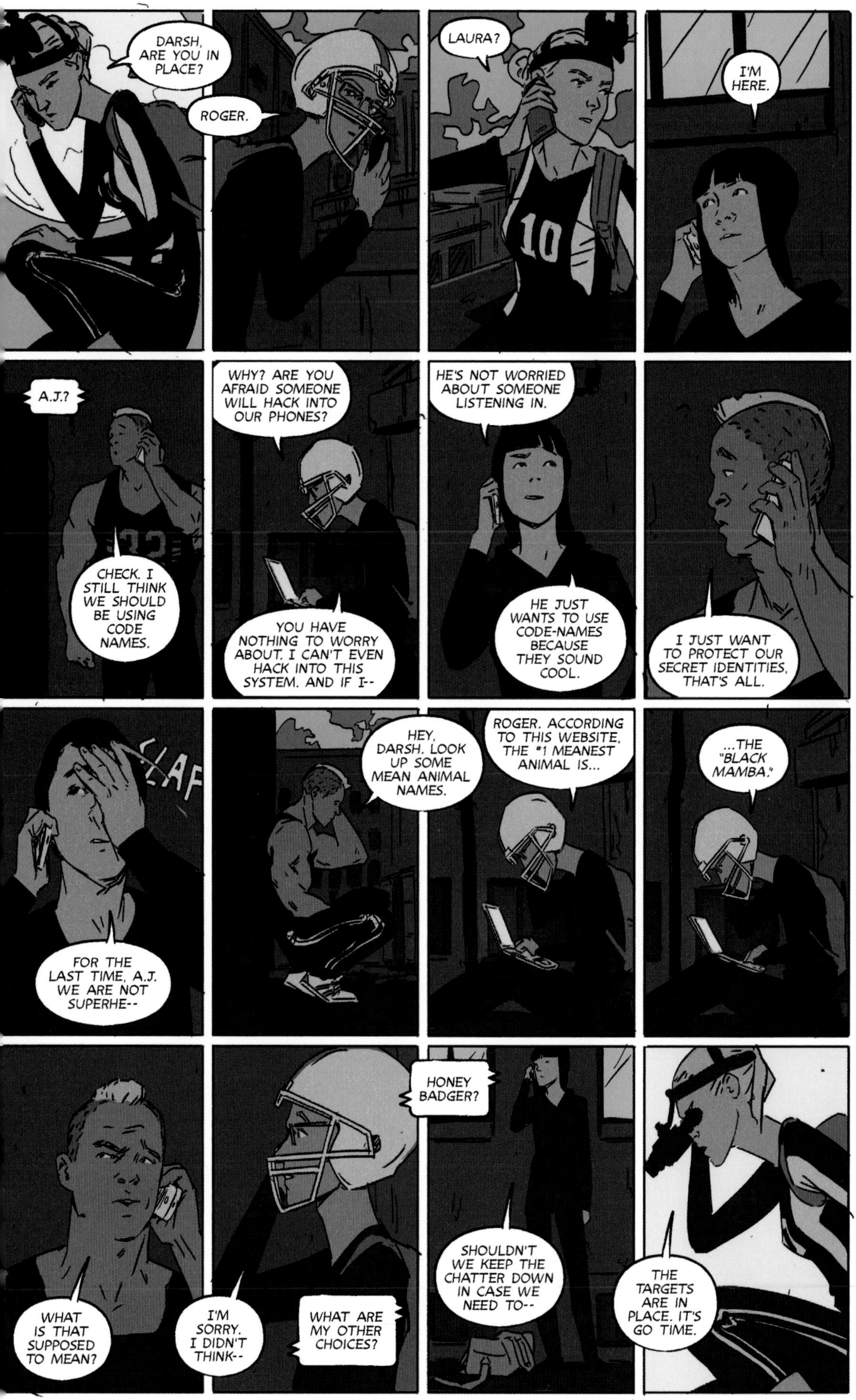
DARSH, ARE YOU IN PLACE?
ROGER.
LAURA?
I'M HERE.
A.J.?
CHECK. I STILL THINK WE SHOULD BE USING CODE NAMES.
WHY? ARE YOU AFRAID SOMEONE WILL HACK INTO OUR PHONES?
YOU HAVE NOTHING TO WORRY ABOUT. I CAN'T EVEN HACK INTO THIS SYSTEM. AND IF I--
HE'S NOT WORRIED ABOUT SOMEONE LISTENING IN.
HE JUST WANTS TO USE CODE-NAMES BECAUSE THEY SOUND COOL.
I JUST WANT TO PROTECT OUR SECRET IDENTITIES, THAT'S ALL.
SLAP
FOR THE LAST TIME, A.J. WE ARE NOT SUPERHE--
HEY, DARSH. LOOK UP SOME MEAN ANIMAL NAMES.
ROGER. ACCORDING TO THIS WEBSITE, THE #1 MEANEST ANIMAL IS...
...THE "BLACK MAMBA."
WHAT IS THAT SUPPOSED TO MEAN?
I'M SORRY. I DIDN'T THINK--
WHAT ARE MY OTHER CHOICES?
HONEY BADGER?
SHOULDN'T WE KEEP THE CHATTER DOWN IN CASE WE NEED TO--
THE TARGETS ARE IN PLACE. IT'S GO TIME.

OKAY, DARSH. KILL THE LIGHTS.

ROGER.

GO, LAURA.

DUKSH

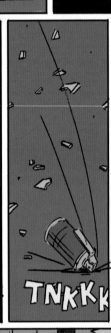

TNKKK

PFFF

GO, A.J.

COUGH COUGH

COUGH COUGH

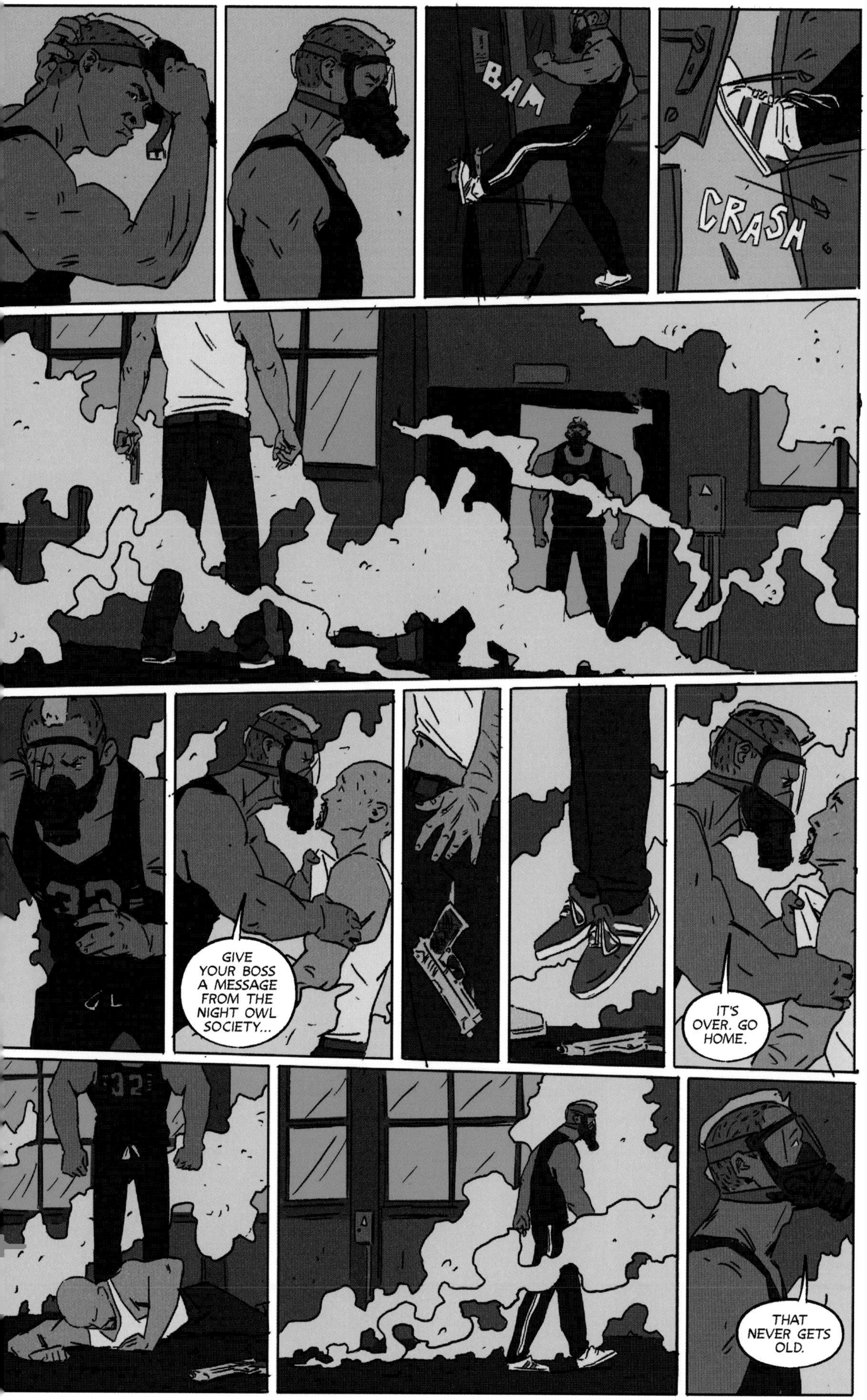
BAM
CRASH
GIVE YOUR BOSS A MESSAGE FROM THE NIGHT OWL SOCIETY...
IT'S OVER. GO HOME.
THAT NEVER GETS OLD.

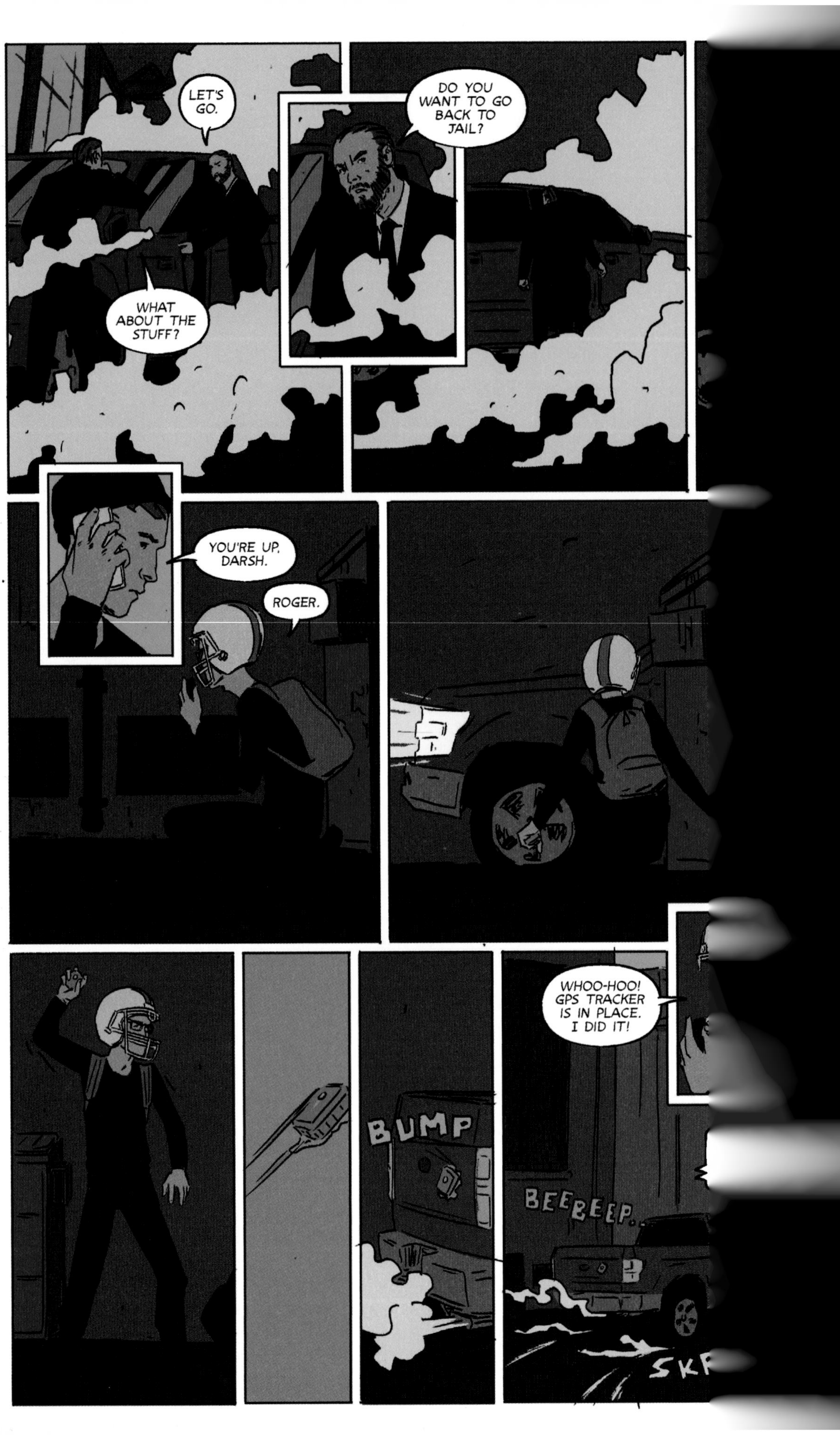
LET'S GO.
WHAT ABOUT THE STUFF?
DO YOU WANT TO GO BACK TO JAIL?
YOU'RE UP, DARSH.
ROGER.
BUMP
WHOO-HOO! GPS TRACKER IS IN PLACE. I DID IT!
BEEBEEP..

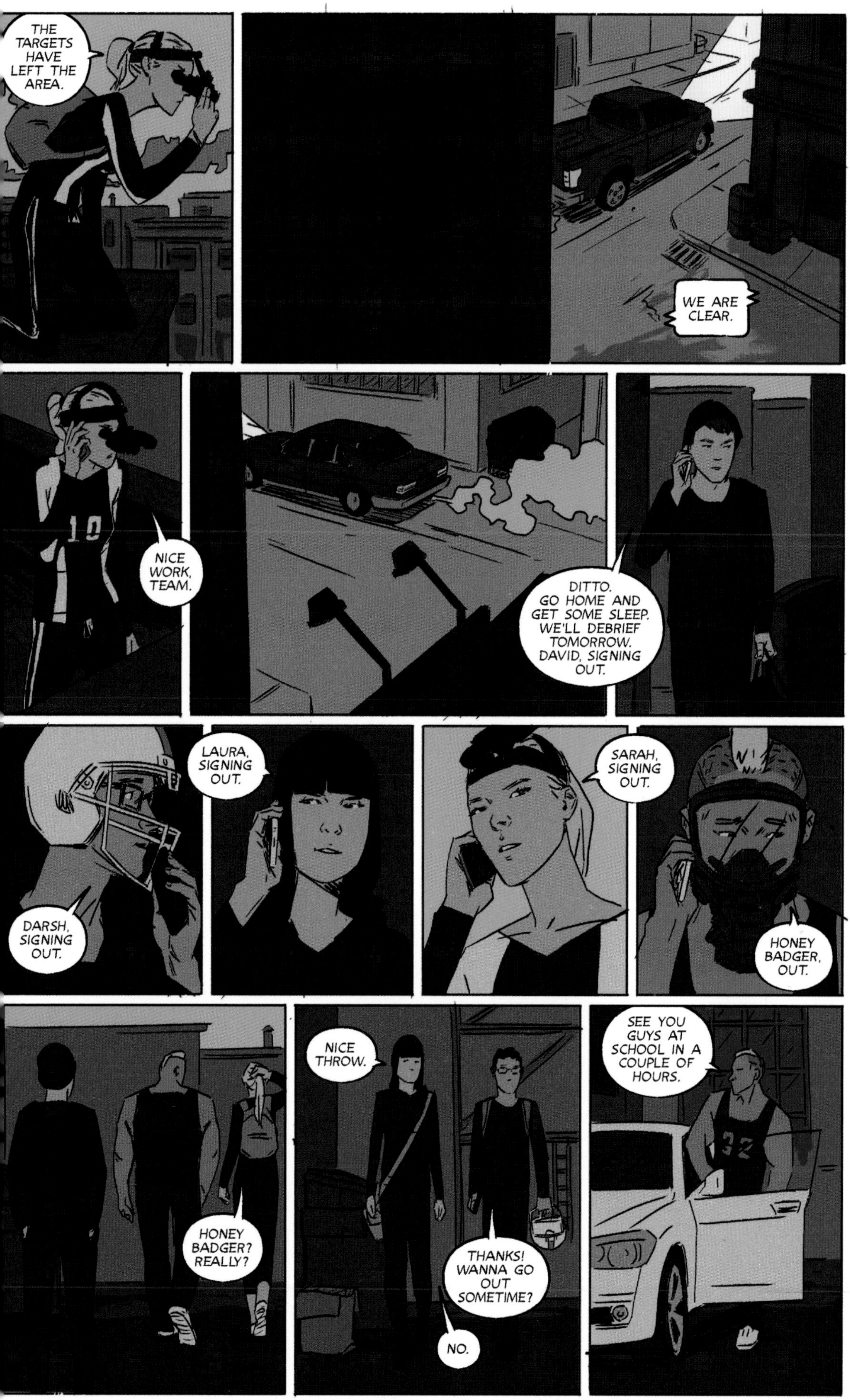
THE TARGETS HAVE LEFT THE AREA.
WE ARE CLEAR.
NICE WORK, TEAM.
DITTO. GO HOME AND GET SOME SLEEP. WE'LL DEBRIEF TOMORROW. DAVID, SIGNING OUT.
DARSH, SIGNING OUT.
LAURA, SIGNING OUT.
SARAH, SIGNING OUT.
HONEY BADGER, OUT.
HONEY BADGER? REALLY?
NICE THROW.
THANKS! WANNA GO OUT SOMETIME?
NO.
SEE YOU GUYS AT SCHOOL IN A COUPLE OF HOURS.

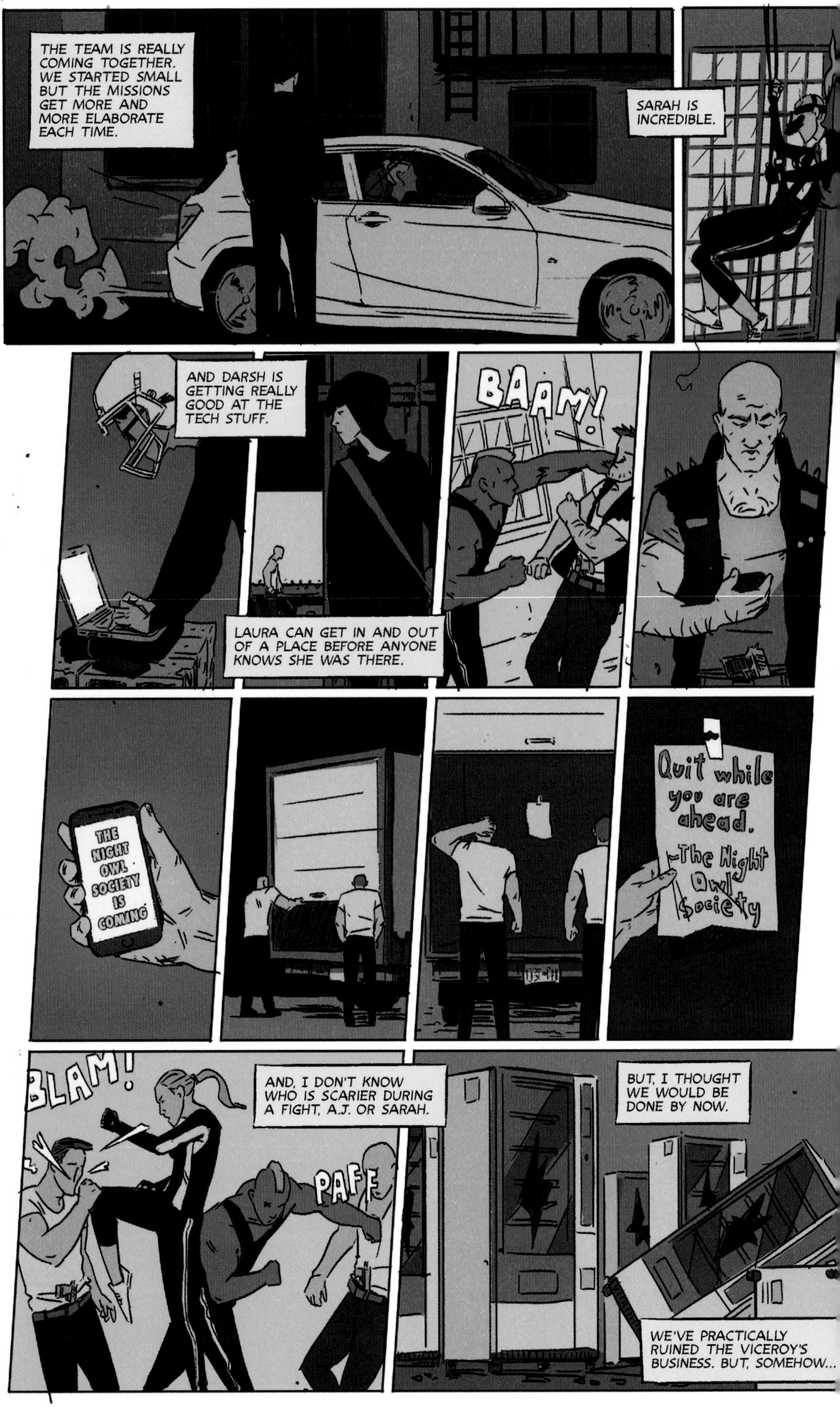
THE TEAM IS REALLY COMING TOGETHER. WE STARTED SMALL BUT THE MISSIONS GET MORE AND MORE ELABORATE EACH TIME.
SARAH IS INCREDIBLE.
AND DARSH IS GETTING REALLY GOOD AT THE TECH STUFF.
LAURA CAN GET IN AND OUT OF A PLACE BEFORE ANYONE KNOWS SHE WAS THERE.
BAAM!
THE NIGHT OWL SOCIETY IS COMING
Quit while you are ahead. -The Night Owl Society
BLAM!
AND, I DON'T KNOW WHO IS SCARIER DURING A FIGHT, A.J. OR SARAH.
PAFF
BUT, I THOUGHT WE WOULD BE DONE BY NOW.
WE'VE PRACTICALLY RUINED THE VICEROY'S BUSINESS. BUT, SOMEHOW...

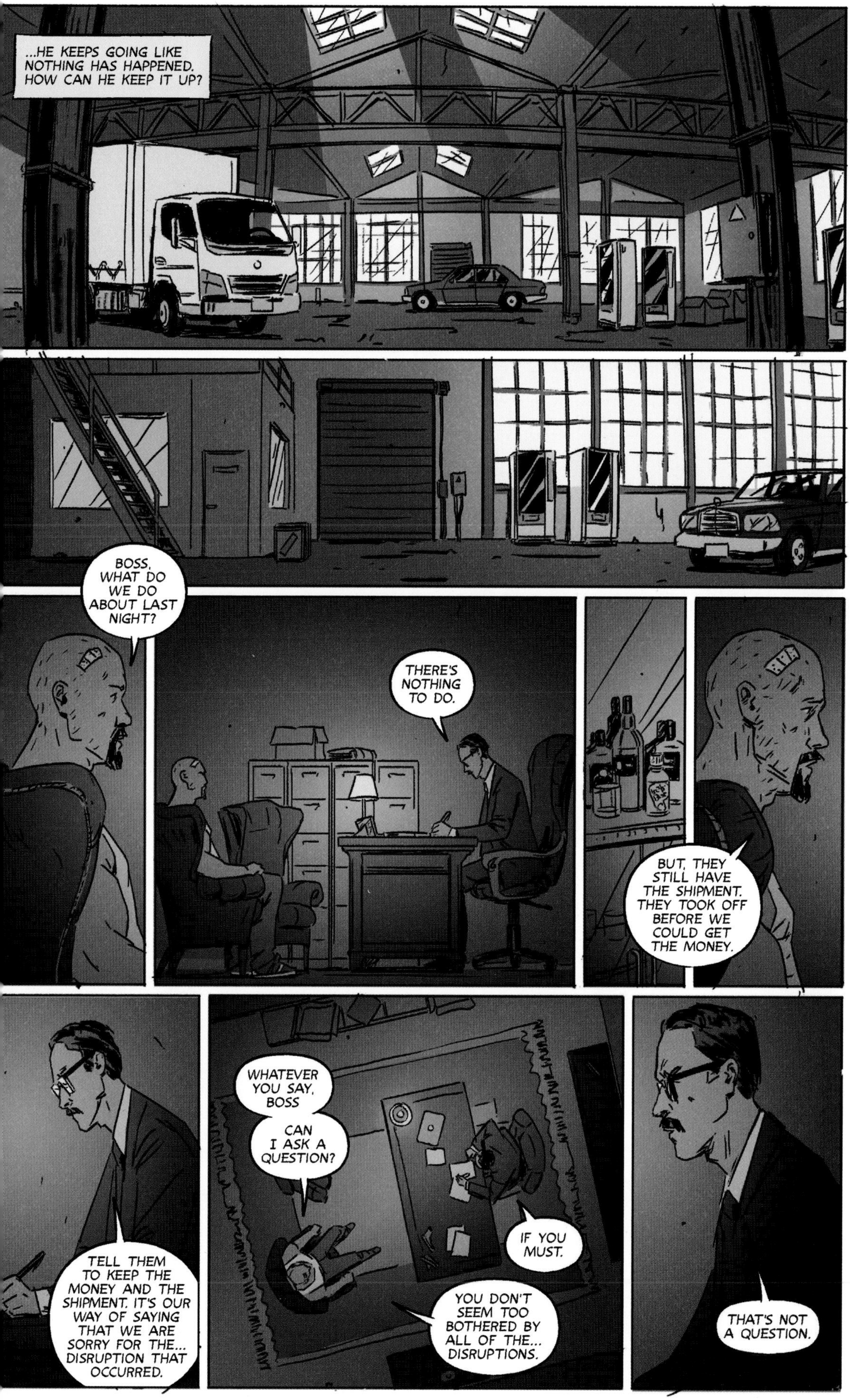
...HE KEEPS GOING LIKE NOTHING HAS HAPPENED. HOW CAN HE KEEP IT UP?
BOSS, WHAT DO WE DO ABOUT LAST NIGHT?
THERE'S NOTHING TO DO.
BUT, THEY STILL HAVE THE SHIPMENT. THEY TOOK OFF BEFORE WE COULD GET THE MONEY.
TELL THEM TO KEEP THE MONEY AND THE SHIPMENT. IT'S OUR WAY OF SAYING THAT WE ARE SORRY FOR THE... DISRUPTION THAT OCCURRED.
WHATEVER YOU SAY, BOSS
CAN I ASK A QUESTION?
IF YOU MUST.
YOU DON'T SEEM TOO BOTHERED BY ALL OF THE... DISRUPTIONS.
THAT'S NOT A QUESTION.

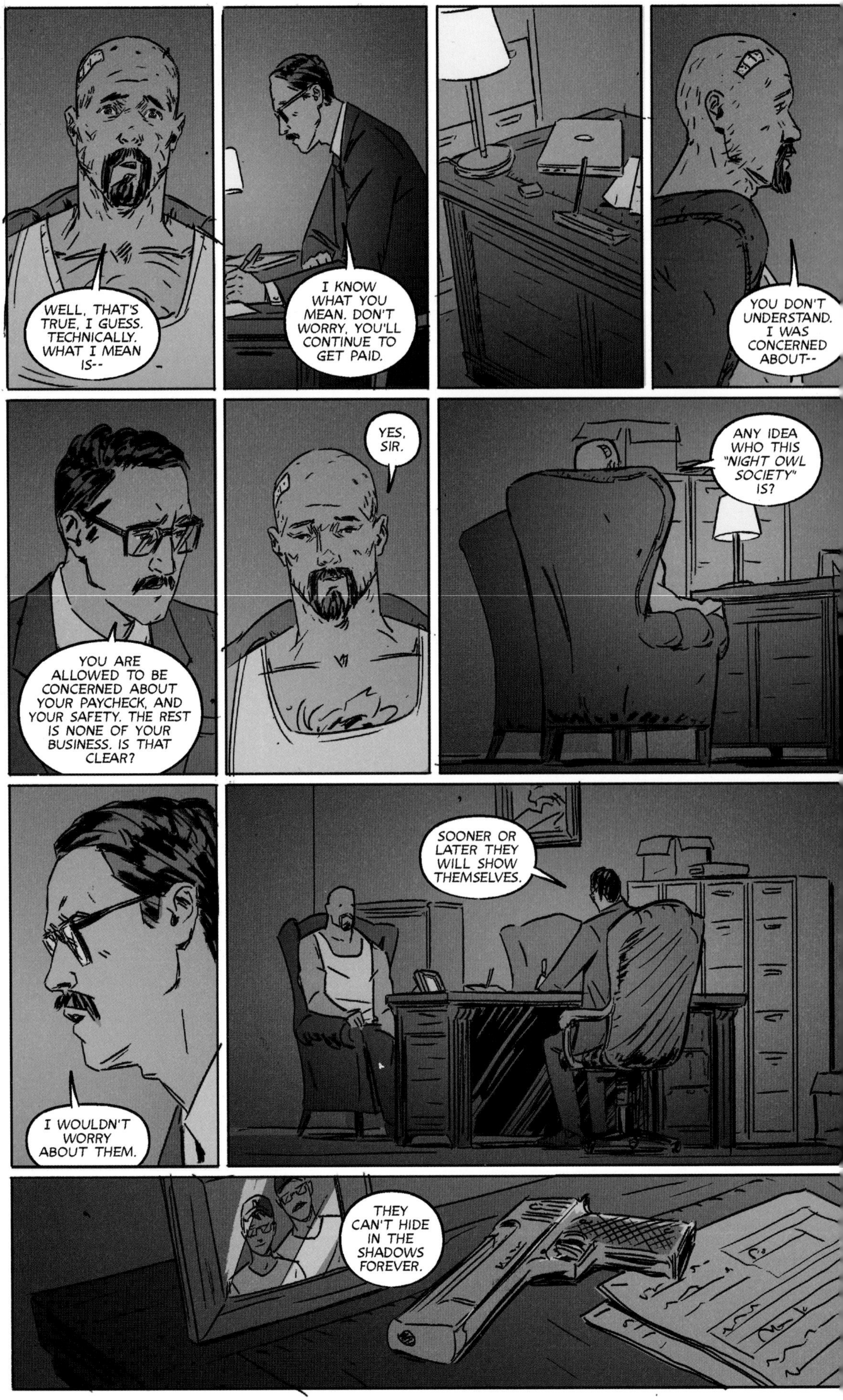
WELL, THAT'S TRUE, I GUESS. TECHNICALLY. WHAT I MEAN IS--
I KNOW WHAT YOU MEAN. DON'T WORRY, YOU'LL CONTINUE TO GET PAID.
YOU DON'T UNDERSTAND. I WAS CONCERNED ABOUT--
YOU ARE ALLOWED TO BE CONCERNED ABOUT YOUR PAYCHECK, AND YOUR SAFETY. THE REST IS NONE OF YOUR BUSINESS. IS THAT CLEAR?
YES, SIR.
ANY IDEA WHO THIS "NIGHT OWL SOCIETY" IS?
I WOULDN'T WORRY ABOUT THEM.
SOONER OR LATER THEY WILL SHOW THEMSELVES.
THEY CAN'T HIDE IN THE SHADOWS FOREVER.

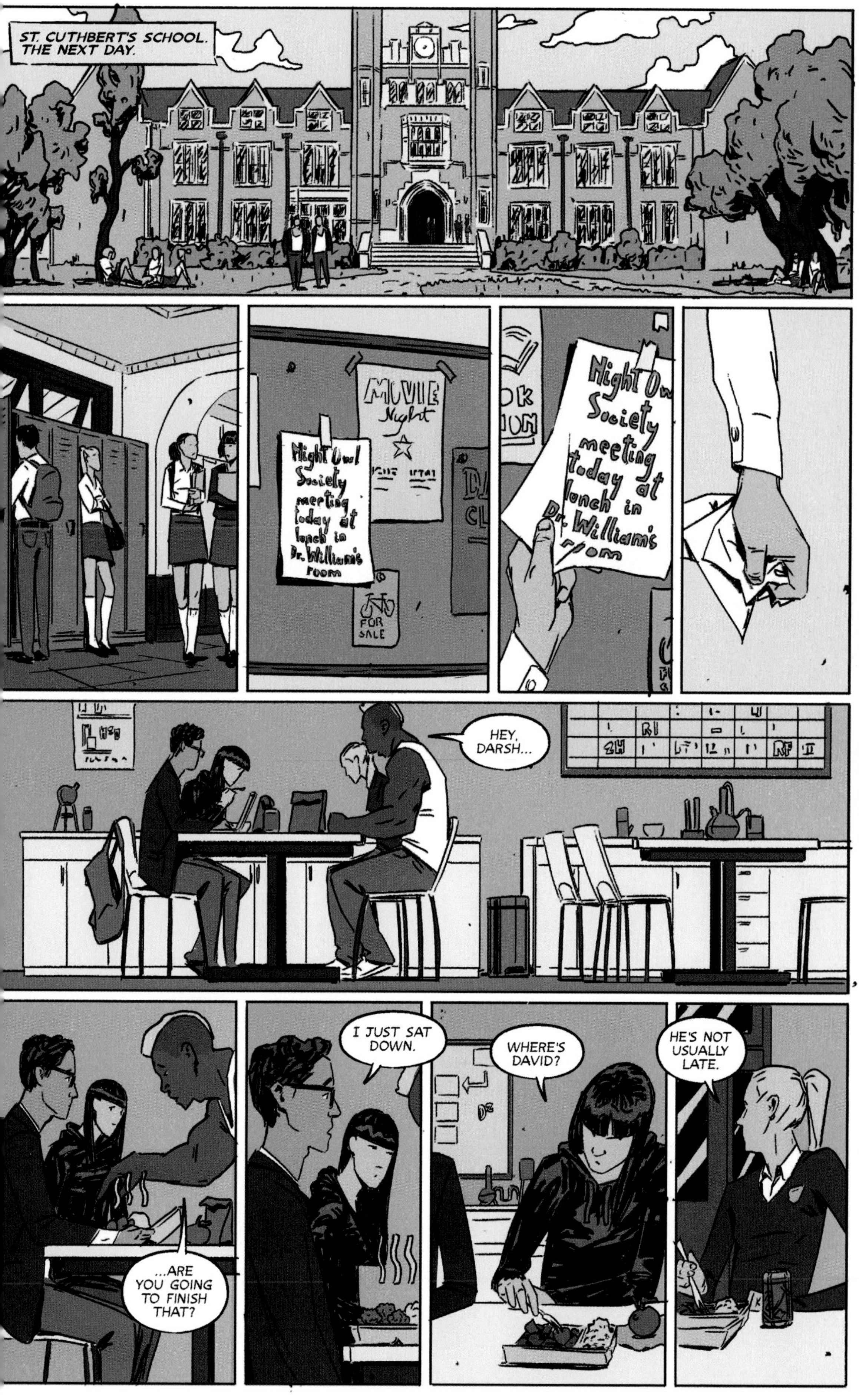

ST. CUTHBERT'S SCHOOL. THE NEXT DAY.
MOVIE Night
Night Owl Society meeting today at lunch in Dr. William's room
FOR SALE
Night Owl Society meeting today at lunch in Dr. William's room
HEY, DARSH...
...ARE YOU GOING TO FINISH THAT?
I JUST SAT DOWN.
WHERE'S DAVID?
HE'S NOT USUALLY LATE.

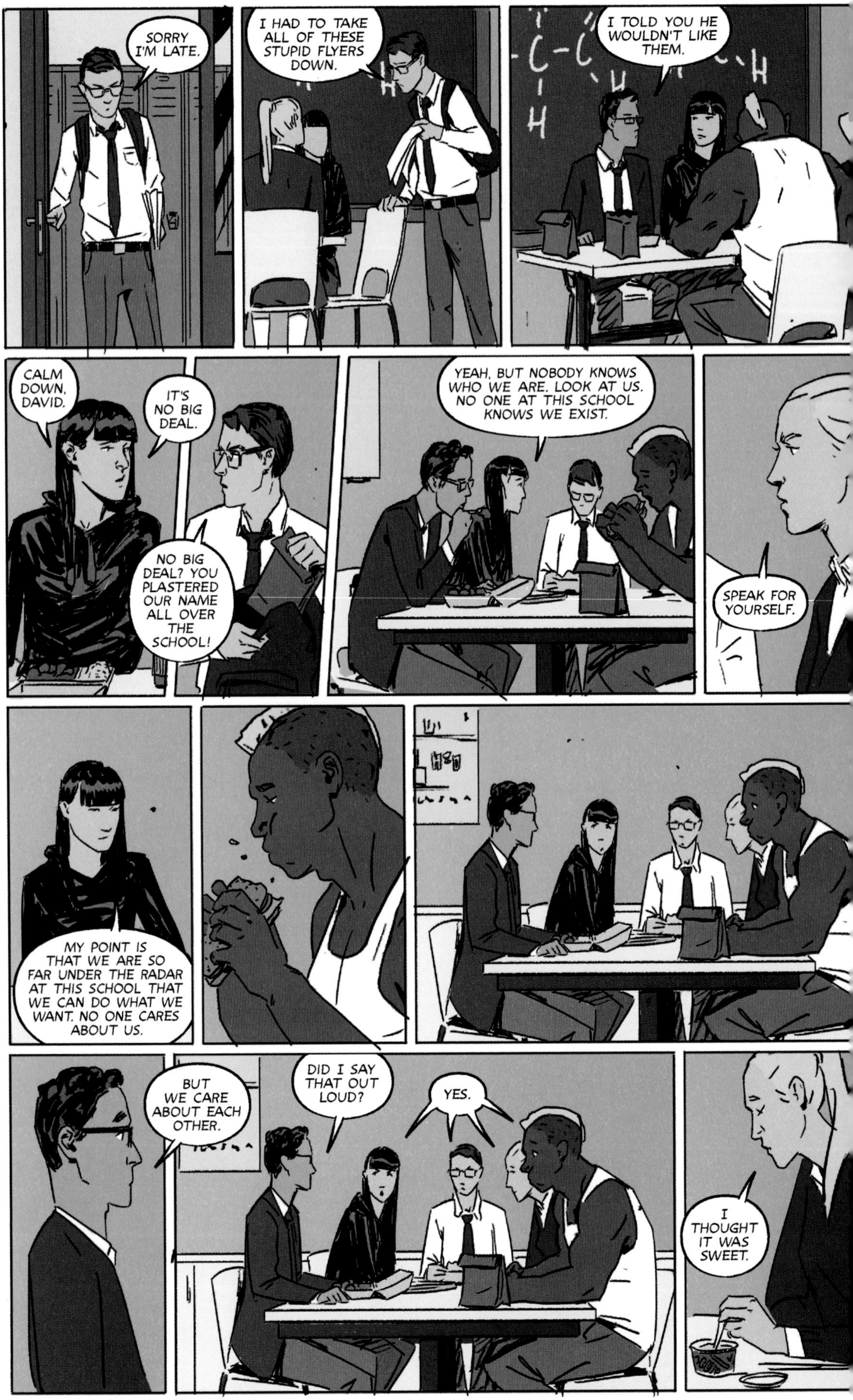
SORRY I'M LATE.
I HAD TO TAKE ALL OF THESE STUPID FLYERS DOWN.
I TOLD YOU HE WOULDN'T LIKE THEM.
CALM DOWN, DAVID.
IT'S NO BIG DEAL.
NO BIG DEAL? YOU PLASTERED OUR NAME ALL OVER THE SCHOOL!
YEAH, BUT NOBODY KNOWS WHO WE ARE. LOOK AT US. NO ONE AT THIS SCHOOL KNOWS WE EXIST.
SPEAK FOR YOURSELF.
MY POINT IS THAT WE ARE SO FAR UNDER THE RADAR AT THIS SCHOOL THAT WE CAN DO WHAT WE WANT. NO ONE CARES ABOUT US.
BUT WE CARE ABOUT EACH OTHER.
DID I SAY THAT OUT LOUD?
YES.
I THOUGHT IT WAS SWEET.

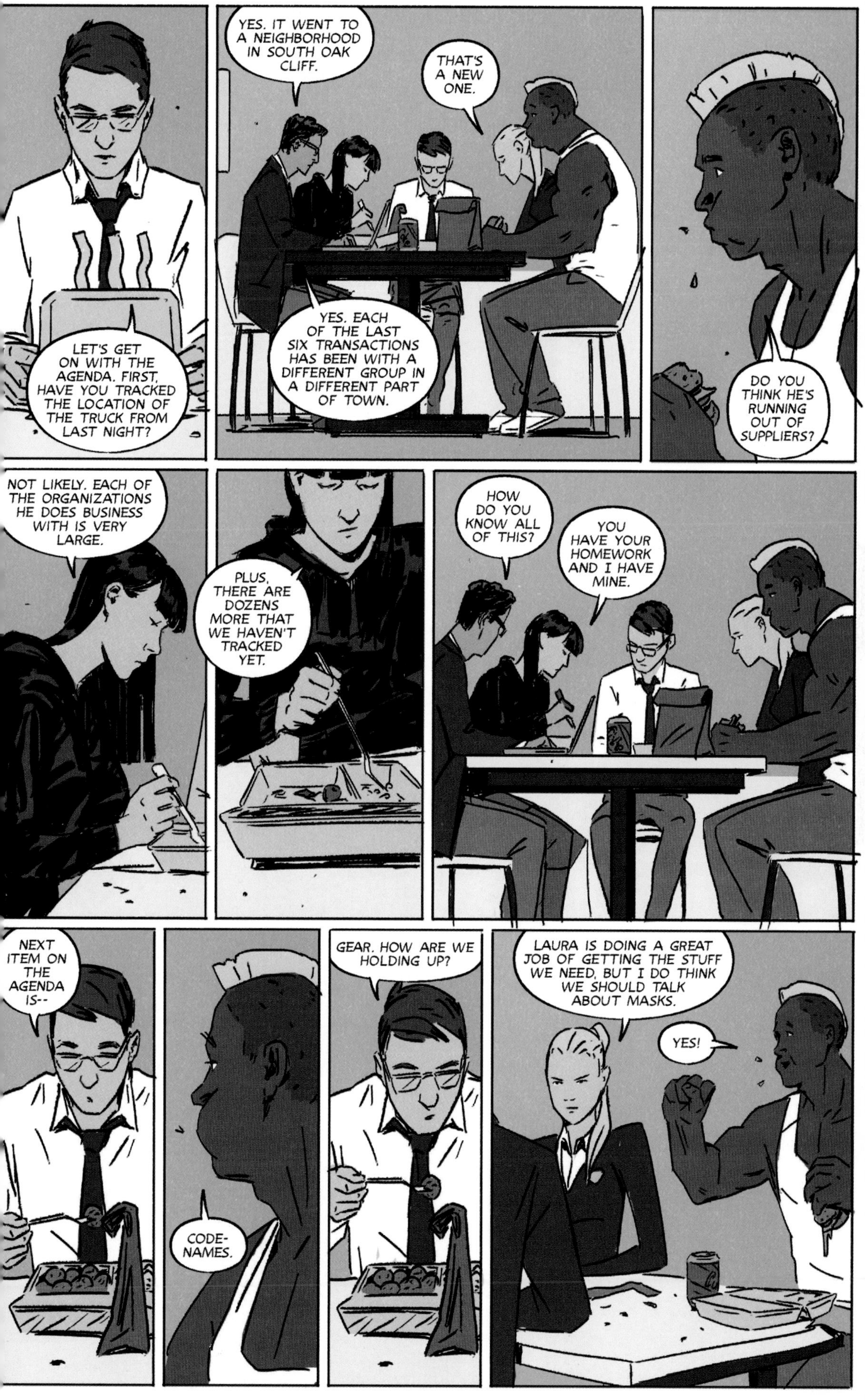
LET'S GET ON WITH THE AGENDA. FIRST, HAVE YOU TRACKED THE LOCATION OF THE TRUCK FROM LAST NIGHT?
YES. IT WENT TO A NEIGHBORHOOD IN SOUTH OAK CLIFF.
THAT'S A NEW ONE.
YES. EACH OF THE LAST SIX TRANSACTIONS HAS BEEN WITH A DIFFERENT GROUP IN A DIFFERENT PART OF TOWN.
DO YOU THINK HE'S RUNNING OUT OF SUPPLIERS?
NOT LIKELY. EACH OF THE ORGANIZATIONS HE DOES BUSINESS WITH IS VERY LARGE.
PLUS, THERE ARE DOZENS MORE THAT WE HAVEN'T TRACKED YET.
HOW DO YOU KNOW ALL OF THIS?
YOU HAVE YOUR HOMEWORK AND I HAVE MINE.
NEXT ITEM ON THE AGENDA IS--
CODE-NAMES.
GEAR. HOW ARE WE HOLDING UP?
LAURA IS DOING A GREAT JOB OF GETTING THE STUFF WE NEED, BUT I DO THINK WE SHOULD TALK ABOUT MASKS.
YES!

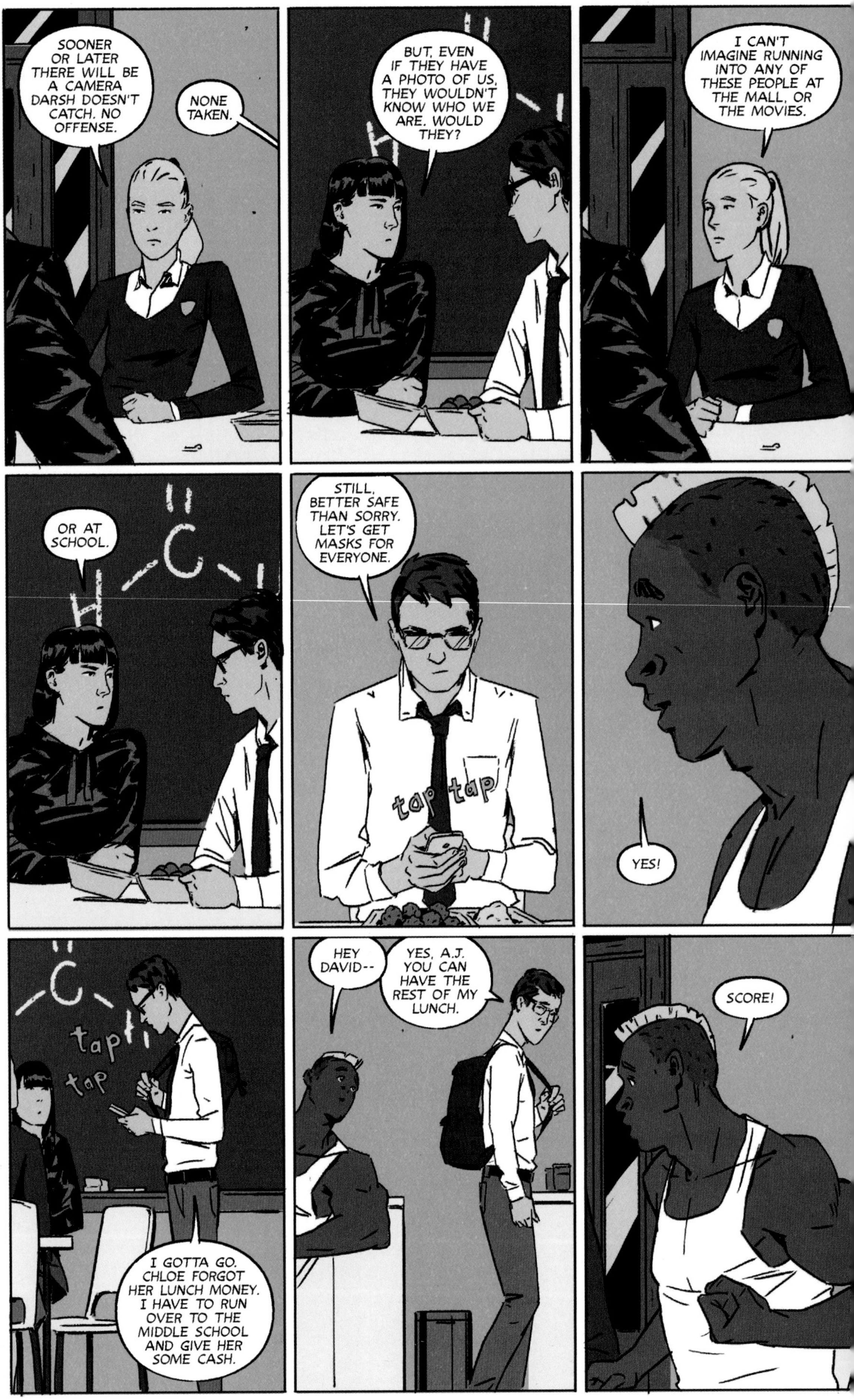
SOONER OR LATER THERE WILL BE A CAMERA DARSH DOESN'T CATCH. NO OFFENSE.
NONE TAKEN.
BUT, EVEN IF THEY HAVE A PHOTO OF US, THEY WOULDN'T KNOW WHO WE ARE. WOULD THEY?
I CAN'T IMAGINE RUNNING INTO ANY OF THESE PEOPLE AT THE MALL, OR THE MOVIES.
OR AT SCHOOL.
STILL, BETTER SAFE THAN SORRY. LET'S GET MASKS FOR EVERYONE.
tap tap
YES!
tap
tap
I GOTTA GO. CHLOE FORGOT HER LUNCH MONEY. I HAVE TO RUN OVER TO THE MIDDLE SCHOOL AND GIVE HER SOME CASH.
HEY DAVID--
YES, A.J. YOU CAN HAVE THE REST OF MY LUNCH.
SCORE!

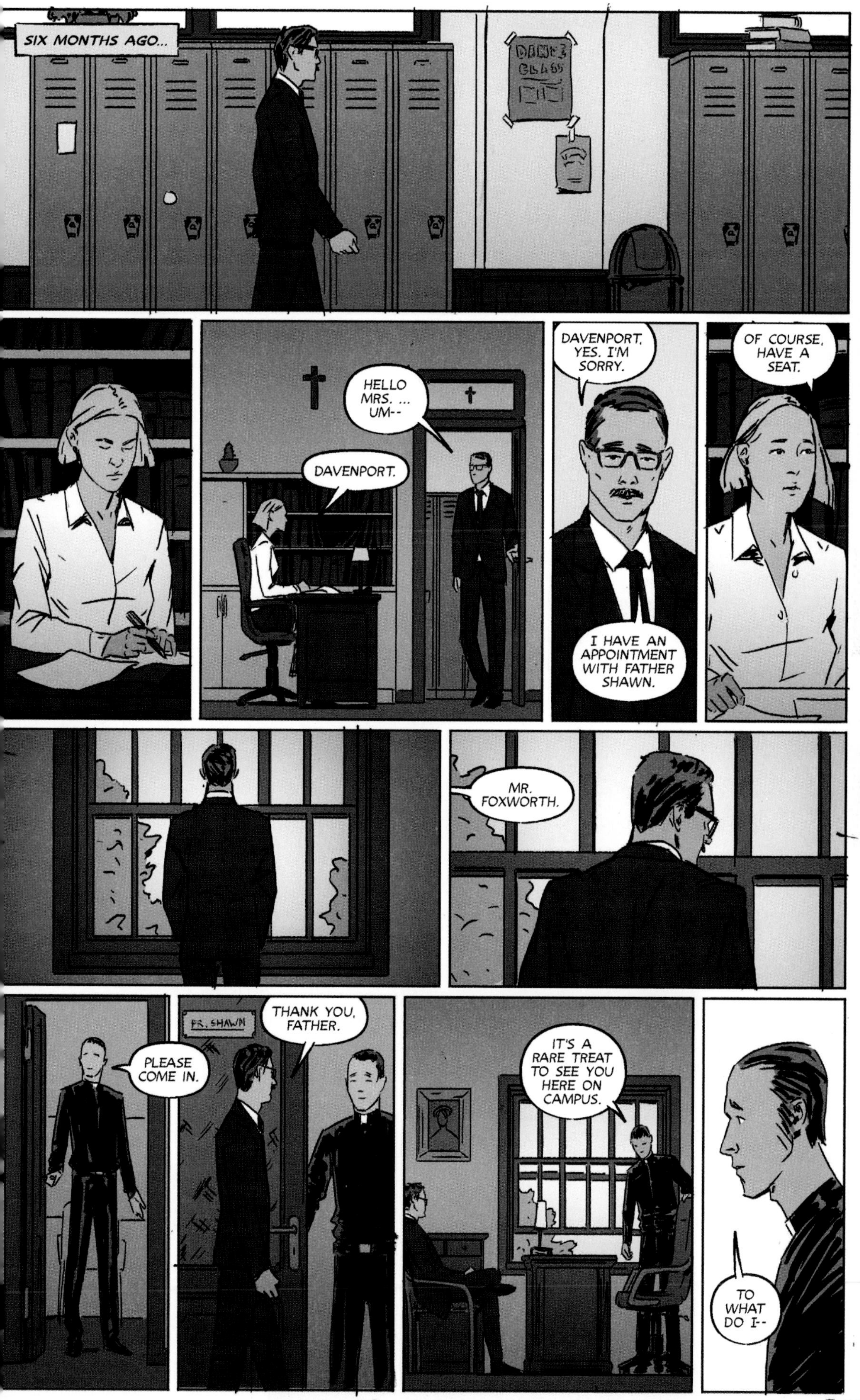
SIX MONTHS AGO...
DANCE CLASS
HELLO MRS. ... UM--
DAVENPORT.
DAVENPORT, YES. I'M SORRY.
I HAVE AN APPOINTMENT WITH FATHER SHAWN.
OF COURSE, HAVE A SEAT.
MR. FOXWORTH.
PLEASE COME IN.
FR. SHAWN
THANK YOU, FATHER.
IT'S A RARE TREAT TO SEE YOU HERE ON CAMPUS.
TO WHAT DO I--

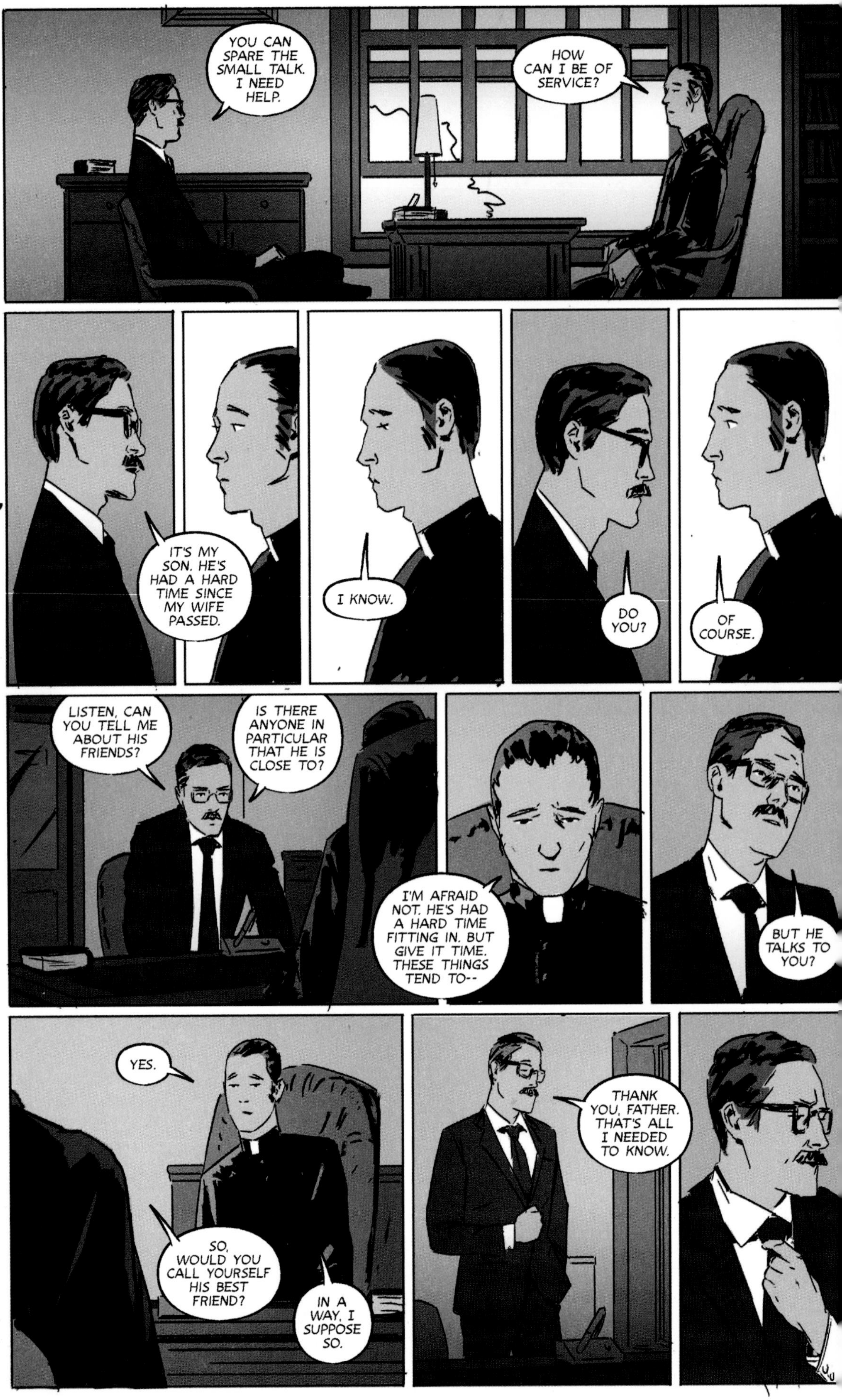
YOU CAN SPARE THE SMALL TALK. I NEED HELP.
HOW CAN I BE OF SERVICE?
IT'S MY SON. HE'S HAD A HARD TIME SINCE MY WIFE PASSED.
I KNOW.
DO YOU?
OF COURSE.
LISTEN, CAN YOU TELL ME ABOUT HIS FRIENDS?
IS THERE ANYONE IN PARTICULAR THAT HE IS CLOSE TO?
I'M AFRAID NOT. HE'S HAD A HARD TIME FITTING IN. BUT GIVE IT TIME. THESE THINGS TEND TO--
BUT HE TALKS TO YOU?
YES.
SO, WOULD YOU CALL YOURSELF HIS BEST FRIEND?
IN A WAY, I SUPPOSE SO.
THANK YOU, FATHER. THAT'S ALL I NEEDED TO KNOW.

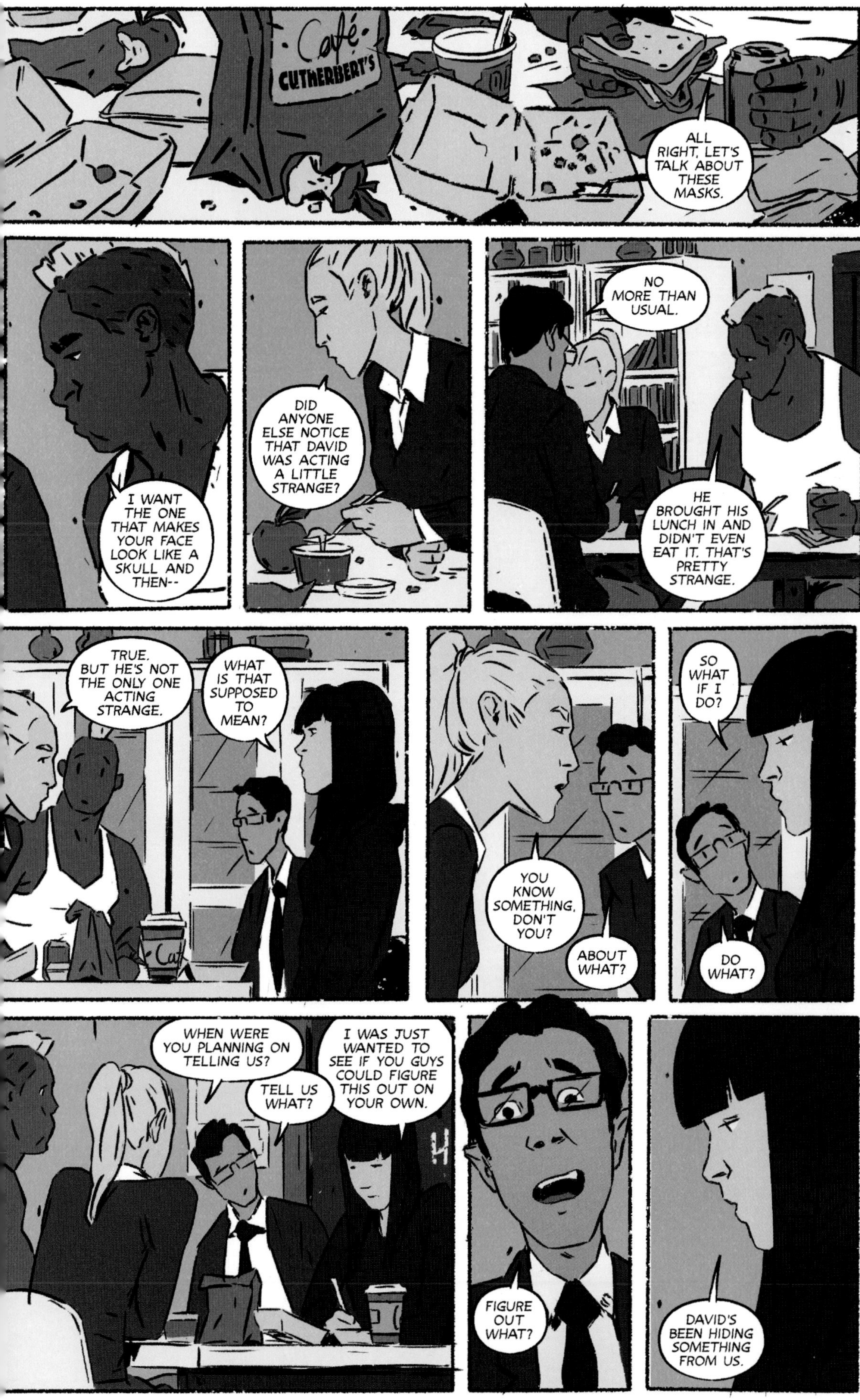
Café CUTHERBERT'S
ALL RIGHT, LET'S TALK ABOUT THESE MASKS.
I WANT THE ONE THAT MAKES YOUR FACE LOOK LIKE A SKULL AND THEN--
DID ANYONE ELSE NOTICE THAT DAVID WAS ACTING A LITTLE STRANGE?
NO MORE THAN USUAL.
HE BROUGHT HIS LUNCH IN AND DIDN'T EVEN EAT IT. THAT'S PRETTY STRANGE.
TRUE. BUT HE'S NOT THE ONLY ONE ACTING STRANGE.
WHAT IS THAT SUPPOSED TO MEAN?
YOU KNOW SOMETHING, DON'T YOU?
ABOUT WHAT?
SO WHAT IF I DO?
DO WHAT?
WHEN WERE YOU PLANNING ON TELLING US?
TELL US WHAT?
I WAS JUST WANTED TO SEE IF YOU GUYS COULD FIGURE THIS OUT ON YOUR OWN.
FIGURE OUT WHAT?
DAVID'S BEEN HIDING SOMETHING FROM US.

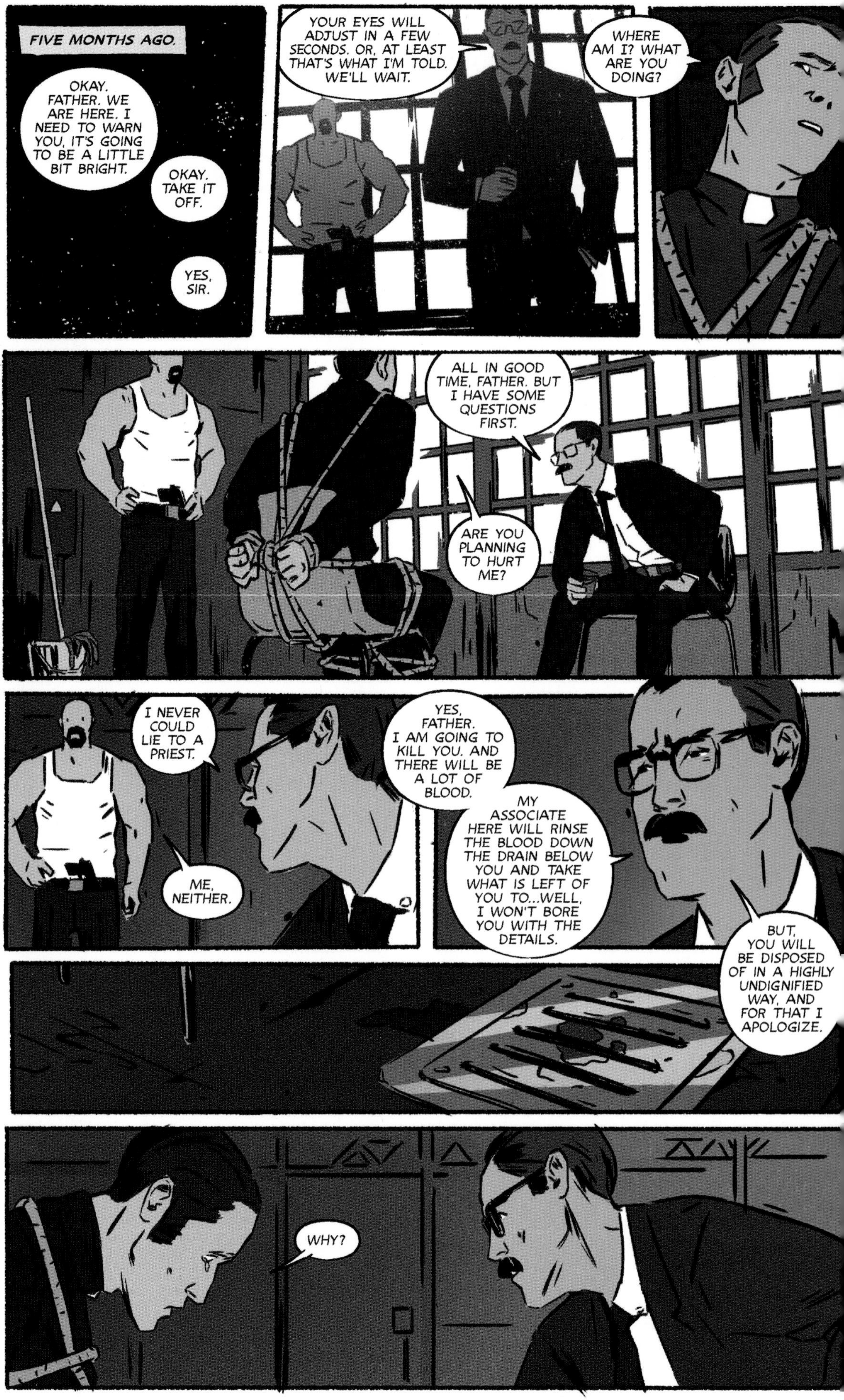
FIVE MONTHS AGO.
OKAY. FATHER. WE ARE HERE. I NEED TO WARN YOU, IT'S GOING TO BE A LITTLE BIT BRIGHT.
OKAY. TAKE IT OFF.
YES, SIR.
YOUR EYES WILL ADJUST IN A FEW SECONDS. OR, AT LEAST THAT'S WHAT I'M TOLD. WE'LL WAIT.
WHERE AM I? WHAT ARE YOU DOING?
ALL IN GOOD TIME, FATHER. BUT I HAVE SOME QUESTIONS FIRST.
ARE YOU PLANNING TO HURT ME?
I NEVER COULD LIE TO A PRIEST.
ME, NEITHER.
YES, FATHER. I AM GOING TO KILL YOU. AND THERE WILL BE A LOT OF BLOOD.
MY ASSOCIATE HERE WILL RINSE THE BLOOD DOWN THE DRAIN BELOW YOU AND TAKE WHAT IS LEFT OF YOU TO...WELL, I WON'T BORE YOU WITH THE DETAILS.
BUT, YOU WILL BE DISPOSED OF IN A HIGHLY UNDIGNIFIED WAY, AND FOR THAT I APOLOGIZE.
WHY?

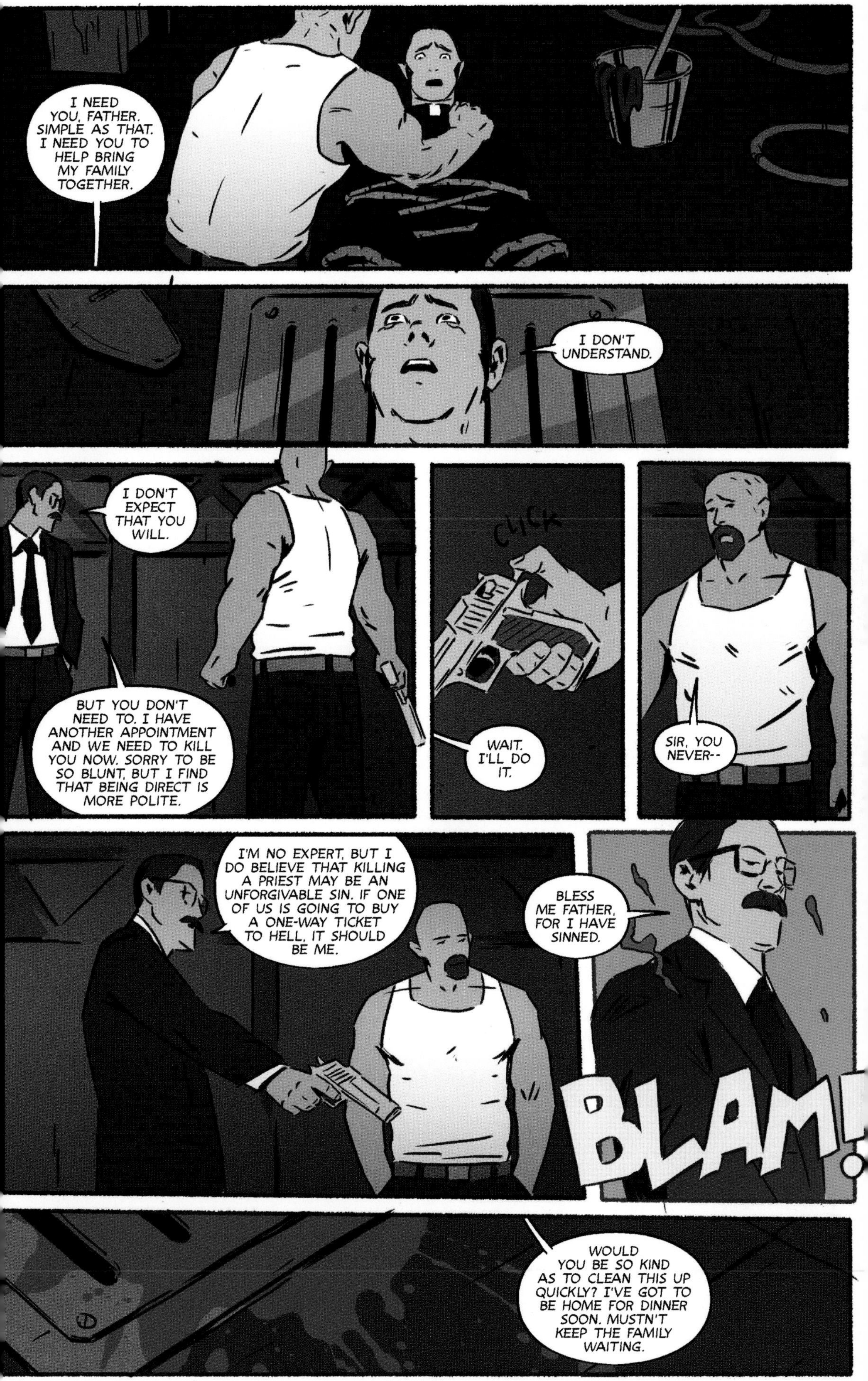
I NEED YOU, FATHER. SIMPLE AS THAT. I NEED YOU TO HELP BRING MY FAMILY TOGETHER.
I DON'T UNDERSTAND.
I DON'T EXPECT THAT YOU WILL.
BUT YOU DON'T NEED TO. I HAVE ANOTHER APPOINTMENT AND WE NEED TO KILL YOU NOW. SORRY TO BE SO BLUNT, BUT I FIND THAT BEING DIRECT IS MORE POLITE.
CLICK
WAIT. I'LL DO IT.
SIR, YOU NEVER--
I'M NO EXPERT, BUT I DO BELIEVE THAT KILLING A PRIEST MAY BE AN UNFORGIVABLE SIN. IF ONE OF US IS GOING TO BUY A ONE-WAY TICKET TO HELL, IT SHOULD BE ME.
BLESS ME FATHER, FOR I HAVE SINNED.
BLAM!
WOULD YOU BE SO KIND AS TO CLEAN THIS UP QUICKLY? I'VE GOT TO BE HOME FOR DINNER SOON. MUSTN'T KEEP THE FAMILY WAITING.

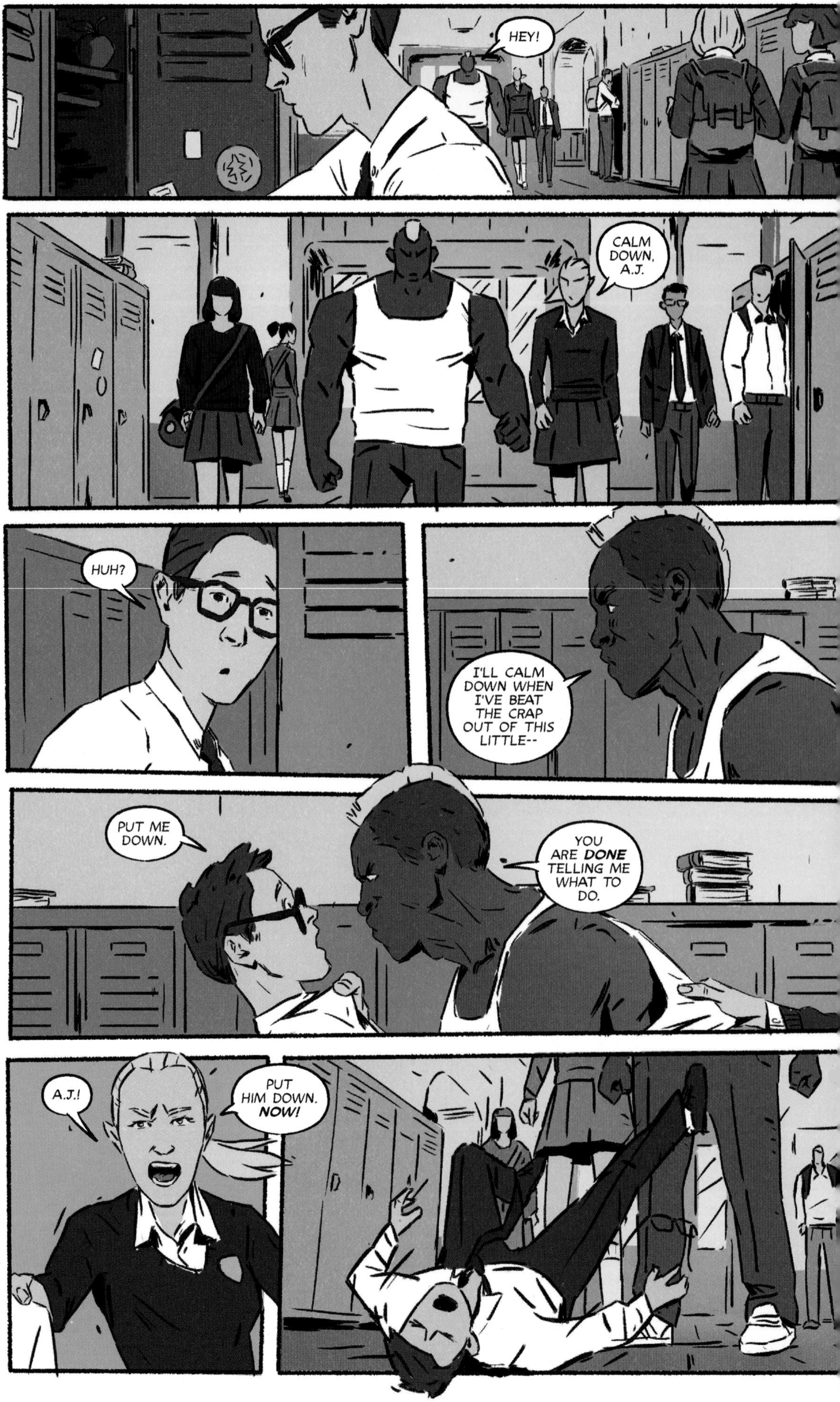
HEY!
CALM DOWN, A.J.
HUH?
I'LL CALM DOWN WHEN I'VE BEAT THE CRAP OUT OF THIS LITTLE--
PUT ME DOWN.
YOU ARE **DONE** TELLING ME WHAT TO DO.
A.J.!
PUT HIM DOWN. ***NOW!***

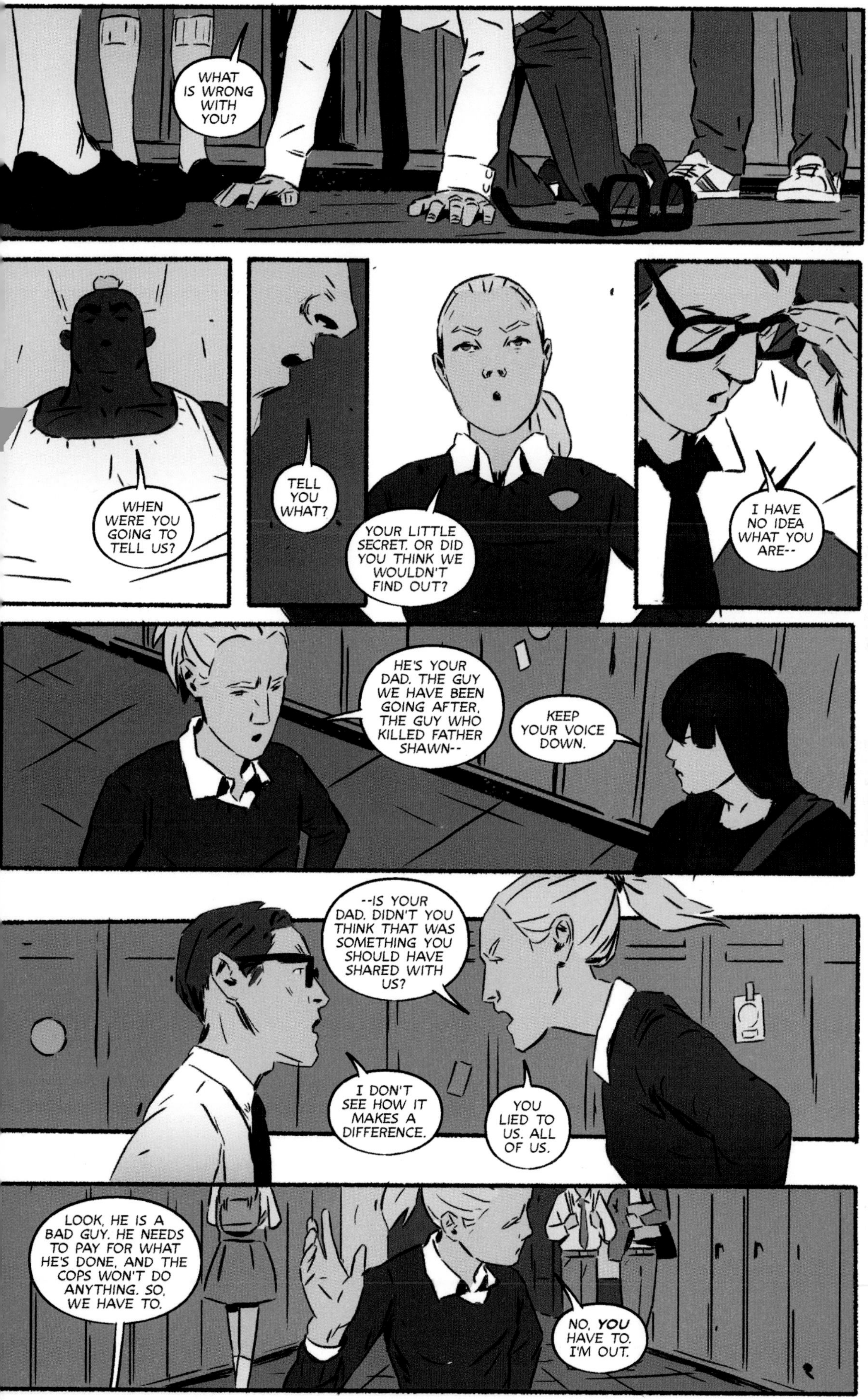
WHAT IS WRONG WITH YOU?
WHEN WERE YOU GOING TO TELL US?
TELL YOU WHAT?
YOUR LITTLE SECRET. OR DID YOU THINK WE WOULDN'T FIND OUT?
I HAVE NO IDEA WHAT YOU ARE--
HE'S YOUR DAD. THE GUY WE HAVE BEEN GOING AFTER, THE GUY WHO KILLED FATHER SHAWN--
KEEP YOUR VOICE DOWN.
--IS YOUR DAD. DIDN'T YOU THINK THAT WAS SOMETHING YOU SHOULD HAVE SHARED WITH US?
I DON'T SEE HOW IT MAKES A DIFFERENCE.
YOU LIED TO US. ALL OF US.
LOOK, HE IS A BAD GUY. HE NEEDS TO PAY FOR WHAT HE'S DONE, AND THE COPS WON'T DO ANYTHING. SO, WE HAVE TO.
NO, YOU HAVE TO. I'M OUT.

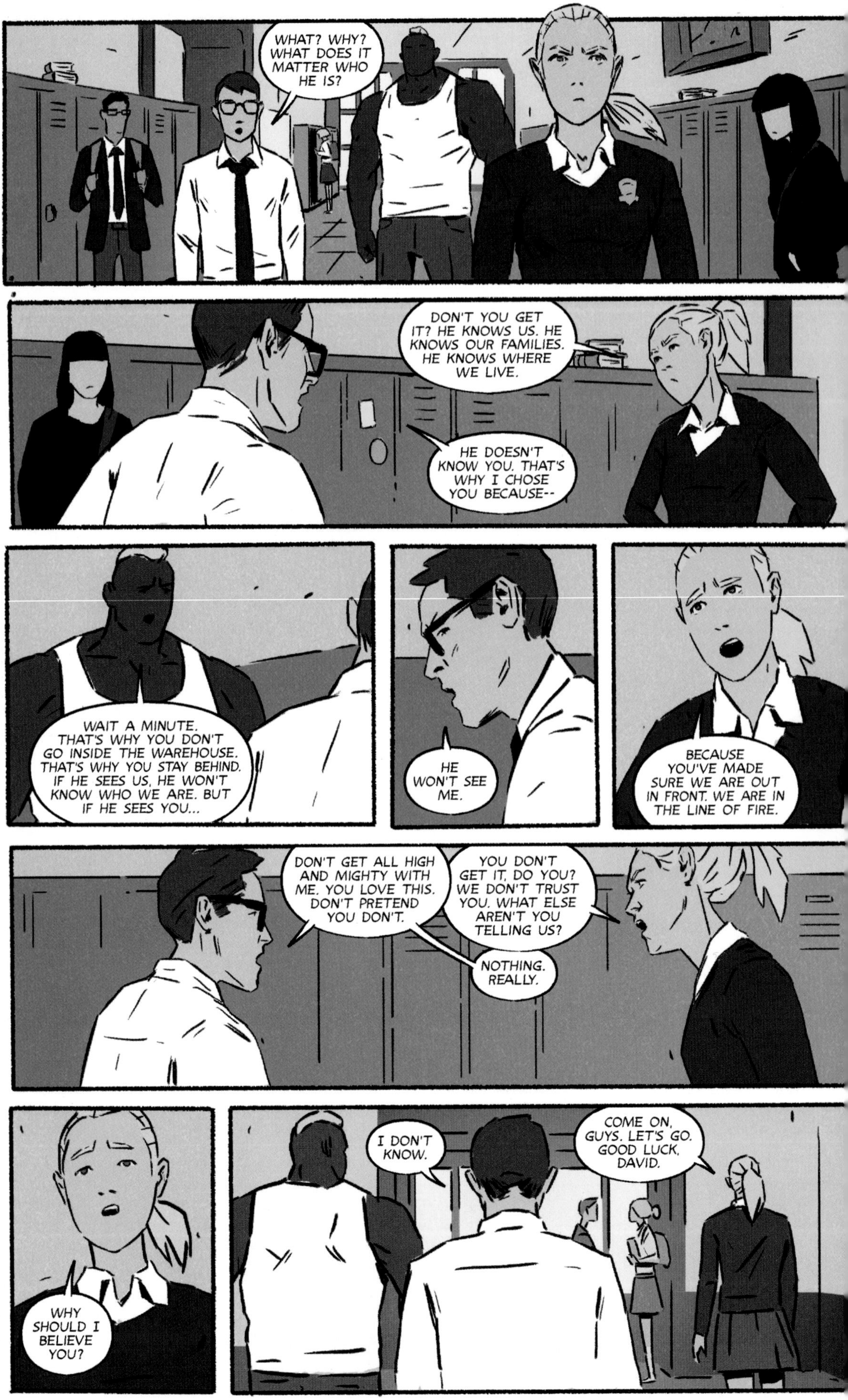
WHAT? WHY? WHAT DOES IT MATTER WHO HE IS?
DON'T YOU GET IT? HE KNOWS US. HE KNOWS OUR FAMILIES. HE KNOWS WHERE WE LIVE.
HE DOESN'T KNOW YOU. THAT'S WHY I CHOSE YOU BECAUSE--
WAIT A MINUTE. THAT'S WHY YOU DON'T GO INSIDE THE WAREHOUSE. THAT'S WHY YOU STAY BEHIND. IF HE SEES US, HE WON'T KNOW WHO WE ARE. BUT IF HE SEES YOU...
HE WON'T SEE ME.
BECAUSE YOU'VE MADE SURE WE ARE OUT IN FRONT. WE ARE IN THE LINE OF FIRE.
DON'T GET ALL HIGH AND MIGHTY WITH ME. YOU LOVE THIS. DON'T PRETEND YOU DON'T.
YOU DON'T GET IT, DO YOU? WE DON'T TRUST YOU. WHAT ELSE AREN'T YOU TELLING US?
NOTHING. REALLY.
WHY SHOULD I BELIEVE YOU?
I DON'T KNOW.
COME ON, GUYS. LET'S GO. GOOD LUCK, DAVID.

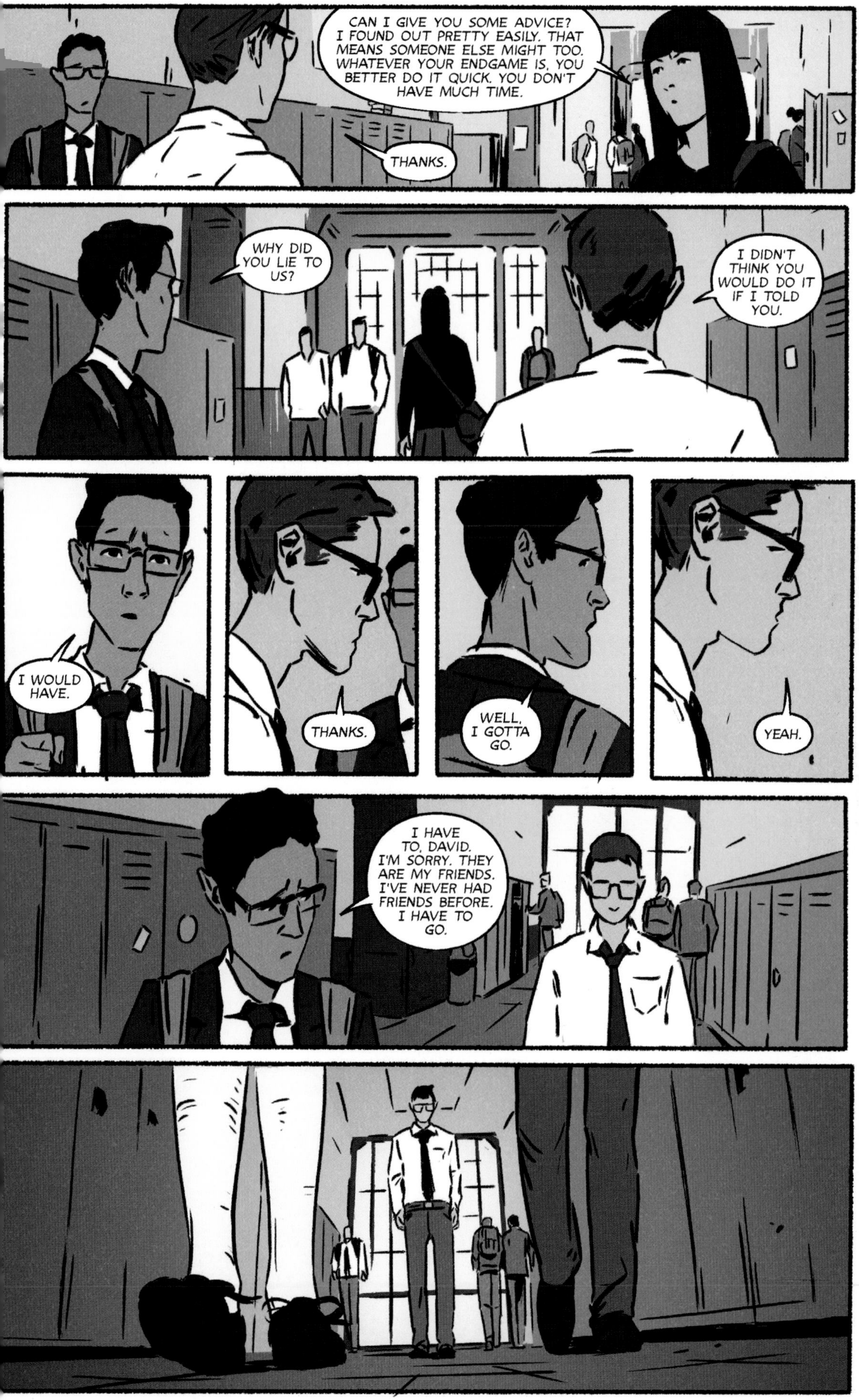
CAN I GIVE YOU SOME ADVICE? I FOUND OUT PRETTY EASILY. THAT MEANS SOMEONE ELSE MIGHT TOO. WHATEVER YOUR ENDGAME IS, YOU BETTER DO IT QUICK. YOU DON'T HAVE MUCH TIME.
THANKS.
WHY DID YOU LIE TO US?
I DIDN'T THINK YOU WOULD DO IT IF I TOLD YOU.
I WOULD HAVE.
THANKS.
WELL, I GOTTA GO.
YEAH.
I HAVE TO, DAVID. I'M SORRY. THEY ARE MY FRIENDS. I'VE NEVER HAD FRIENDS BEFORE. I HAVE TO GO.

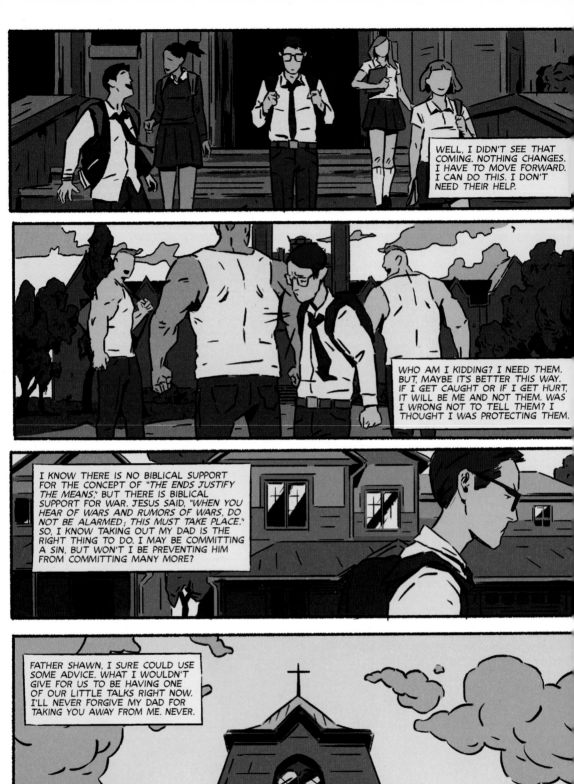

WELL, I DIDN'T SEE THAT COMING. NOTHING CHANGES. I HAVE TO MOVE FORWARD. I CAN DO THIS. I DON'T NEED THEIR HELP.

WHO AM I KIDDING? I NEED THEM. BUT, MAYBE IT'S BETTER THIS WAY. IF I GET CAUGHT OR IF I GET HURT, IT WILL BE ME AND NOT THEM. WAS I WRONG NOT TO TELL THEM? I THOUGHT I WAS PROTECTING THEM.

I KNOW THERE IS NO BIBLICAL SUPPORT FOR THE CONCEPT OF *"THE ENDS JUSTIFY THE MEANS,"* BUT THERE IS BIBLICAL SUPPORT FOR WAR. JESUS SAID, *"WHEN YOU HEAR OF WARS AND RUMORS OF WARS, DO NOT BE ALARMED; THIS MUST TAKE PLACE."* SO, I KNOW TAKING OUT MY DAD IS THE RIGHT THING TO DO. I MAY BE COMMITTING A SIN, BUT WON'T I BE PREVENTING HIM FROM COMMITTING MANY MORE?

FATHER SHAWN, I SURE COULD USE SOME ADVICE. WHAT I WOULDN'T GIVE FOR US TO BE HAVING ONE OF OUR LITTLE TALKS RIGHT NOW. I'LL NEVER FORGIVE MY DAD FOR TAKING YOU AWAY FROM ME. NEVER.

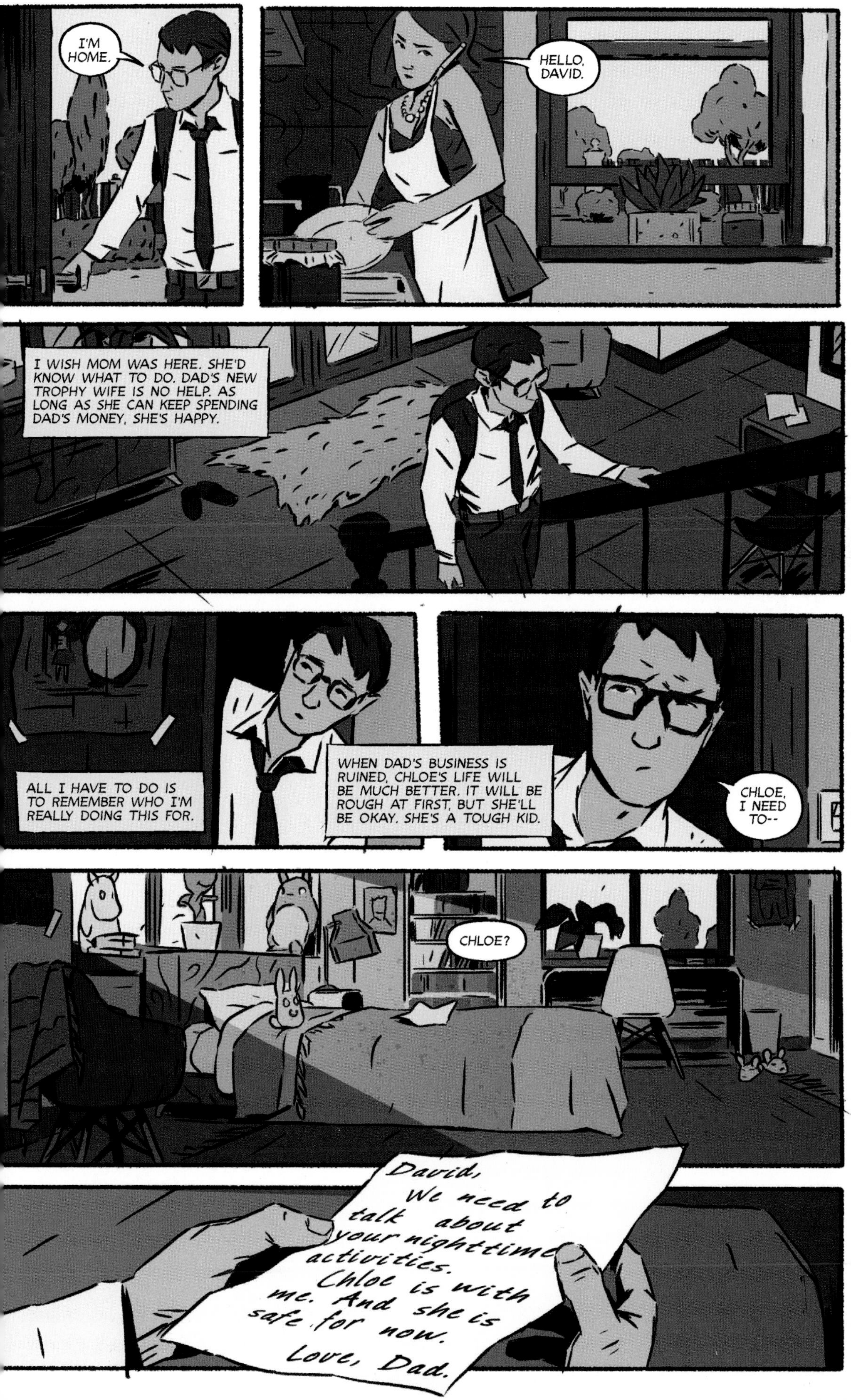

I'M HOME.
HELLO, DAVID.
I WISH MOM WAS HERE. SHE'D KNOW WHAT TO DO. DAD'S NEW TROPHY WIFE IS NO HELP. AS LONG AS SHE CAN KEEP SPENDING DAD'S MONEY, SHE'S HAPPY.
ALL I HAVE TO DO IS TO REMEMBER WHO I'M REALLY DOING THIS FOR.
WHEN DAD'S BUSINESS IS RUINED, CHLOE'S LIFE WILL BE MUCH BETTER. IT WILL BE ROUGH AT FIRST, BUT SHE'LL BE OKAY. SHE'S A TOUGH KID.
CHLOE, I NEED TO--
CHLOE?
David, We need to talk about your nighttime activities. Chloe is with me. And she is safe for now. Love, Dad.

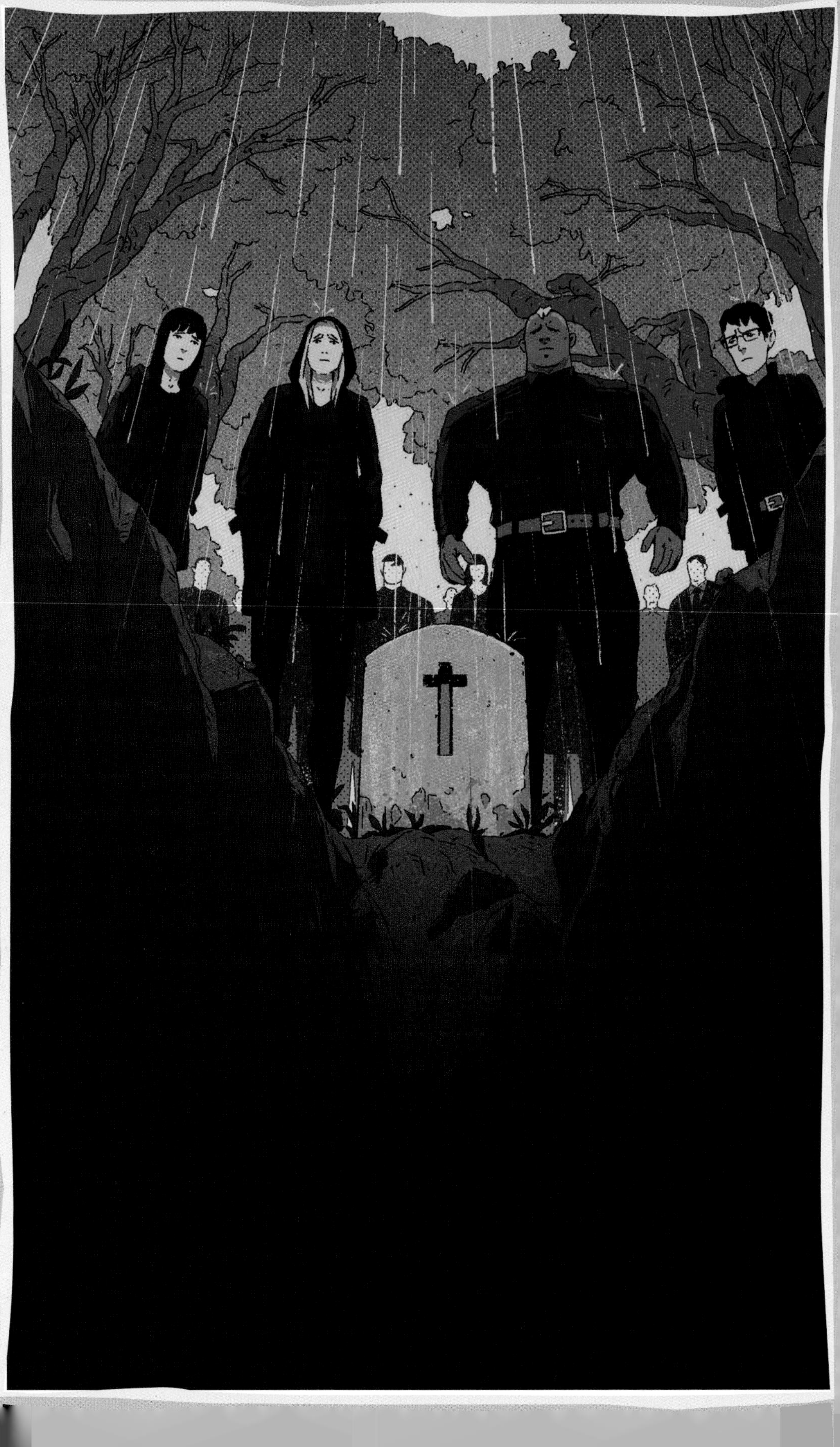

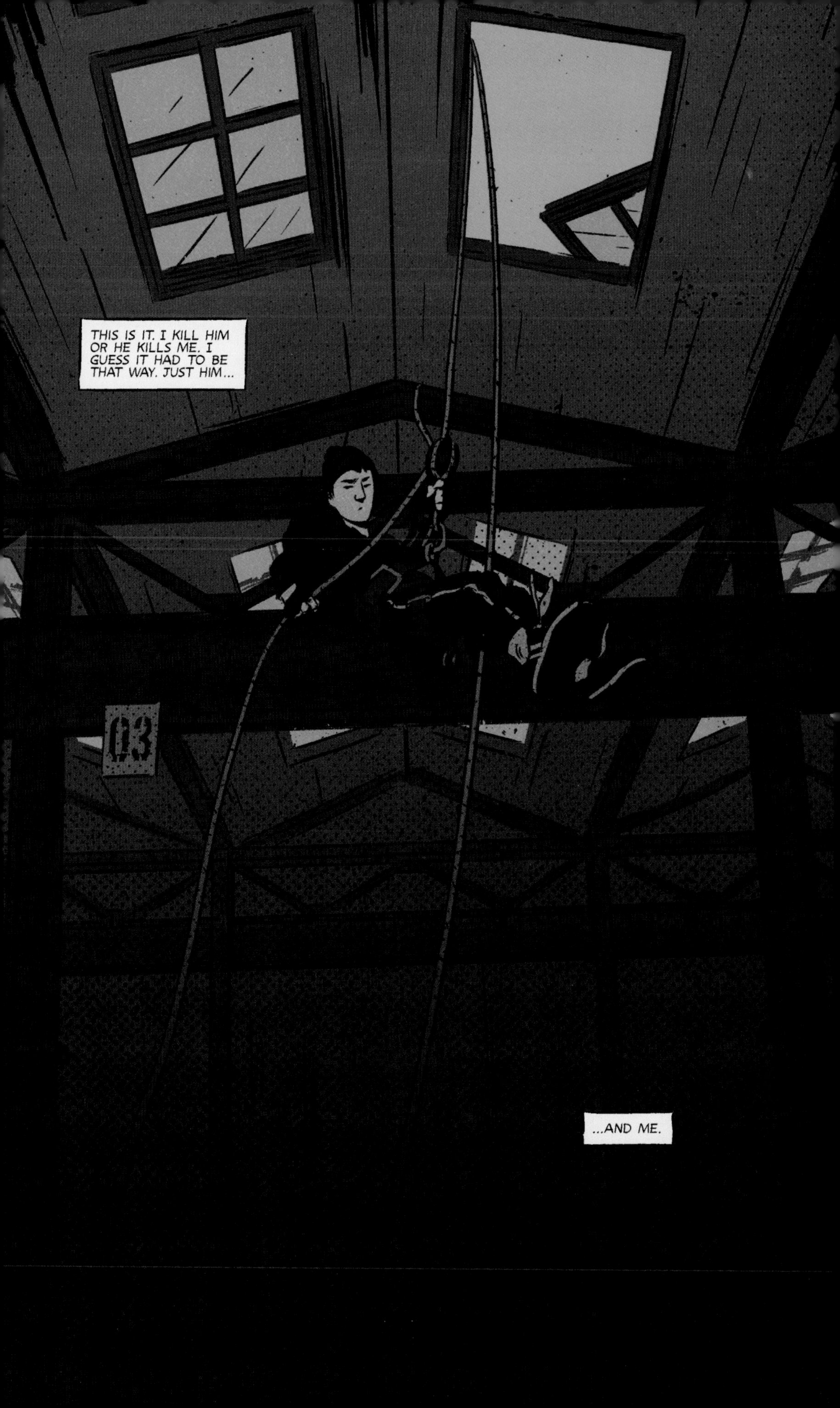
THIS IS IT. I KILL HIM OR HE KILLS ME. I GUESS IT HAD TO BE THAT WAY. JUST HIM...
03
...AND ME.

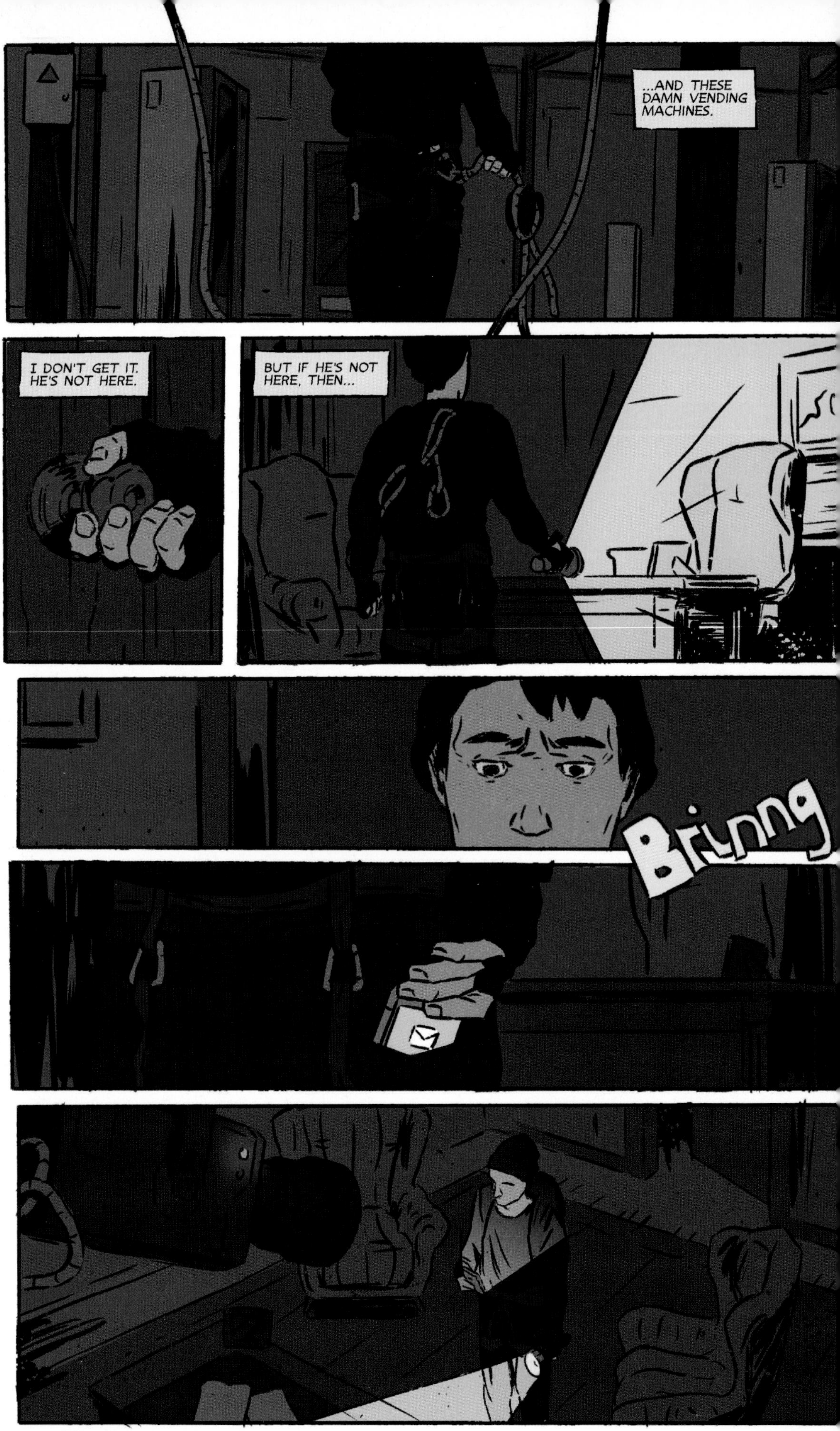
...AND THESE DAMN VENDING MACHINES.
I DON'T GET IT. HE'S NOT HERE.
BUT IF HE'S NOT HERE, THEN...
Brinng

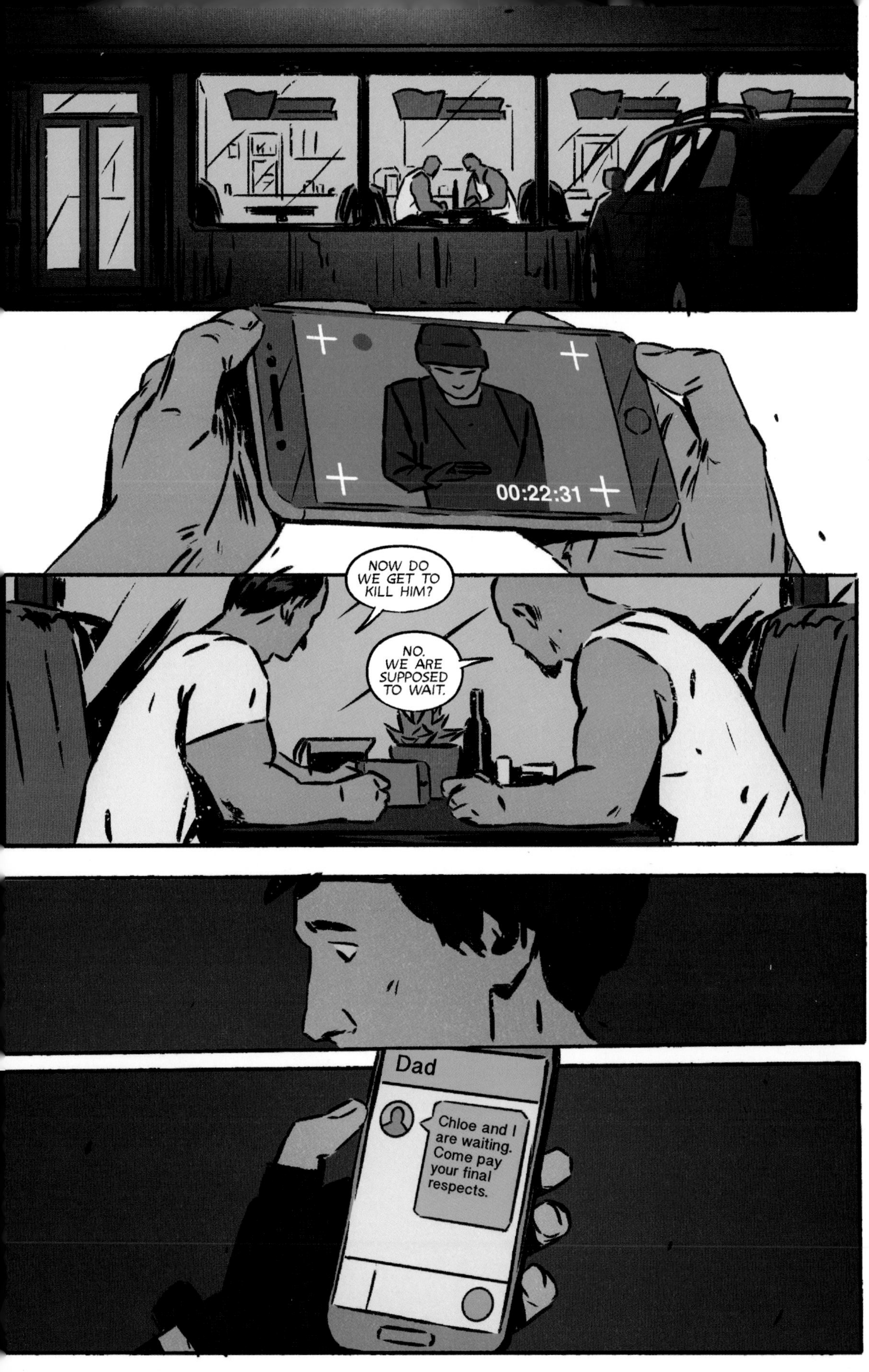
00:22:31
NOW DO WE GET TO KILL HIM?
NO. WE ARE SUPPOSED TO WAIT.
Dad
Chloe and I are waiting. Come pay your final respects.

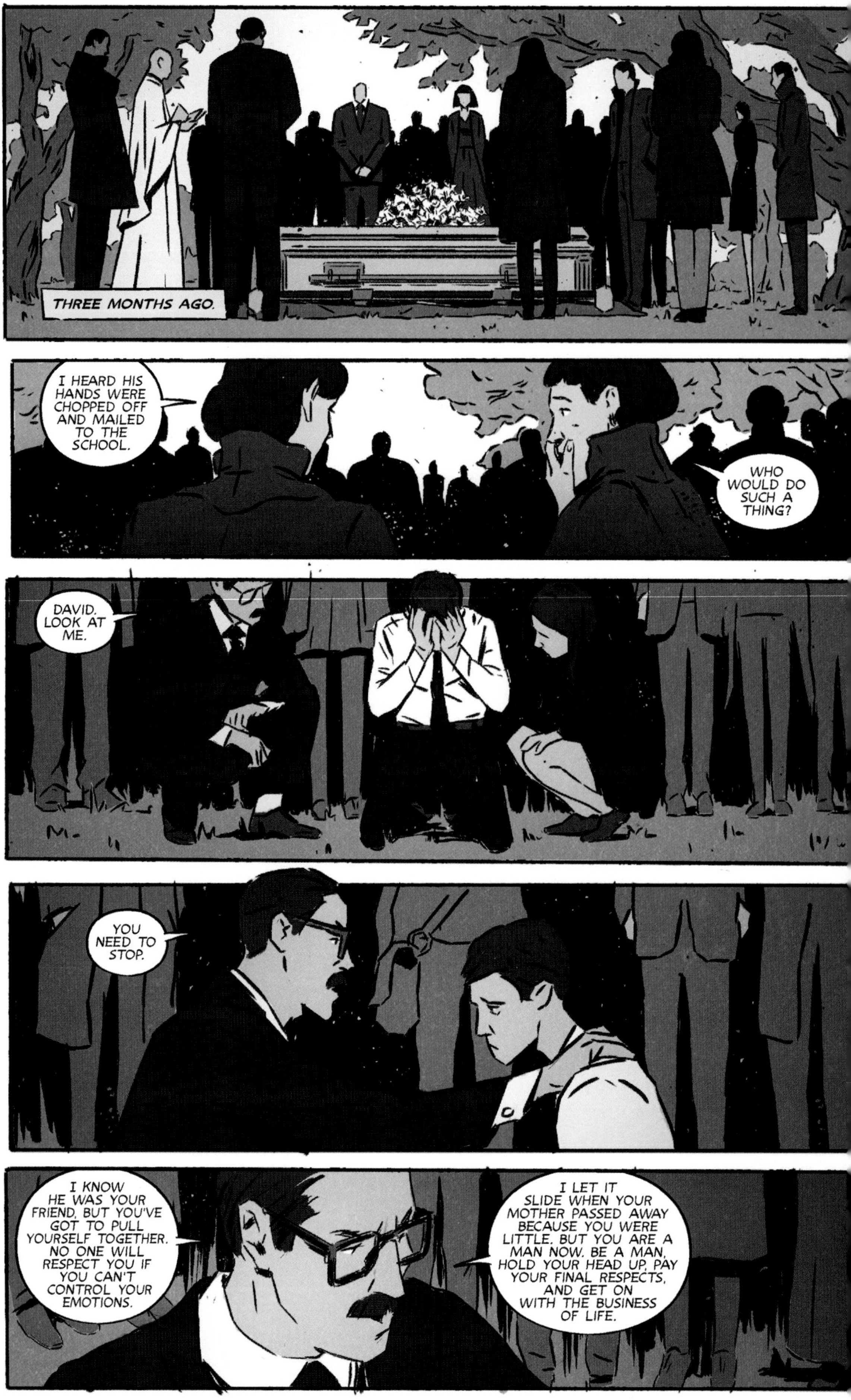
THREE MONTHS AGO.
I HEARD HIS HANDS WERE CHOPPED OFF AND MAILED TO THE SCHOOL.
WHO WOULD DO SUCH A THING?
DAVID. LOOK AT ME.
YOU NEED TO STOP.
I KNOW HE WAS YOUR FRIEND, BUT YOU'VE GOT TO PULL YOURSELF TOGETHER. NO ONE WILL RESPECT YOU IF YOU CAN'T CONTROL YOUR EMOTIONS.
I LET IT SLIDE WHEN YOUR MOTHER PASSED AWAY BECAUSE YOU WERE LITTLE. BUT YOU ARE A MAN NOW. BE A MAN, HOLD YOUR HEAD UP, PAY YOUR FINAL RESPECTS, AND GET ON WITH THE BUSINESS OF LIFE.

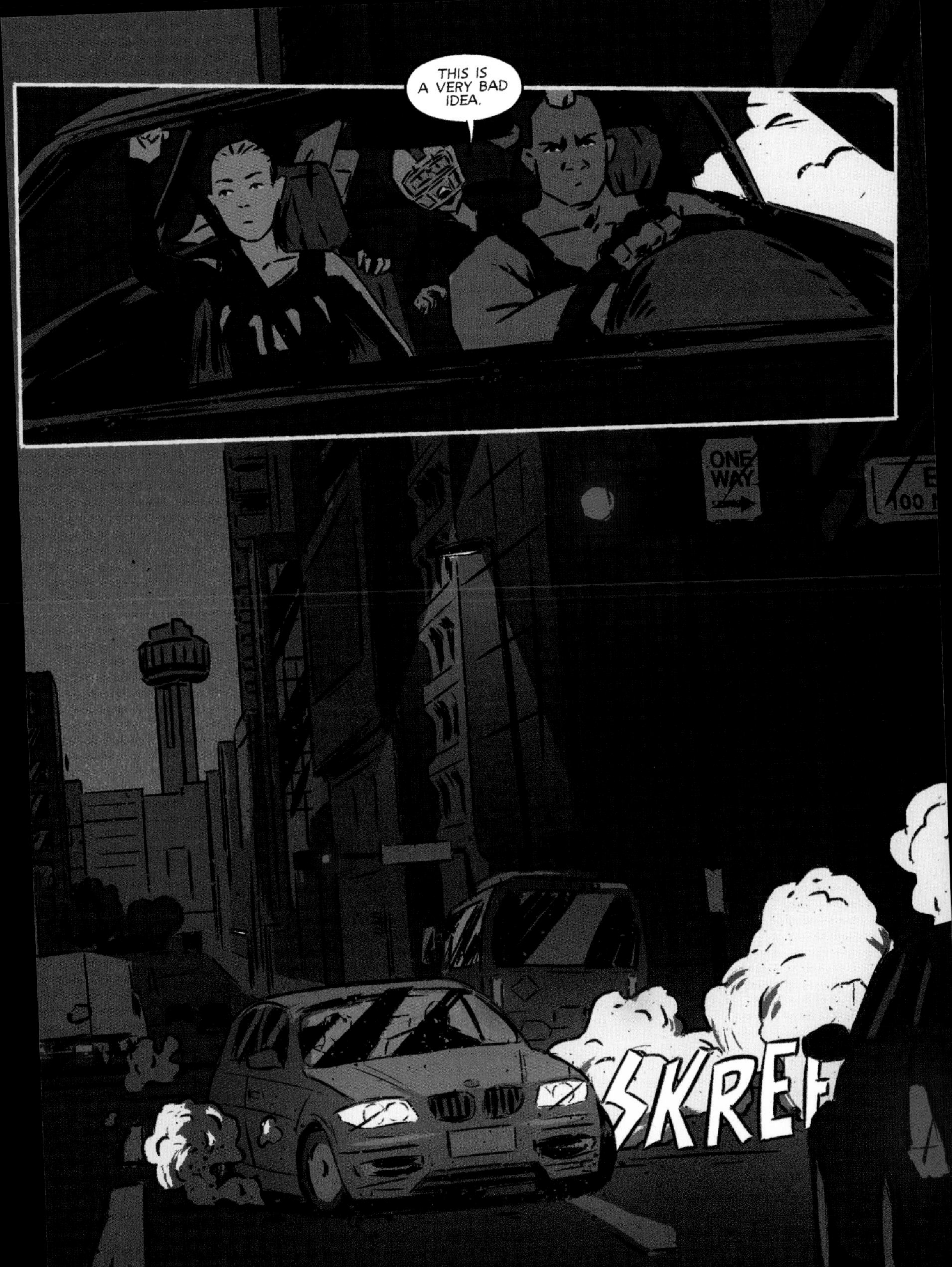
THIS IS A VERY BAD IDEA.
ONE WAY
SKREE

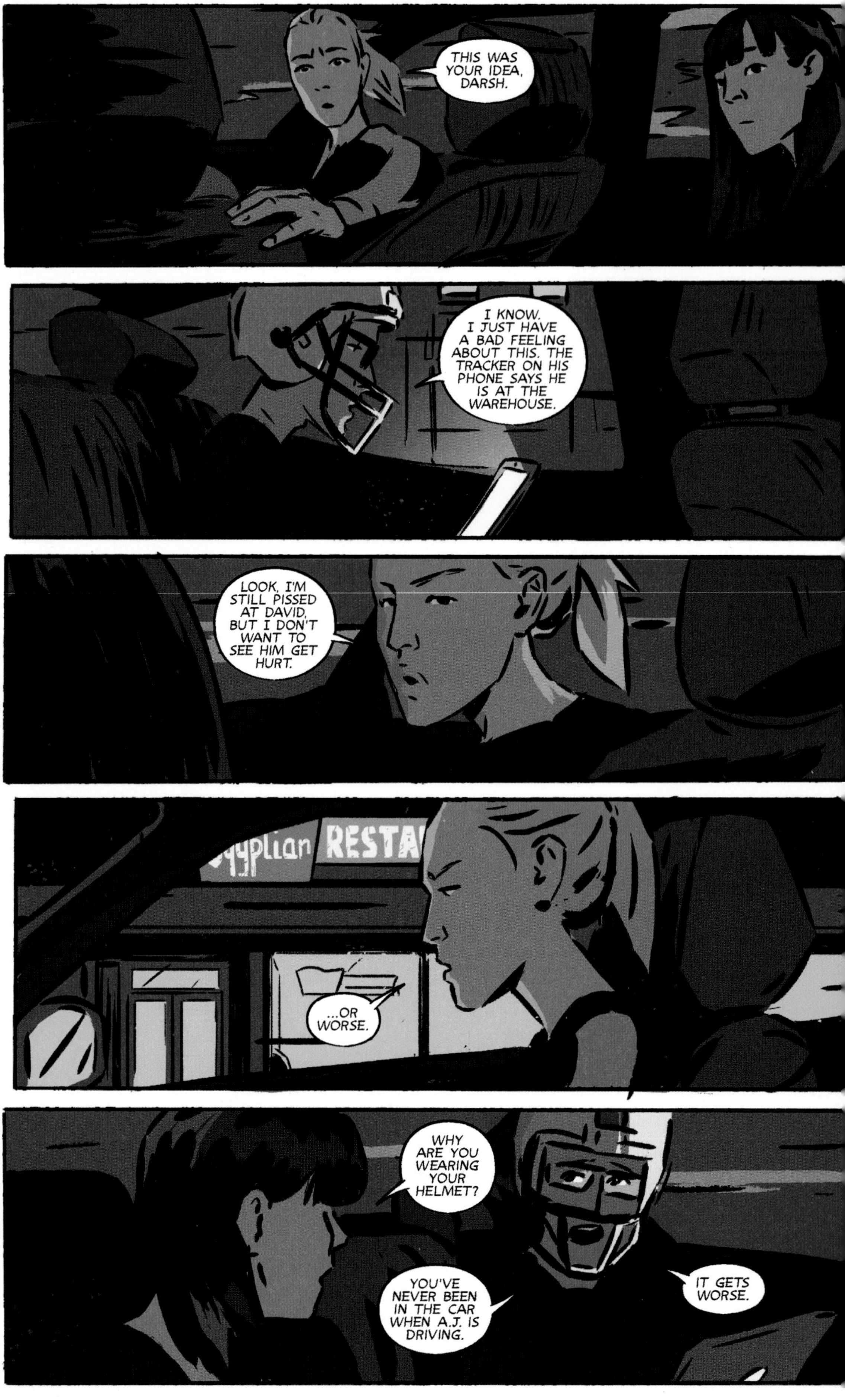
THIS WAS YOUR IDEA, DARSH.
I KNOW. I JUST HAVE A BAD FEELING ABOUT THIS. THE TRACKER ON HIS PHONE SAYS HE IS AT THE WAREHOUSE.
LOOK, I'M STILL PISSED AT DAVID, BUT I DON'T WANT TO SEE HIM GET HURT.
RESTA
...OR WORSE.
WHY ARE YOU WEARING YOUR HELMET?
YOU'VE NEVER BEEN IN THE CAR WHEN A.J. IS DRIVING.
IT GETS WORSE.

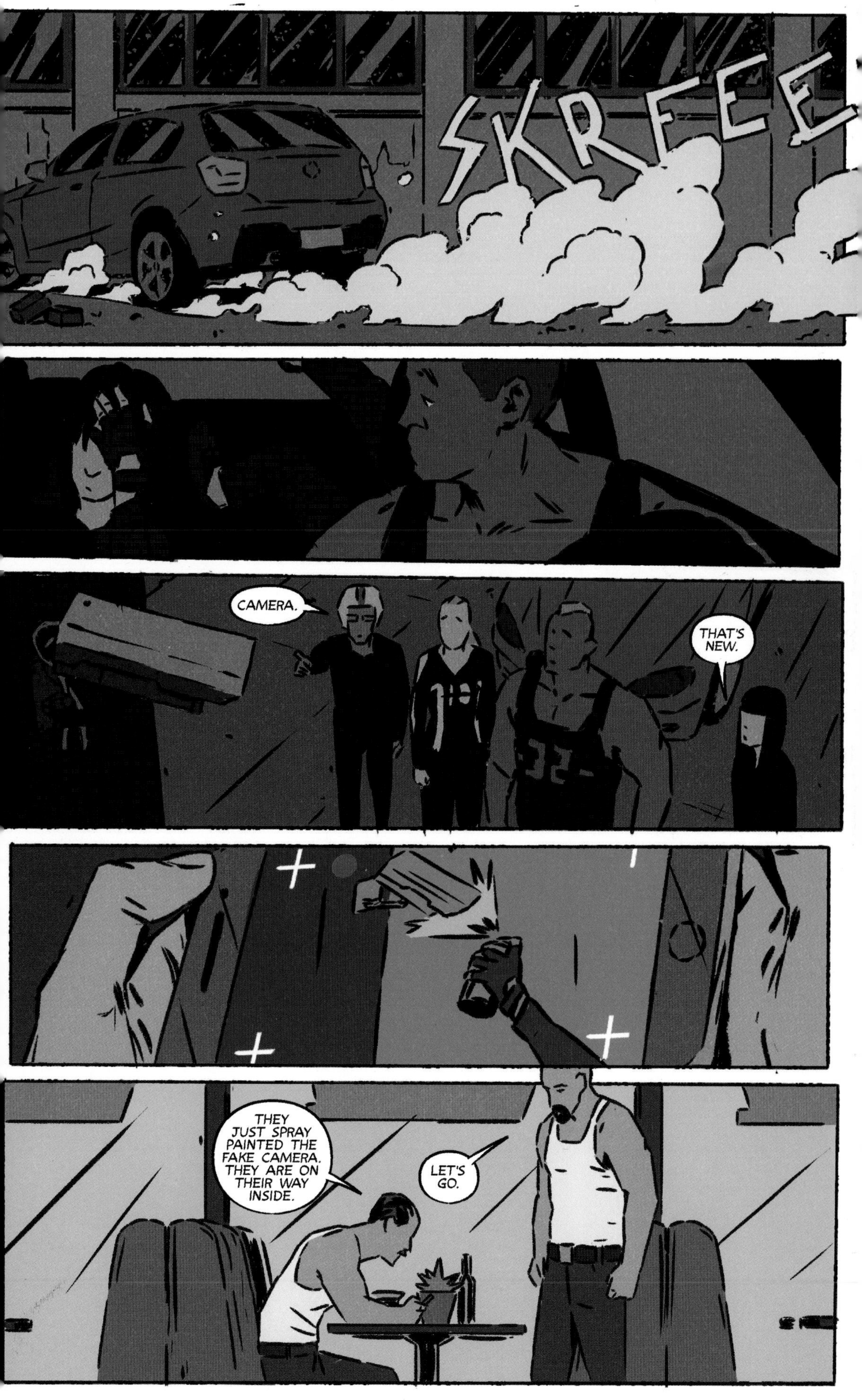
SKREEE
CAMERA.
THAT'S NEW.
THEY JUST SPRAY PAINTED THE FAKE CAMERA. THEY ARE ON THEIR WAY INSIDE.
LET'S GO.

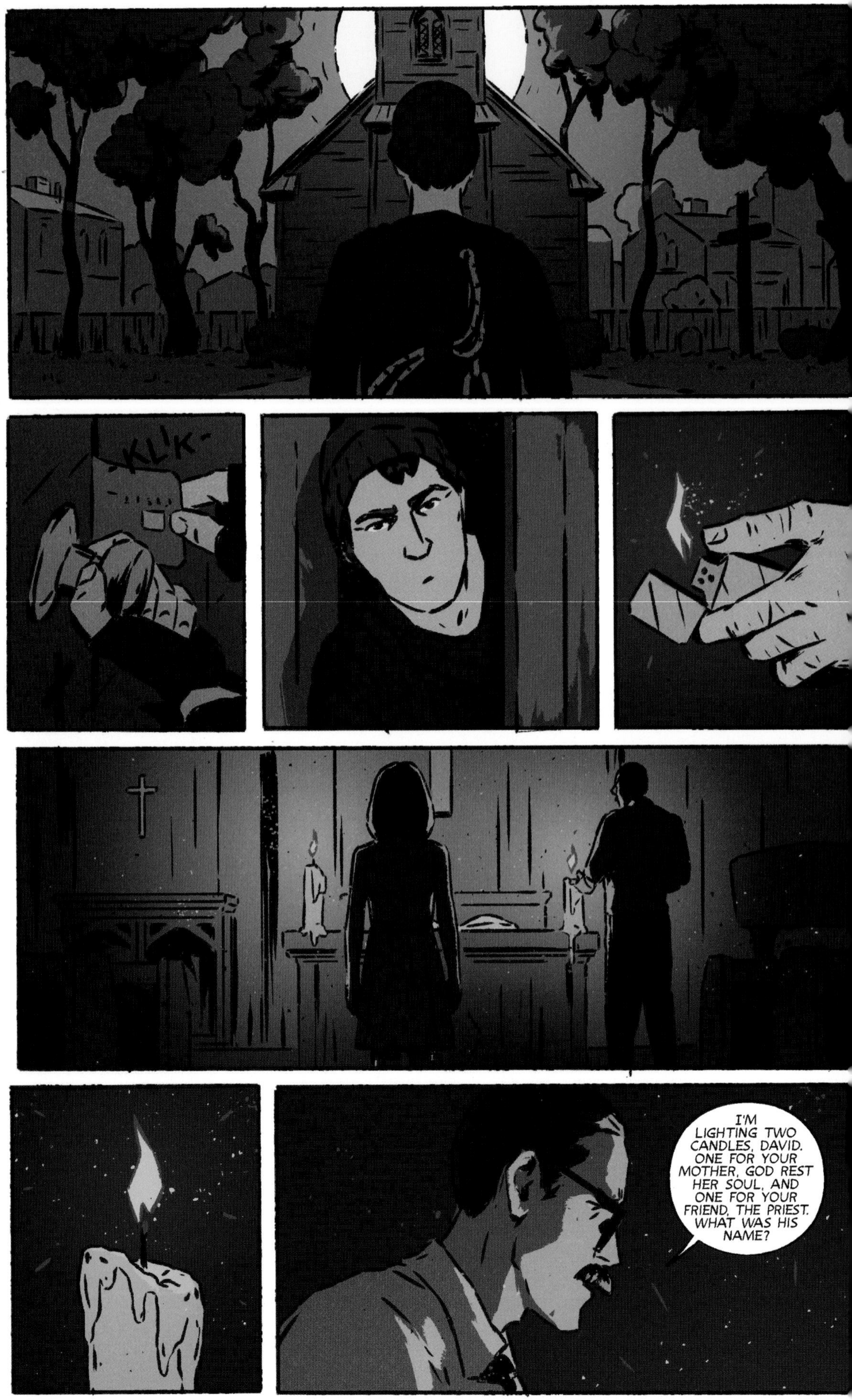
KLIK-
I'M LIGHTING TWO CANDLES, DAVID. ONE FOR YOUR MOTHER, GOD REST HER SOUL, AND ONE FOR YOUR FRIEND, THE PRIEST. WHAT WAS HIS NAME?

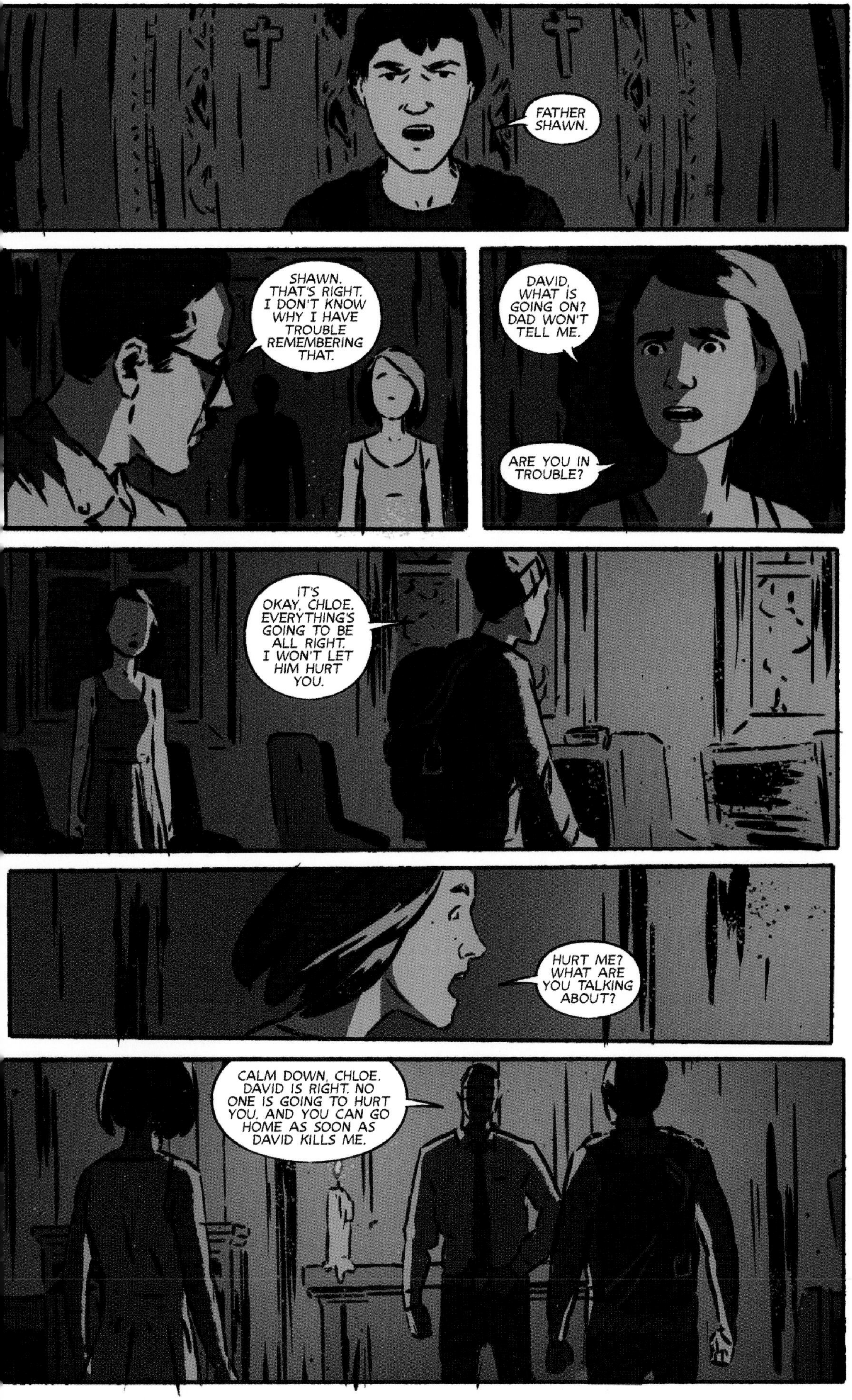
FATHER SHAWN.
SHAWN. THAT'S RIGHT. I DON'T KNOW WHY I HAVE TROUBLE REMEMBERING THAT.
DAVID, WHAT IS GOING ON? DAD WON'T TELL ME.
ARE YOU IN TROUBLE?
IT'S OKAY, CHLOE. EVERYTHING'S GOING TO BE ALL RIGHT. I WON'T LET HIM HURT YOU.
HURT ME? WHAT ARE YOU TALKING ABOUT?
CALM DOWN, CHLOE. DAVID IS RIGHT. NO ONE IS GOING TO HURT YOU. AND YOU CAN GO HOME AS SOON AS DAVID KILLS ME.

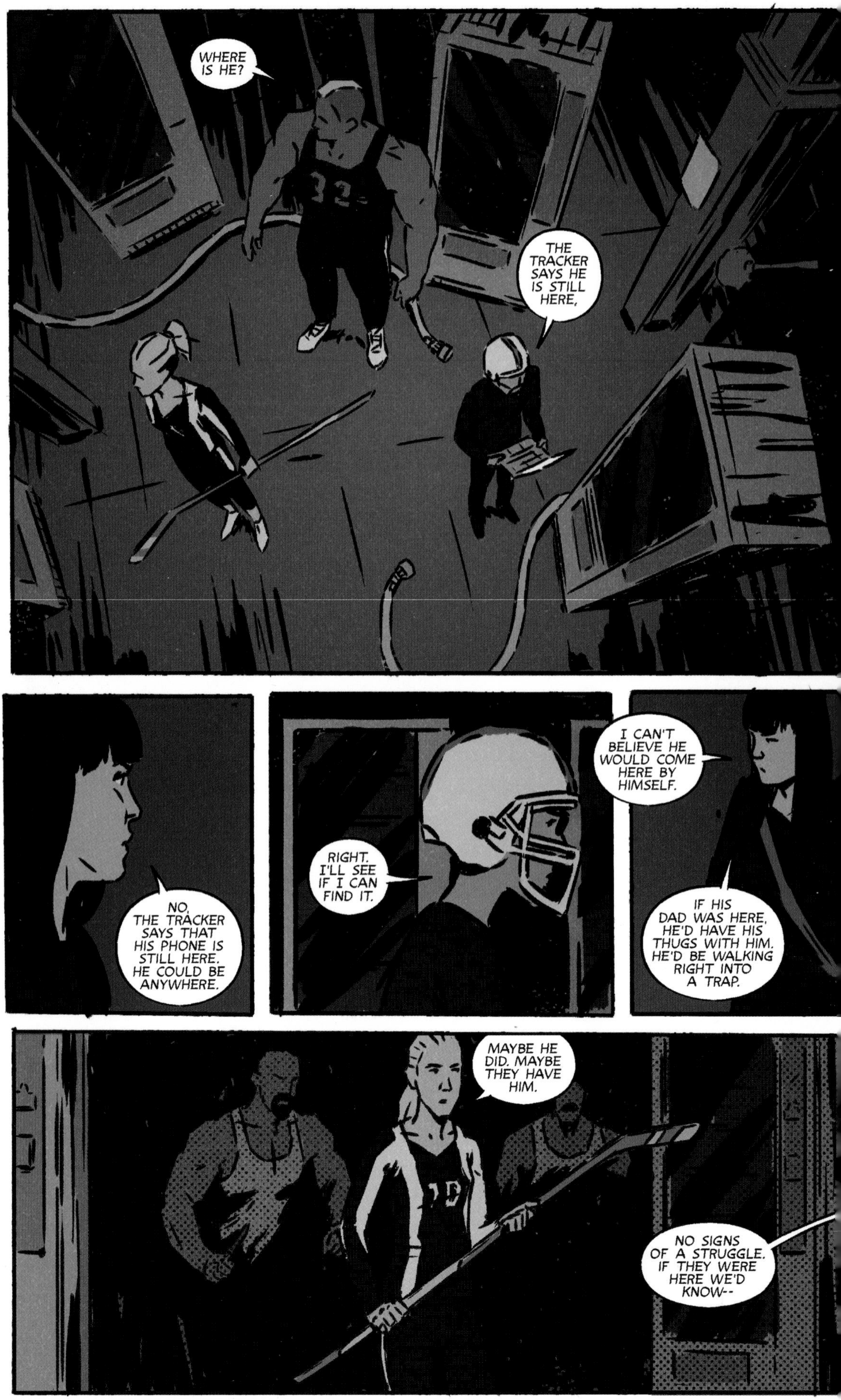
WHERE IS HE?
THE TRACKER SAYS HE IS STILL HERE,
NO, THE TRACKER SAYS THAT HIS PHONE IS STILL HERE. HE COULD BE ANYWHERE.
RIGHT. I'LL SEE IF I CAN FIND IT.
I CAN'T BELIEVE HE WOULD COME HERE BY HIMSELF.
IF HIS DAD WAS HERE, HE'D HAVE HIS THUGS WITH HIM. HE'D BE WALKING RIGHT INTO A TRAP.
MAYBE HE DID. MAYBE THEY HAVE HIM.
NO SIGNS OF A STRUGGLE. IF THEY WERE HERE WE'D KNOW--

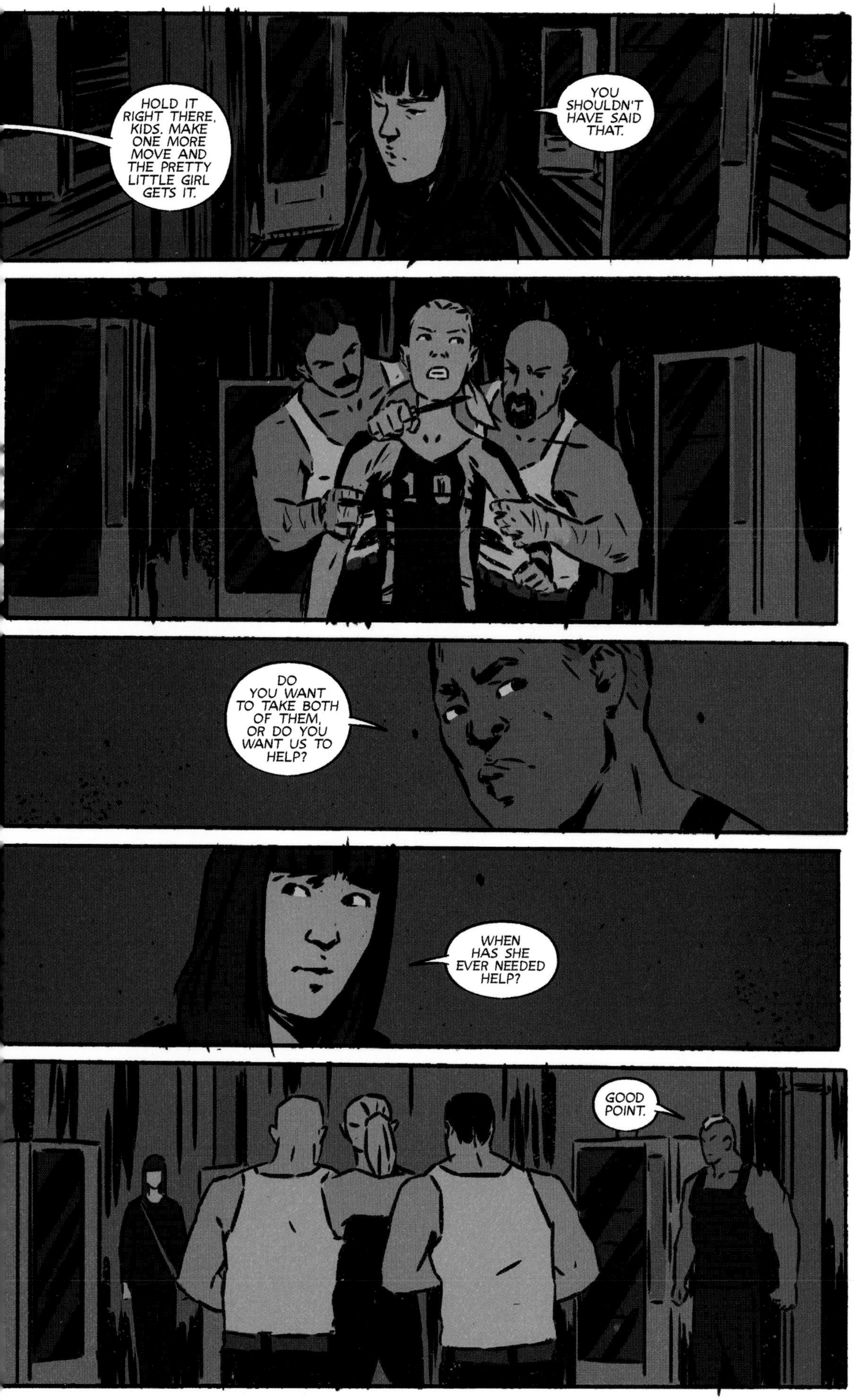
HOLD IT RIGHT THERE, KIDS. MAKE ONE MORE MOVE AND THE PRETTY LITTLE GIRL GETS IT.
YOU SHOULDN'T HAVE SAID THAT.
DO YOU WANT TO TAKE BOTH OF THEM, OR DO YOU WANT US TO HELP?
WHEN HAS SHE EVER NEEDED HELP?
GOOD POINT.

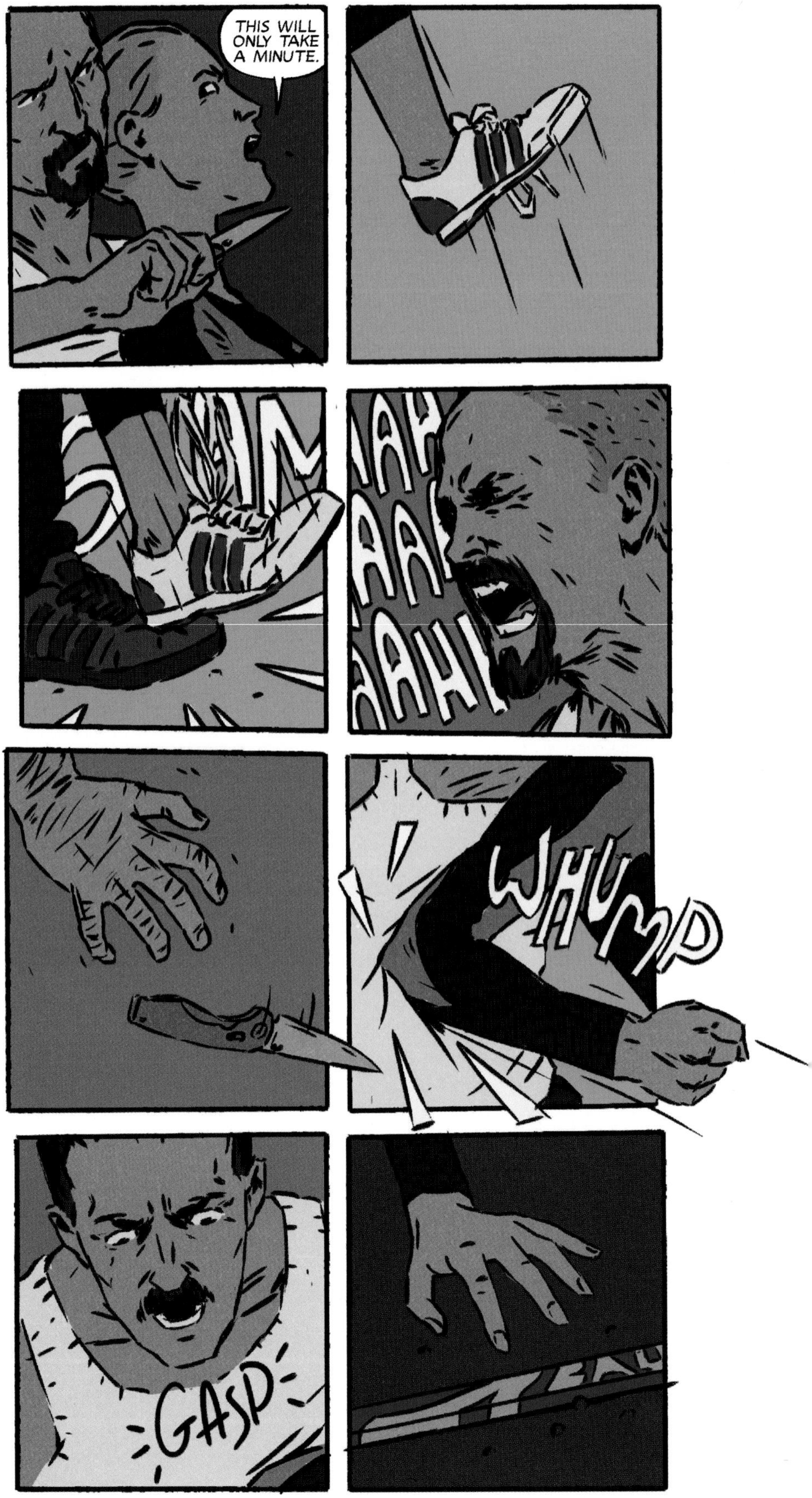
THIS WILL ONLY TAKE A MINUTE.
WHUMP
GASP

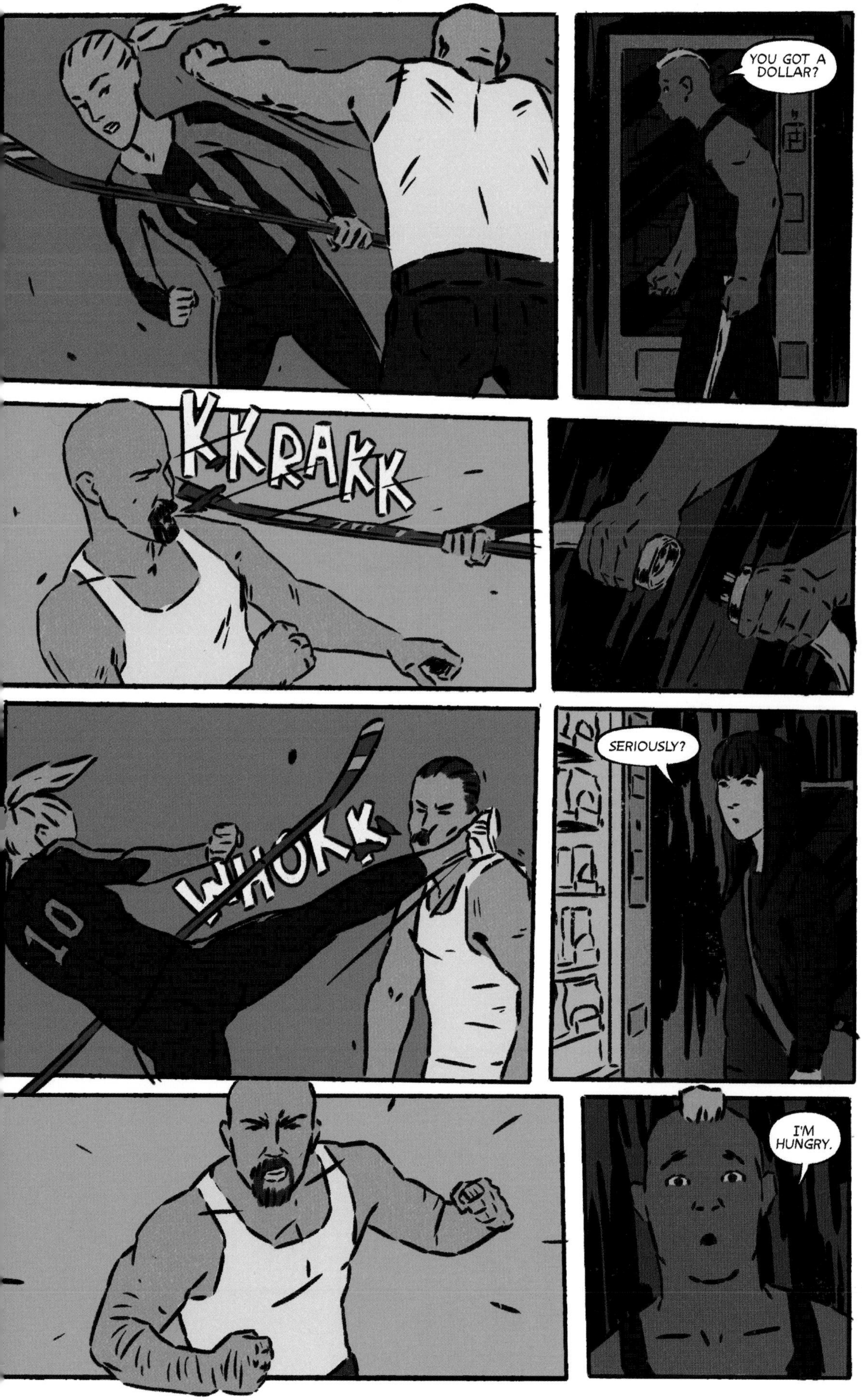
YOU GOT A DOLLAR?
KKRAKK
WHOKK
SERIOUSLY?
I'M HUNGRY.

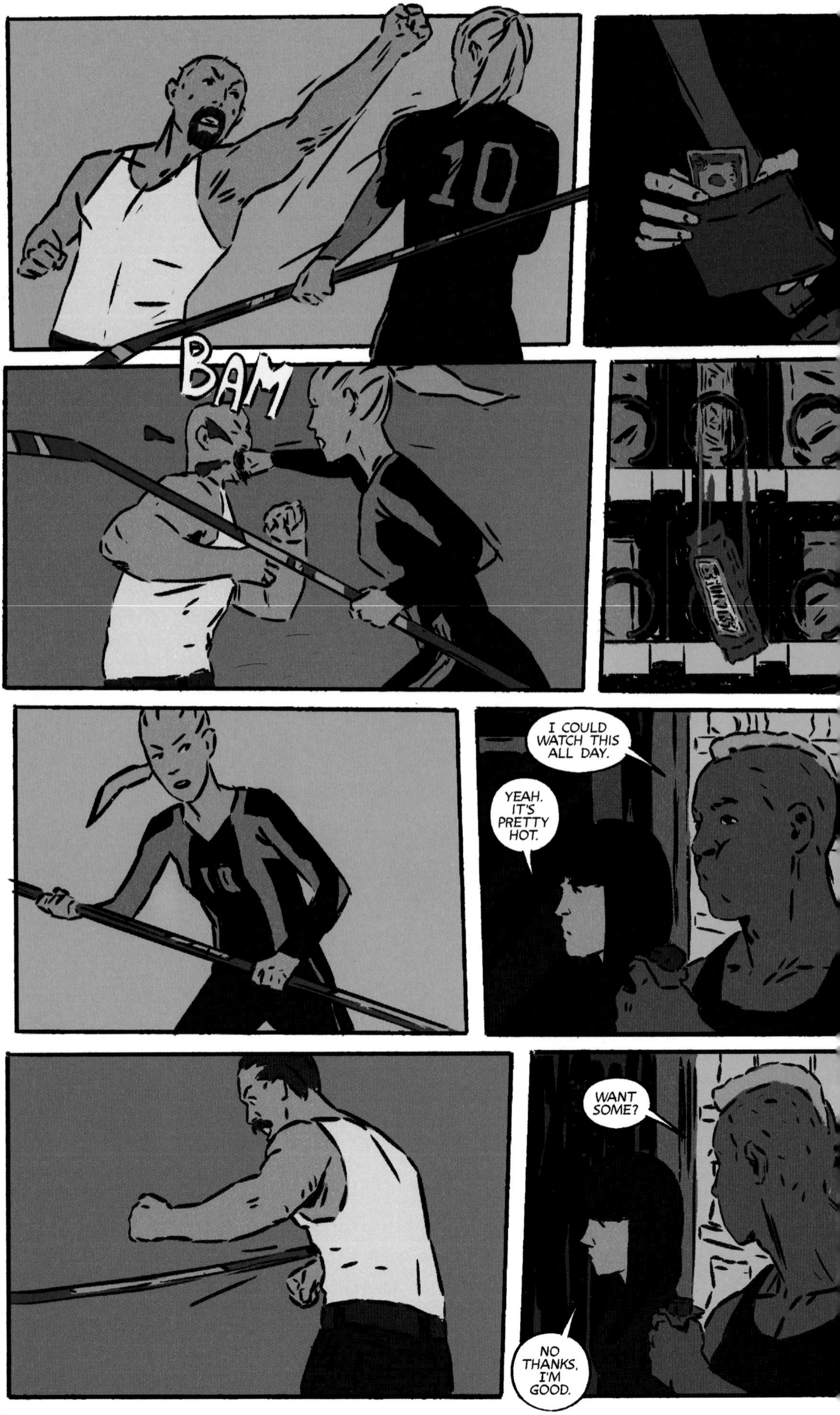
10
BAM
I COULD WATCH THIS ALL DAY.
YEAH. IT'S PRETTY HOT.
WANT SOME?
NO THANKS, I'M GOOD.

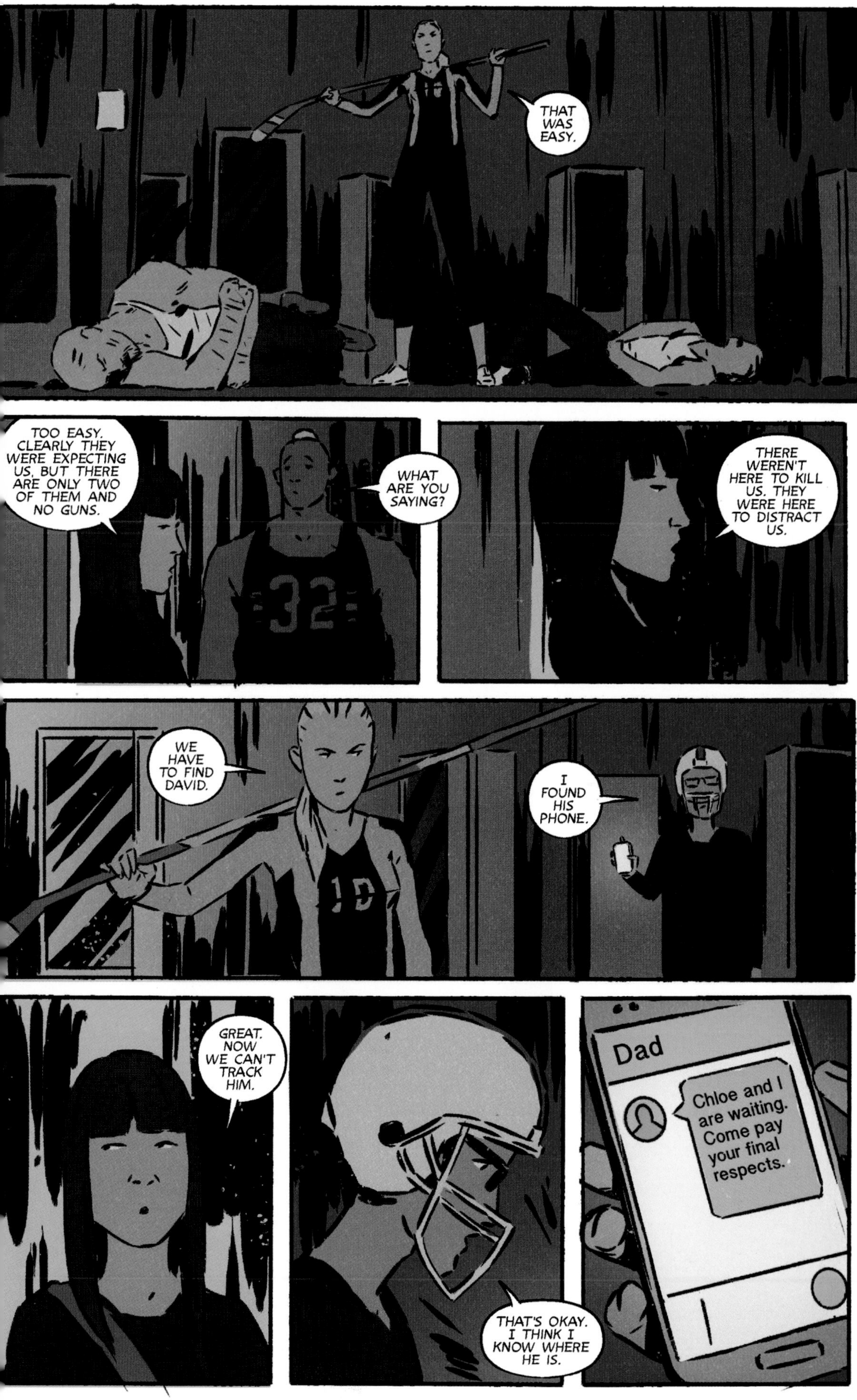
THAT WAS EASY.
TOO EASY. CLEARLY THEY WERE EXPECTING US, BUT THERE ARE ONLY TWO OF THEM AND NO GUNS.
WHAT ARE YOU SAYING?
THERE WEREN'T HERE TO KILL US. THEY WERE HERE TO DISTRACT US.
WE HAVE TO FIND DAVID.
I FOUND HIS PHONE.
GREAT. NOW WE CAN'T TRACK HIM.
THAT'S OKAY. I THINK I KNOW WHERE HE IS.
Dad
Chloe and I are waiting. Come pay your final respects.

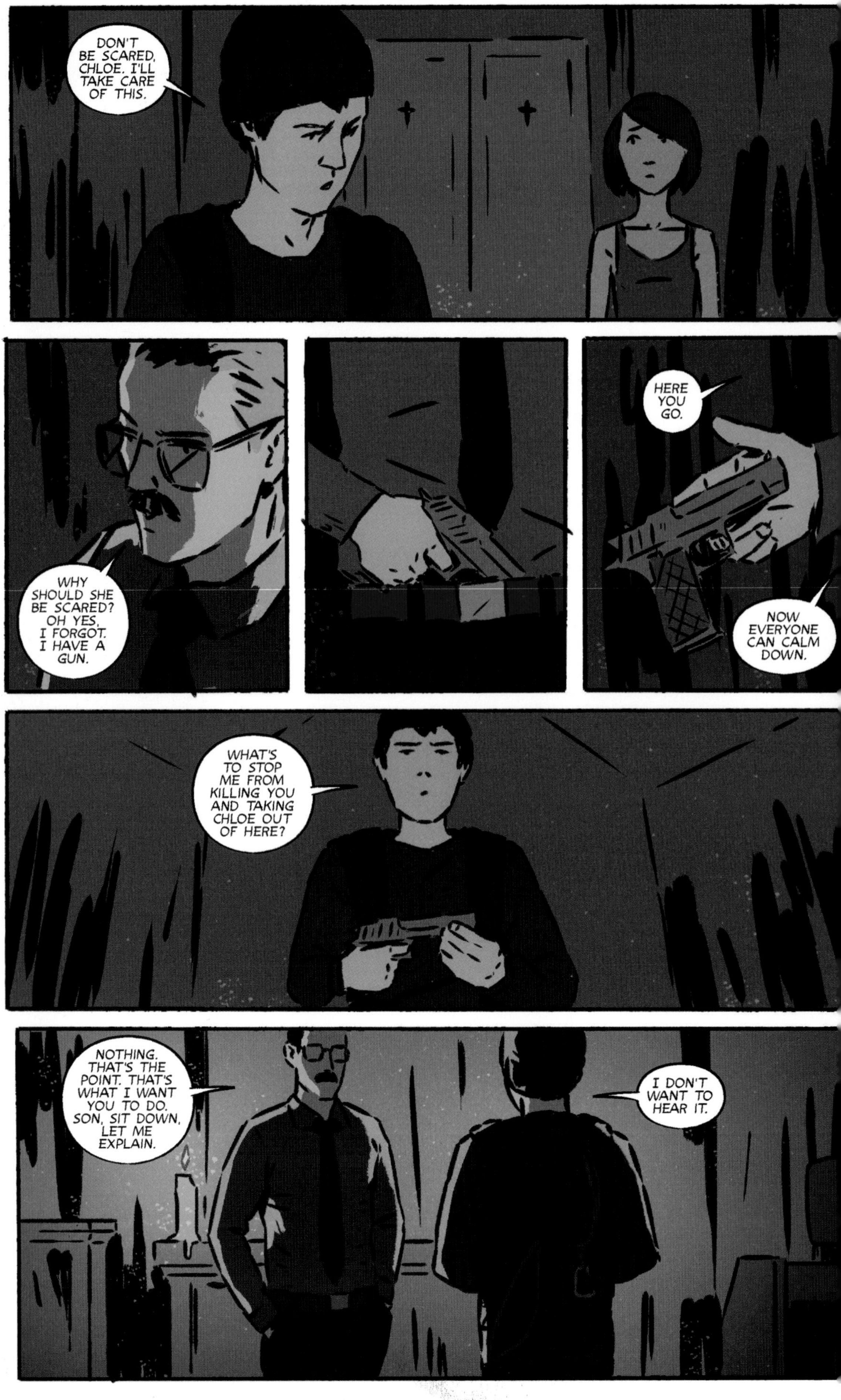
DON'T BE SCARED, CHLOE. I'LL TAKE CARE OF THIS.
WHY SHOULD SHE BE SCARED? OH YES, I FORGOT. I HAVE A GUN.
HERE YOU GO.
NOW EVERYONE CAN CALM DOWN.
WHAT'S TO STOP ME FROM KILLING YOU AND TAKING CHLOE OUT OF HERE?
NOTHING. THAT'S THE POINT. THAT'S WHAT I WANT YOU TO DO. SON, SIT DOWN, LET ME EXPLAIN.
I DON'T WANT TO HEAR IT.

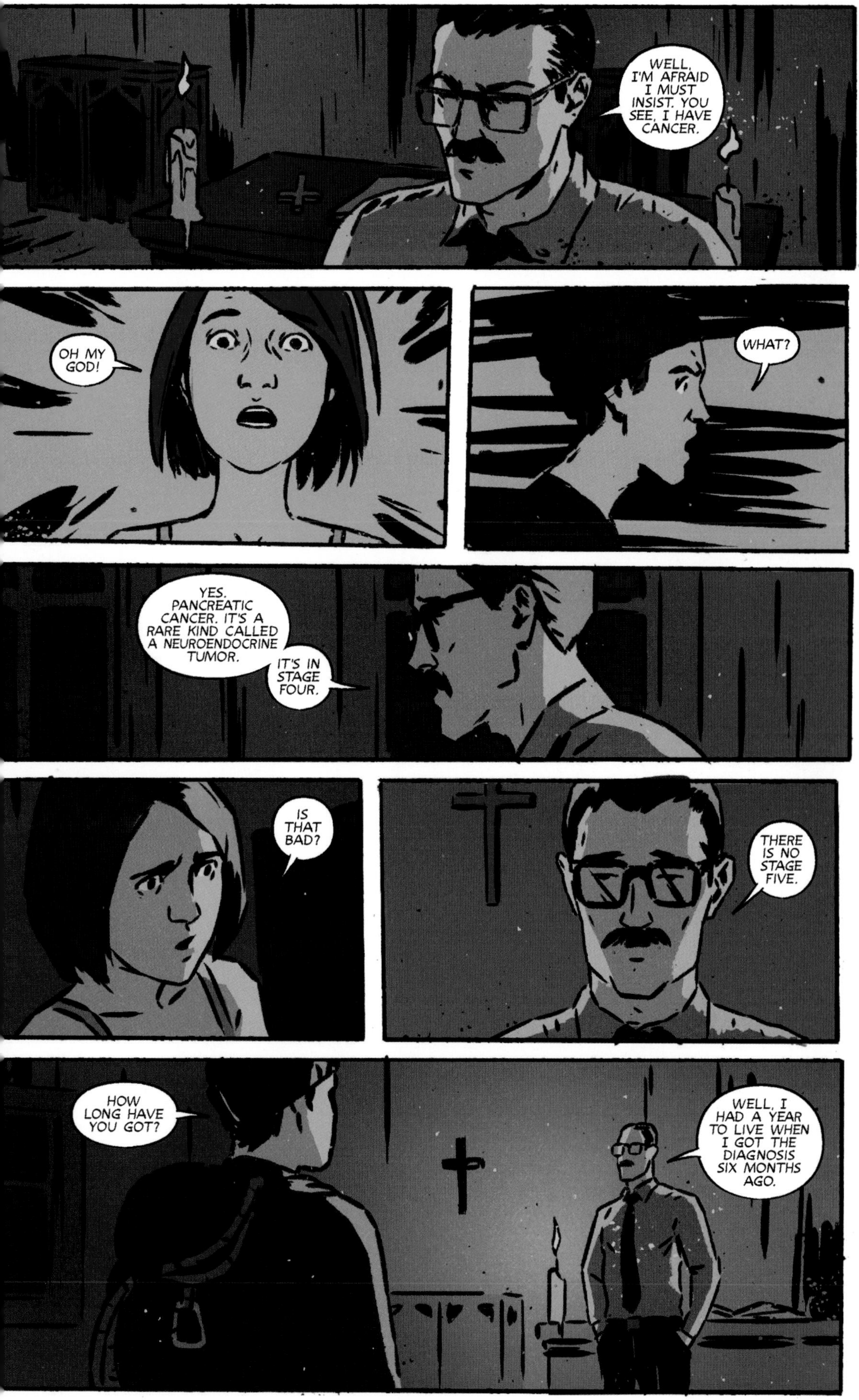
WELL, I'M AFRAID I MUST INSIST. YOU SEE, I HAVE CANCER.
OH MY GOD!
WHAT?
YES. PANCREATIC CANCER. IT'S A RARE KIND CALLED A NEUROENDOCRINE TUMOR.
IT'S IN STAGE FOUR.
IS THAT BAD?
THERE IS NO STAGE FIVE.
HOW LONG HAVE YOU GOT?
WELL, I HAD A YEAR TO LIVE WHEN I GOT THE DIAGNOSIS SIX MONTHS AGO.

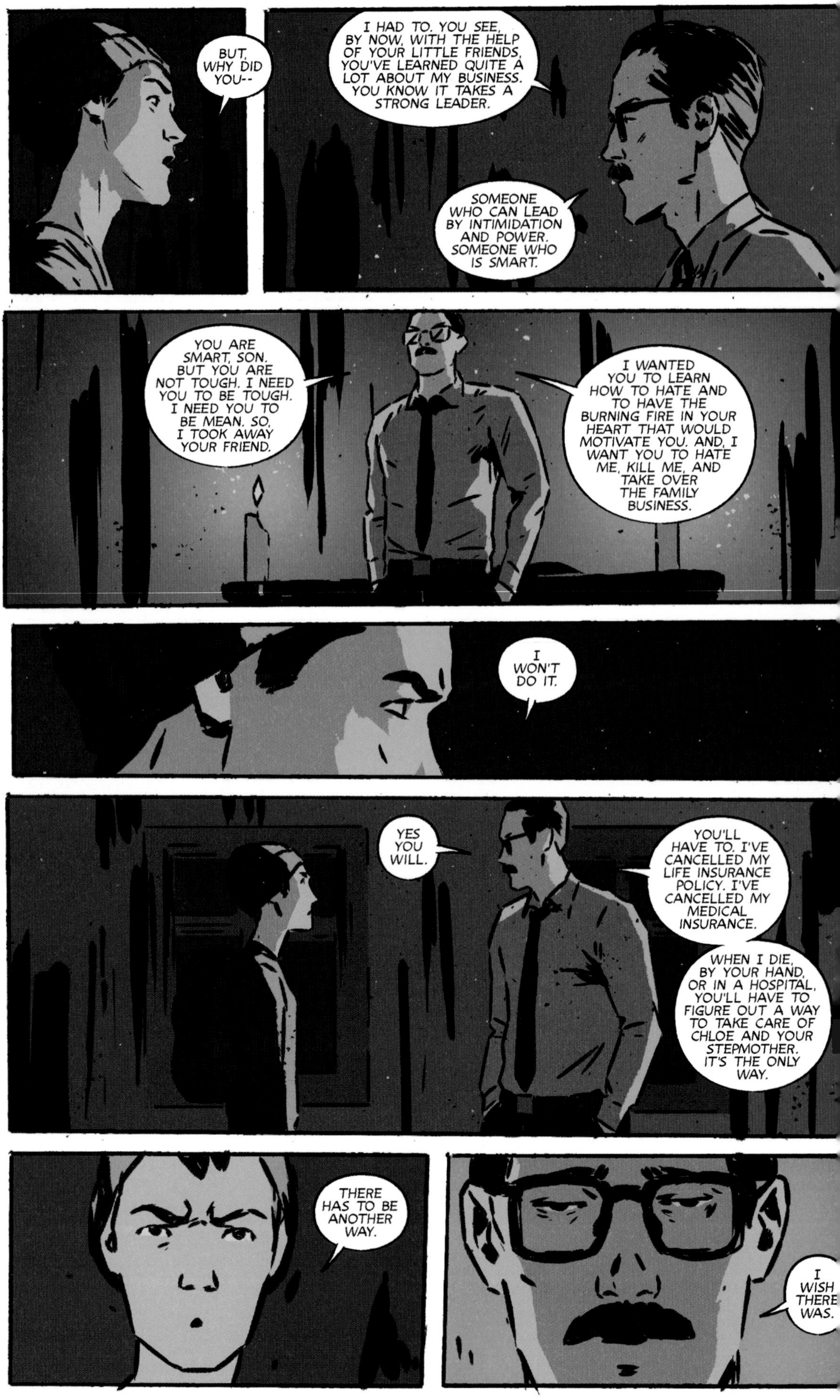
BUT, WHY DID YOU--
I HAD TO. YOU SEE, BY NOW, WITH THE HELP OF YOUR LITTLE FRIENDS, YOU'VE LEARNED QUITE A LOT ABOUT MY BUSINESS. YOU KNOW IT TAKES A STRONG LEADER.
SOMEONE WHO CAN LEAD BY INTIMIDATION AND POWER. SOMEONE WHO IS SMART.
YOU ARE SMART, SON. BUT YOU ARE NOT TOUGH. I NEED YOU TO BE TOUGH. I NEED YOU TO BE MEAN. SO, I TOOK AWAY YOUR FRIEND.
I WANTED YOU TO LEARN HOW TO HATE AND TO HAVE THE BURNING FIRE IN YOUR HEART THAT WOULD MOTIVATE YOU. AND, I WANT YOU TO HATE ME, KILL ME, AND TAKE OVER THE FAMILY BUSINESS.
I WON'T DO IT.
YES YOU WILL.
YOU'LL HAVE TO. I'VE CANCELLED MY LIFE INSURANCE POLICY. I'VE CANCELLED MY MEDICAL INSURANCE.
WHEN I DIE, BY YOUR HAND, OR IN A HOSPITAL, YOU'LL HAVE TO FIGURE OUT A WAY TO TAKE CARE OF CHLOE AND YOUR STEPMOTHER. IT'S THE ONLY WAY.
THERE HAS TO BE ANOTHER WAY.
I WISH THERE WAS.

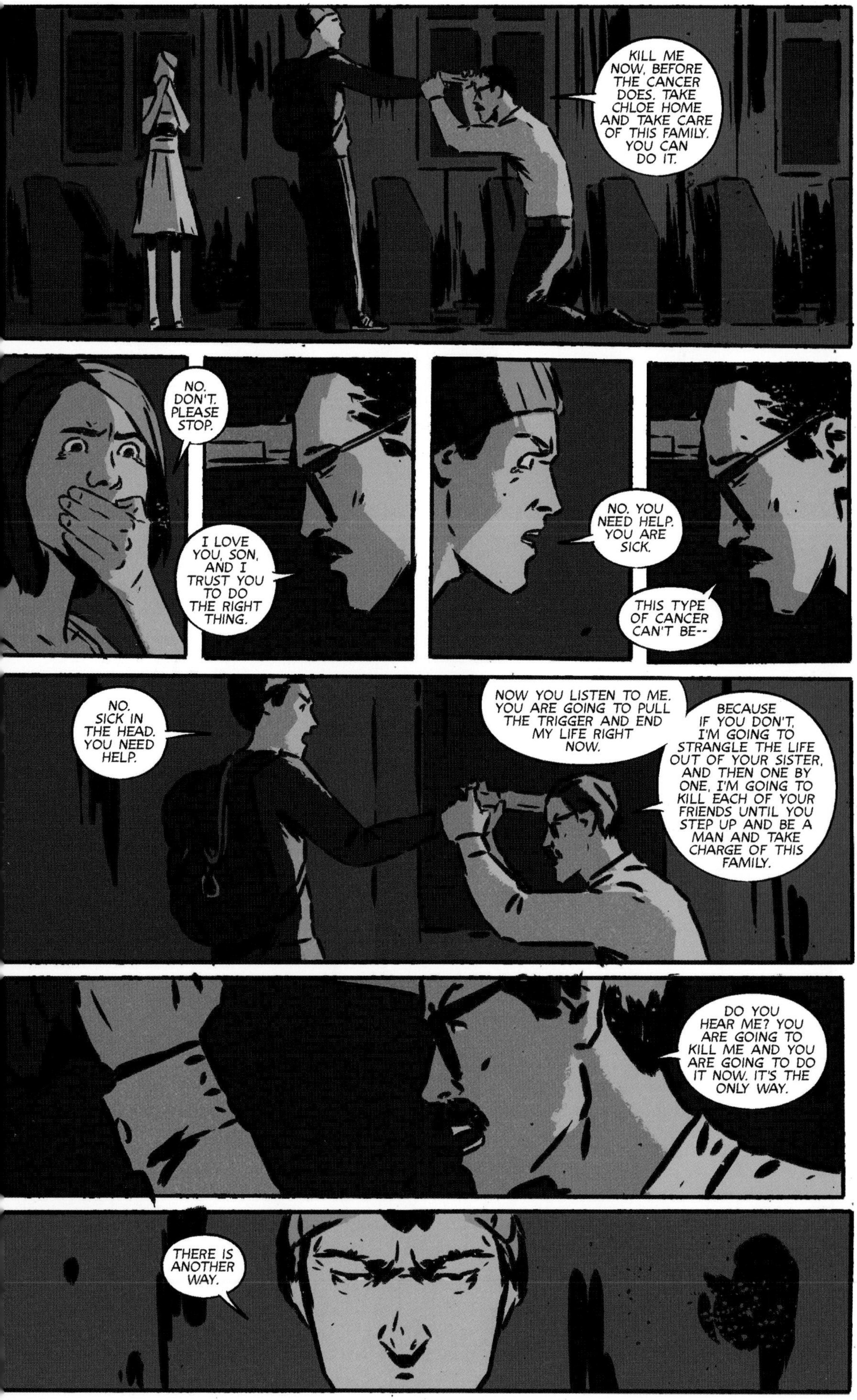
KILL ME NOW, BEFORE THE CANCER DOES. TAKE CHLOE HOME AND TAKE CARE OF THIS FAMILY. YOU CAN DO IT.
NO. DON'T. PLEASE STOP.
I LOVE YOU, SON, AND I TRUST YOU TO DO THE RIGHT THING.
NO. YOU NEED HELP. YOU ARE SICK.
THIS TYPE OF CANCER CAN'T BE--
NO. SICK IN THE HEAD. YOU NEED HELP.
NOW YOU LISTEN TO ME. YOU ARE GOING TO PULL THE TRIGGER AND END MY LIFE RIGHT NOW.
BECAUSE IF YOU DON'T, I'M GOING TO STRANGLE THE LIFE OUT OF YOUR SISTER, AND THEN ONE BY ONE, I'M GOING TO KILL EACH OF YOUR FRIENDS UNTIL YOU STEP UP AND BE A MAN AND TAKE CHARGE OF THIS FAMILY.
DO YOU HEAR ME? YOU ARE GOING TO KILL ME AND YOU ARE GOING TO DO IT NOW. IT'S THE ONLY WAY.
THERE IS ANOTHER WAY.

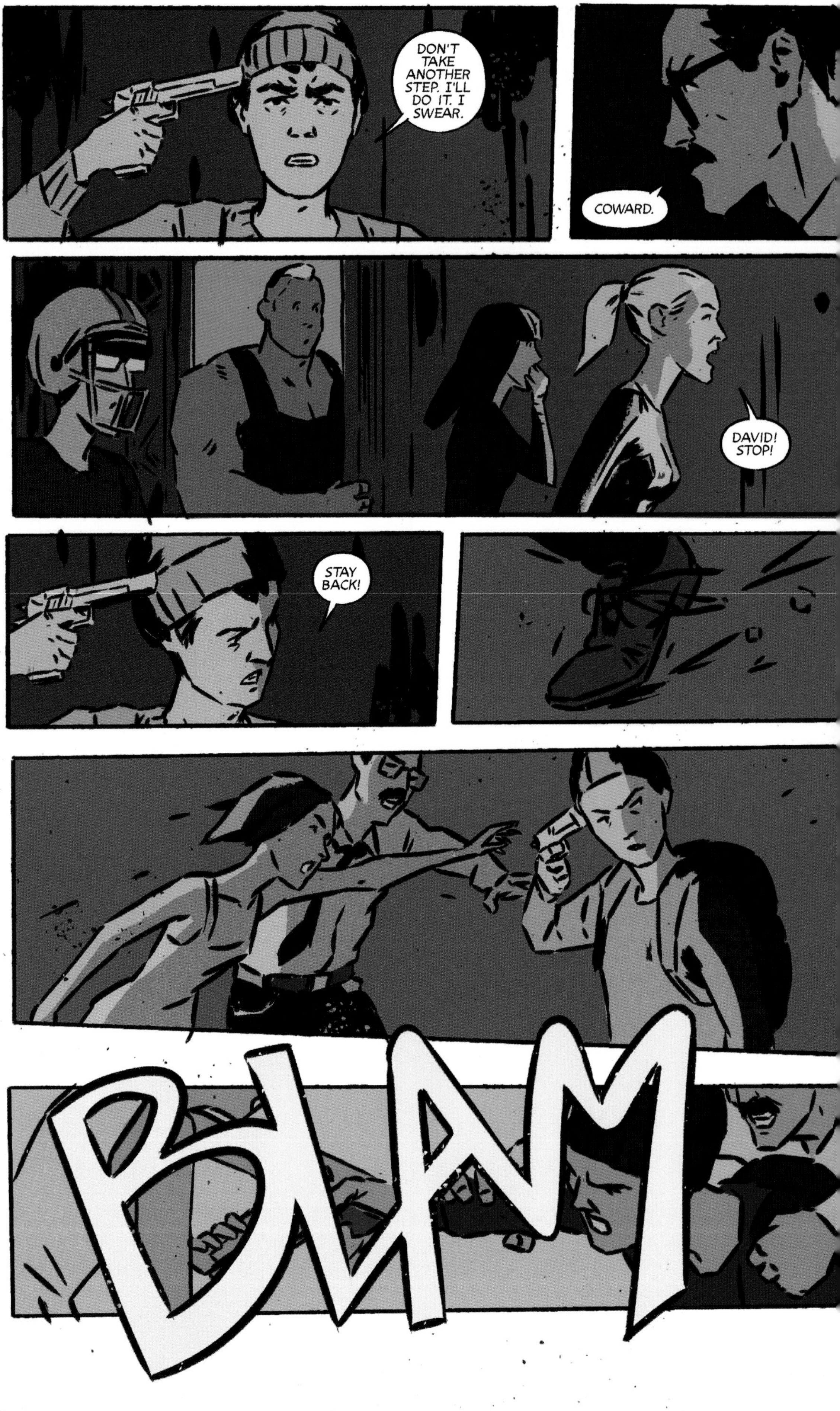
DON'T TAKE ANOTHER STEP. I'LL DO IT. I SWEAR.
COWARD.
DAVID! STOP!
STAY BACK!
BLAM

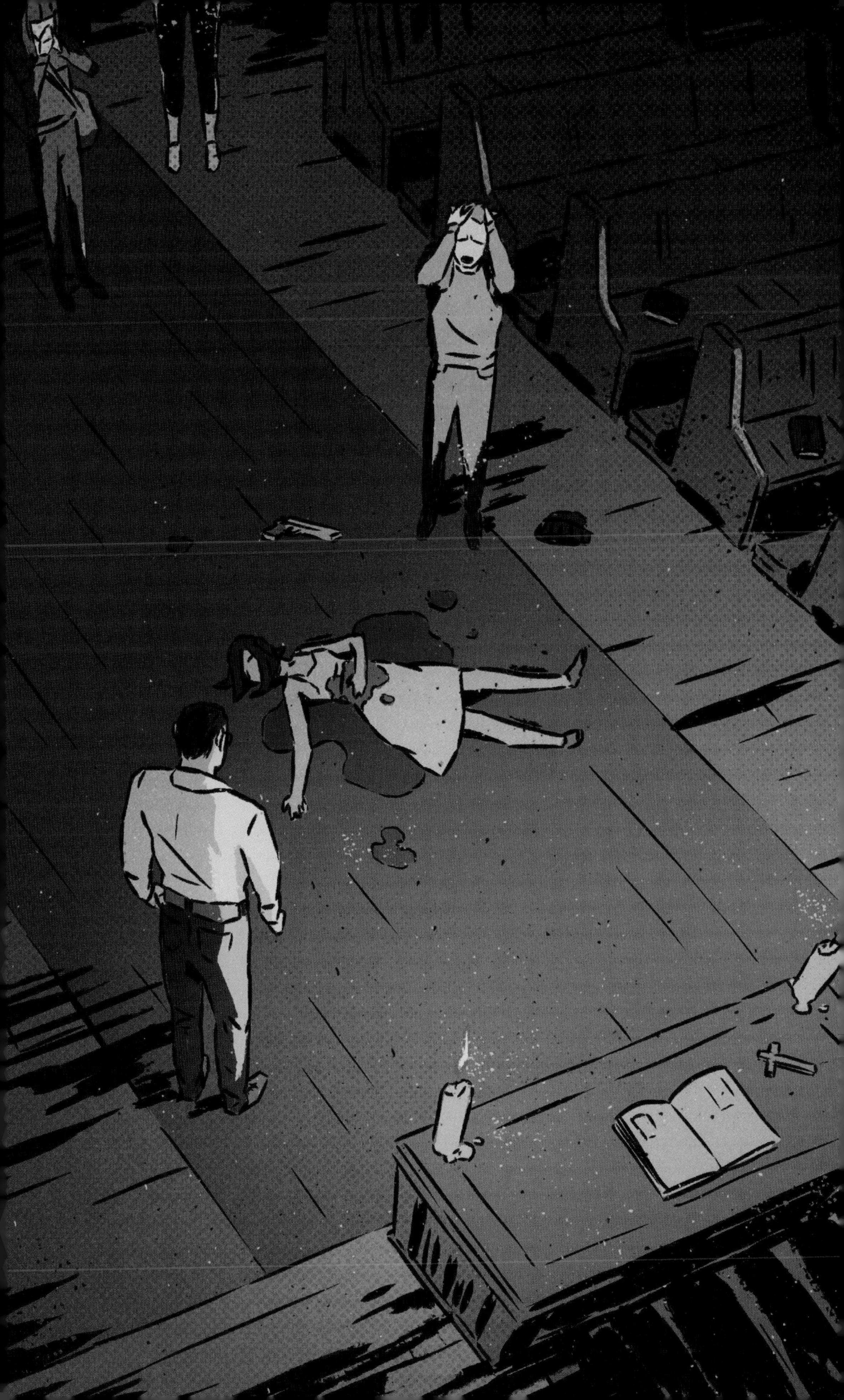

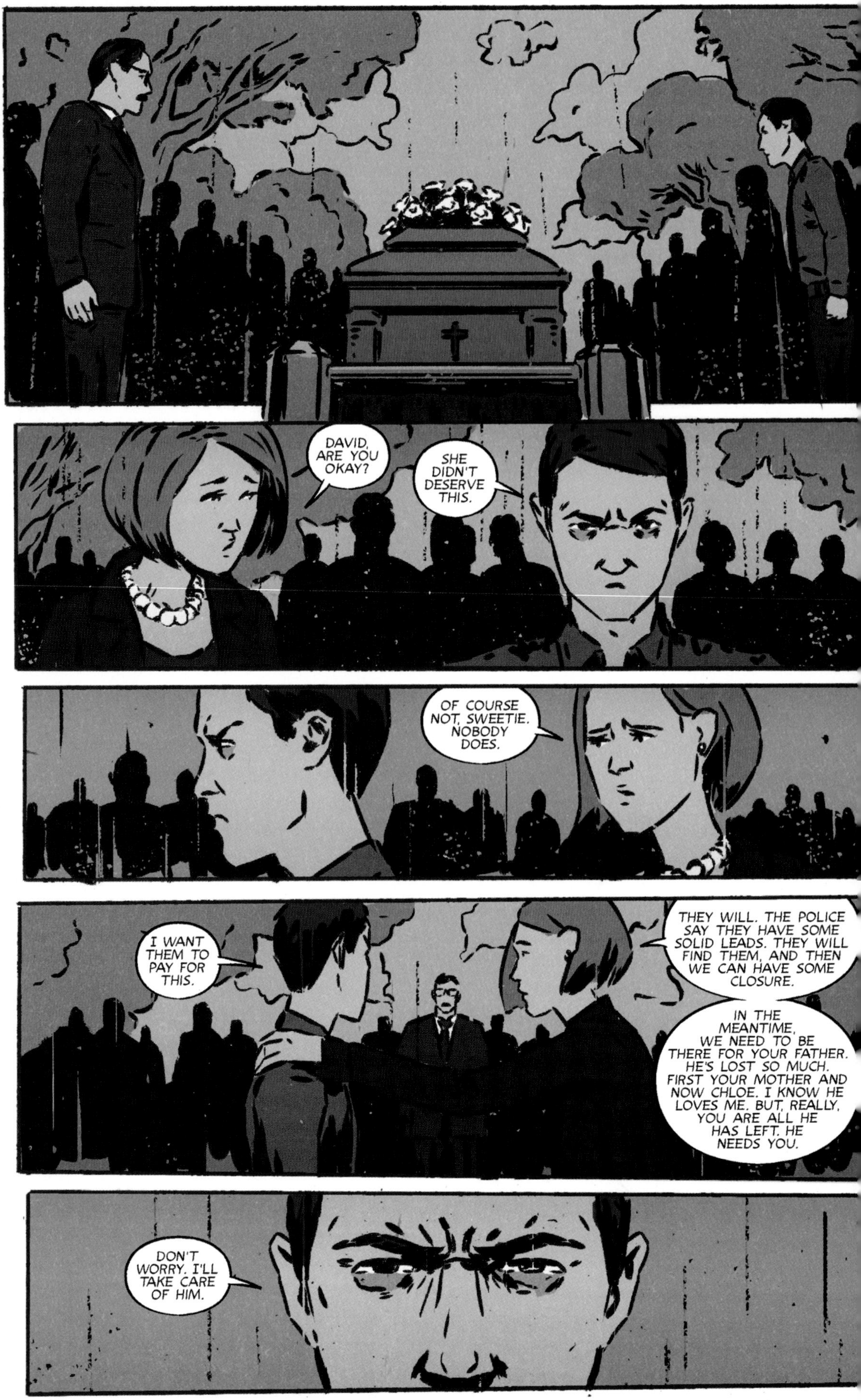
DAVID, ARE YOU OKAY?
SHE DIDN'T DESERVE THIS.
OF COURSE NOT, SWEETIE. NOBODY DOES.
I WANT THEM TO PAY FOR THIS.
THEY WILL. THE POLICE SAY THEY HAVE SOME SOLID LEADS. THEY WILL FIND THEM, AND THEN WE CAN HAVE SOME CLOSURE.
IN THE MEANTIME, WE NEED TO BE THERE FOR YOUR FATHER. HE'S LOST SO MUCH. FIRST YOUR MOTHER AND NOW CHLOE. I KNOW HE LOVES ME. BUT, REALLY, YOU ARE ALL HE HAS LEFT. HE NEEDS YOU.
DON'T WORRY. I'LL TAKE CARE OF HIM.

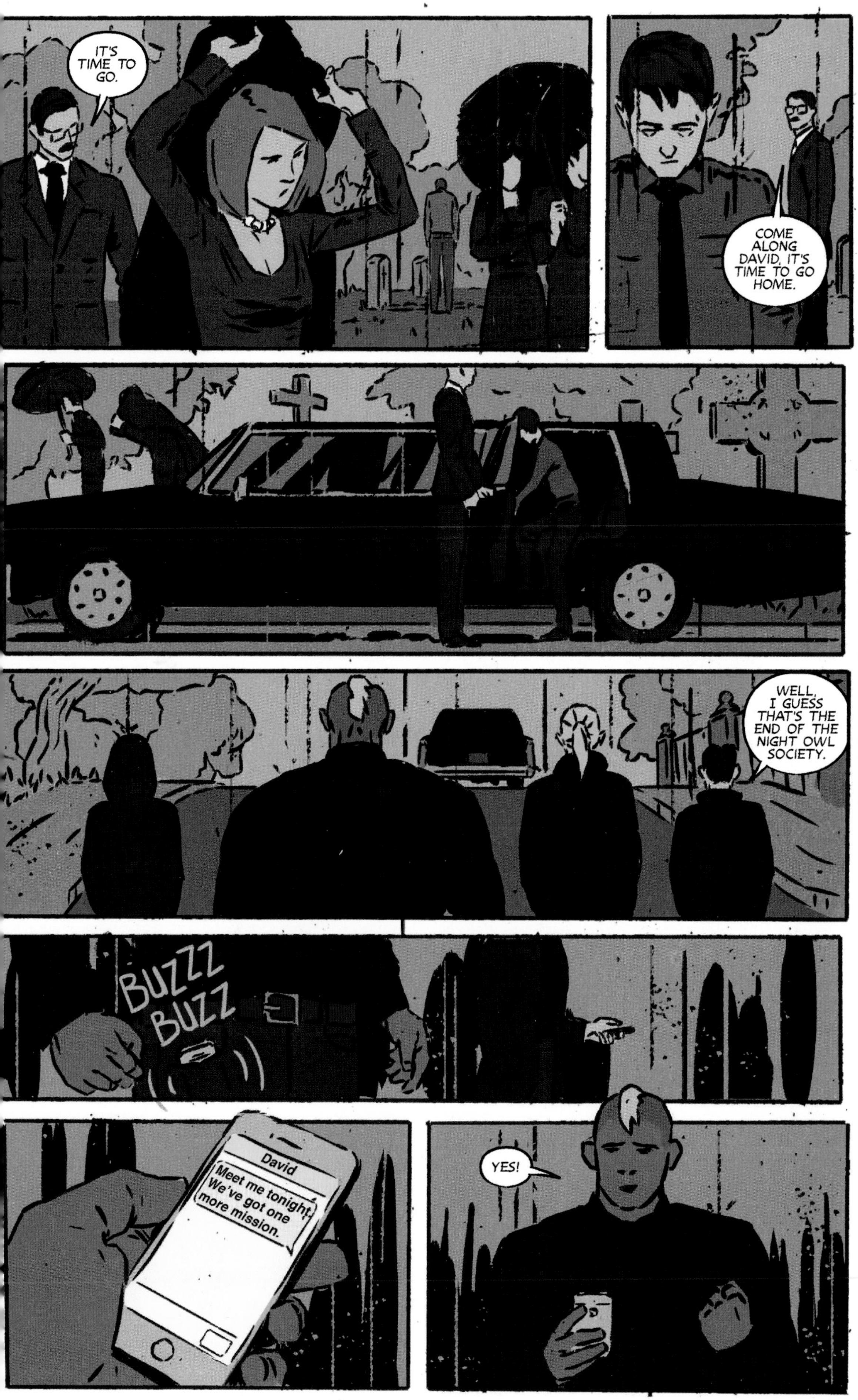
IT'S TIME TO GO.
COME ALONG DAVID, IT'S TIME TO GO HOME.
WELL, I GUESS THAT'S THE END OF THE NIGHT OWL SOCIETY.
BUZZZ BUZZ
David
Meet me tonight. We've got one more mission.
YES!

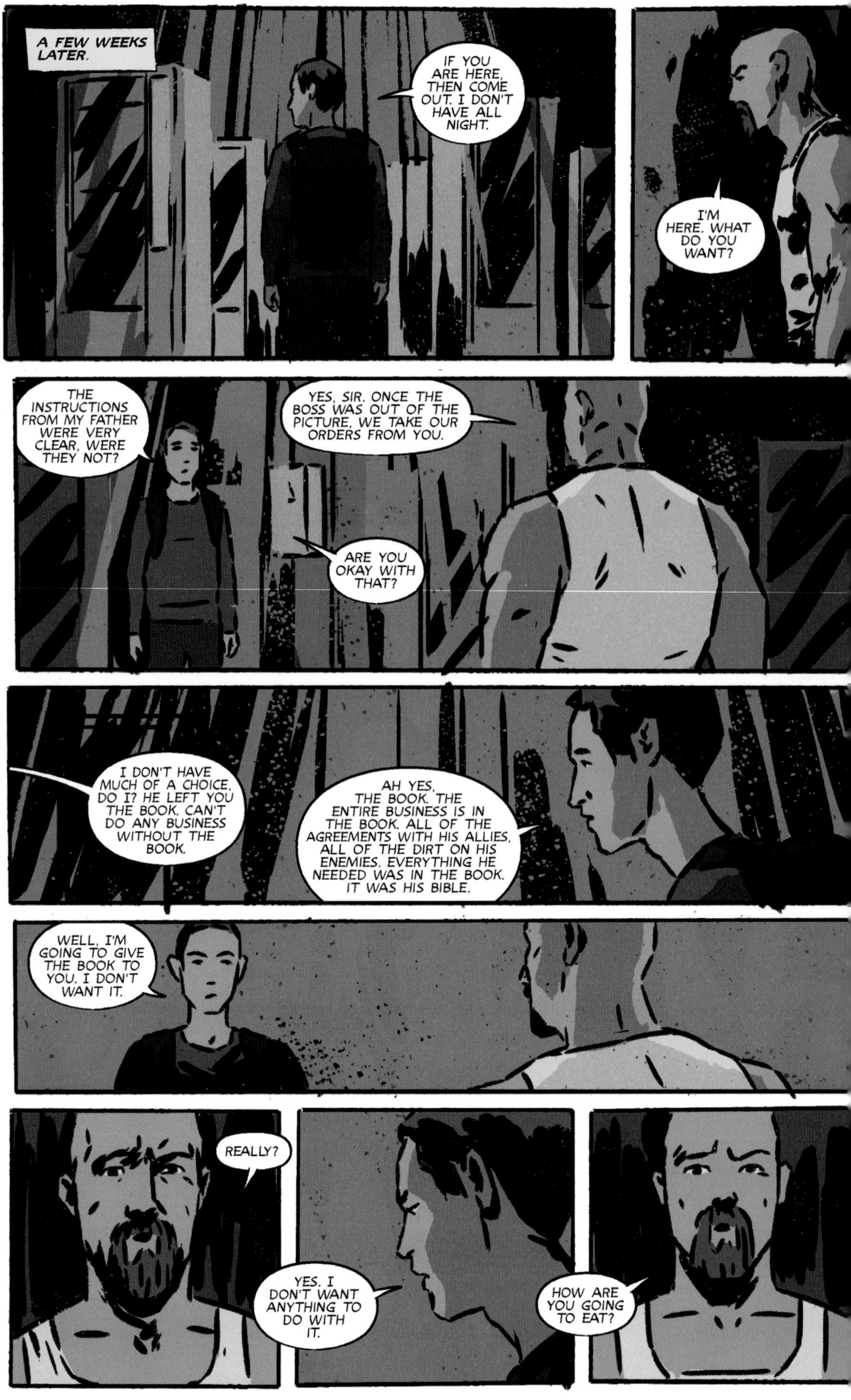
A FEW WEEKS LATER.
IF YOU ARE HERE, THEN COME OUT. I DON'T HAVE ALL NIGHT.
I'M HERE. WHAT DO YOU WANT?
THE INSTRUCTIONS FROM MY FATHER WERE VERY CLEAR, WERE THEY NOT?
YES, SIR. ONCE THE BOSS WAS OUT OF THE PICTURE, WE TAKE OUR ORDERS FROM YOU.
ARE YOU OKAY WITH THAT?
I DON'T HAVE MUCH OF A CHOICE, DO I? HE LEFT YOU THE BOOK. CAN'T DO ANY BUSINESS WITHOUT THE BOOK.
AH YES, THE BOOK. THE ENTIRE BUSINESS IS IN THE BOOK. ALL OF THE AGREEMENTS WITH HIS ALLIES, ALL OF THE DIRT ON HIS ENEMIES. EVERYTHING HE NEEDED WAS IN THE BOOK. IT WAS HIS BIBLE.
WELL, I'M GOING TO GIVE THE BOOK TO YOU. I DON'T WANT IT.
REALLY?
YES. I DON'T WANT ANYTHING TO DO WITH IT.
HOW ARE YOU GOING TO EAT?

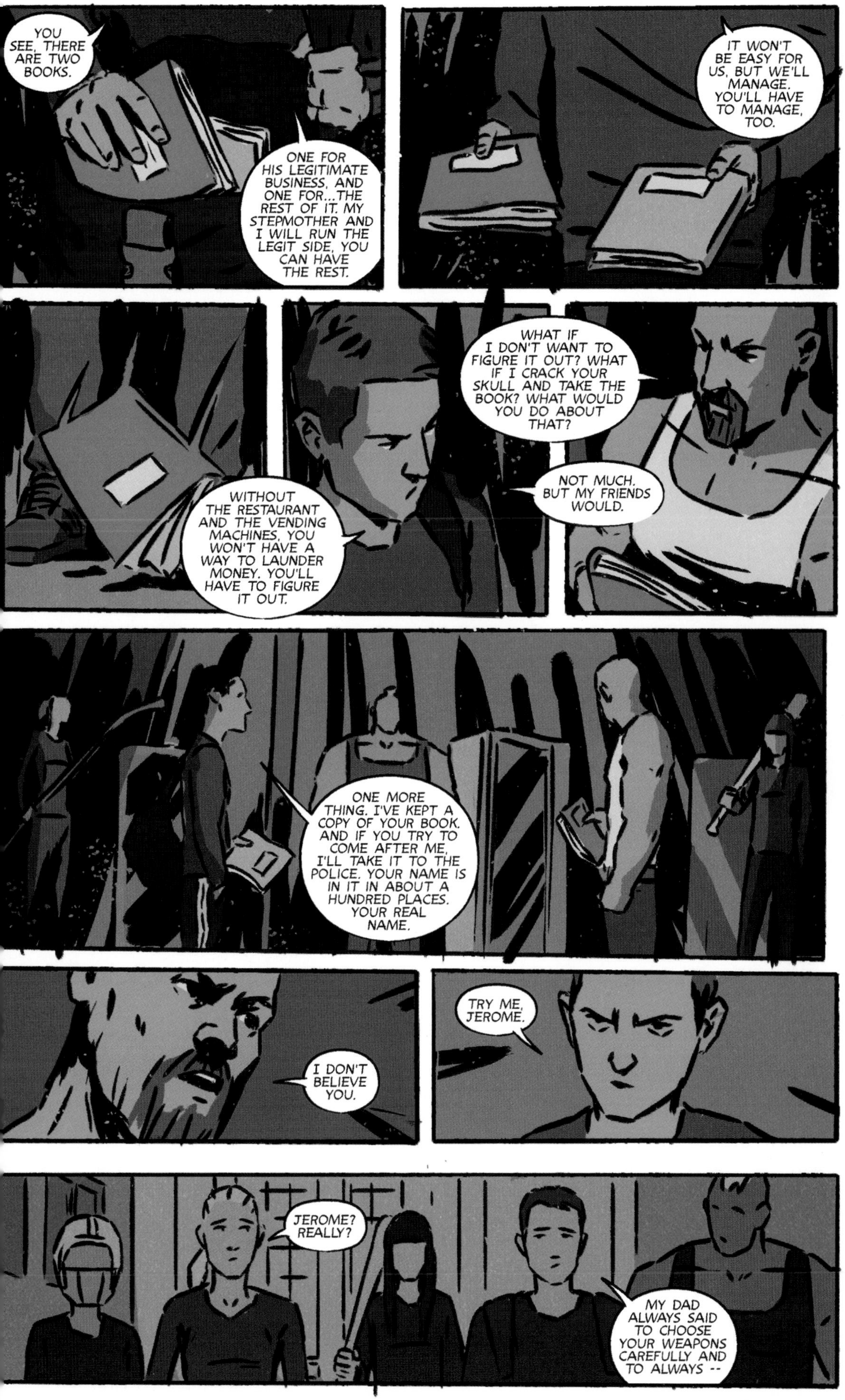
YOU SEE, THERE ARE TWO BOOKS.
ONE FOR HIS LEGITIMATE BUSINESS, AND ONE FOR...THE REST OF IT. MY STEPMOTHER AND I WILL RUN THE LEGIT SIDE, YOU CAN HAVE THE REST.
IT WON'T BE EASY FOR US, BUT WE'LL MANAGE. YOU'LL HAVE TO MANAGE, TOO.
WITHOUT THE RESTAURANT AND THE VENDING MACHINES, YOU WON'T HAVE A WAY TO LAUNDER MONEY. YOU'LL HAVE TO FIGURE IT OUT.
WHAT IF I DON'T WANT TO FIGURE IT OUT? WHAT IF I CRACK YOUR SKULL AND TAKE THE BOOK? WHAT WOULD YOU DO ABOUT THAT?
NOT MUCH. BUT MY FRIENDS WOULD.
ONE MORE THING. I'VE KEPT A COPY OF YOUR BOOK. AND IF YOU TRY TO COME AFTER ME, I'LL TAKE IT TO THE POLICE. YOUR NAME IS IN IT IN ABOUT A HUNDRED PLACES. YOUR REAL NAME.
I DON'T BELIEVE YOU.
TRY ME, JEROME.
JEROME? REALLY?
MY DAD ALWAYS SAID TO CHOOSE YOUR WEAPONS CAREFULLY AND TO ALWAYS --

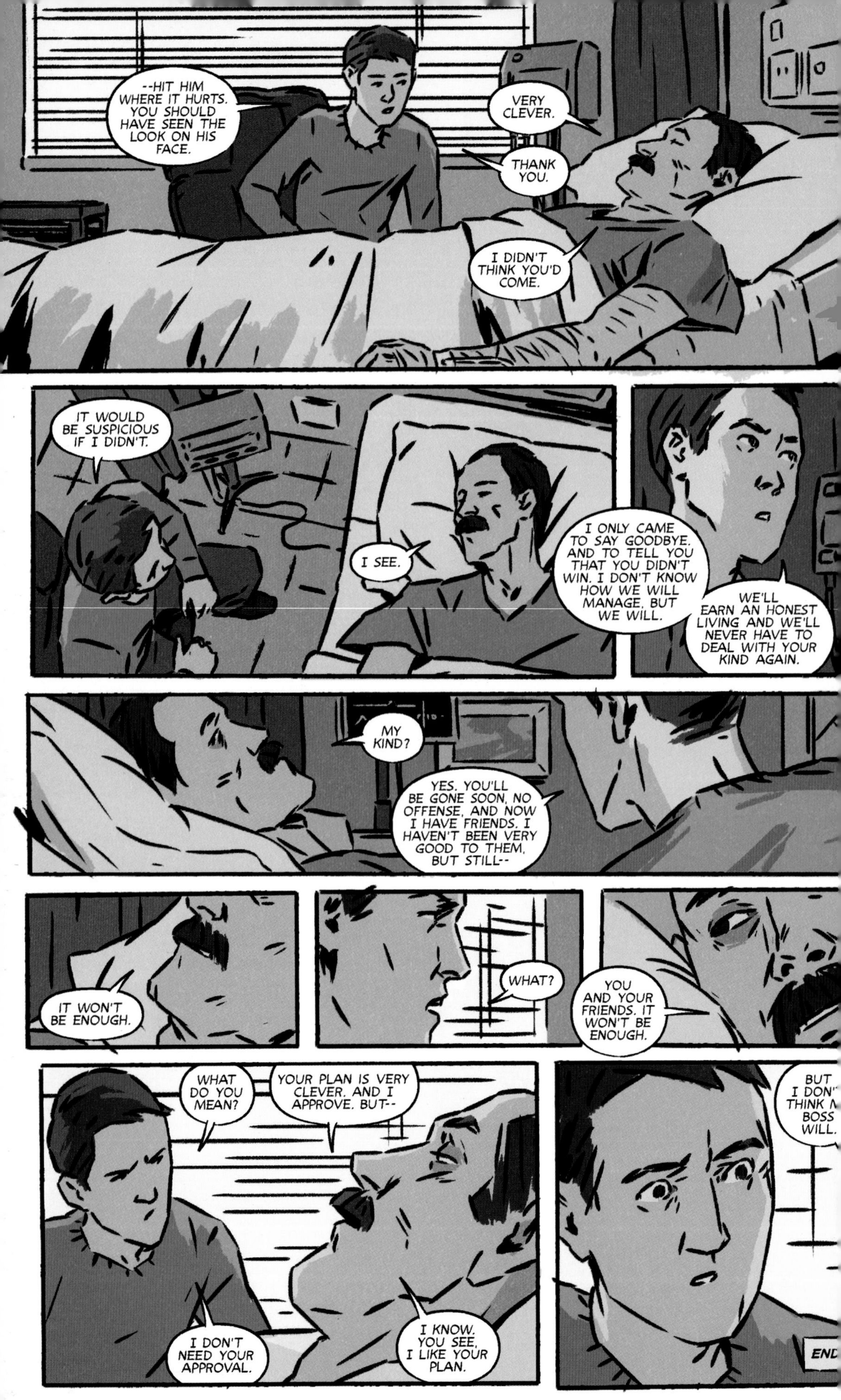
--HIT HIM WHERE IT HURTS. YOU SHOULD HAVE SEEN THE LOOK ON HIS FACE.
VERY CLEVER.
THANK YOU.
I DIDN'T THINK YOU'D COME.
IT WOULD BE SUSPICIOUS IF I DIDN'T.
I SEE.
I ONLY CAME TO SAY GOODBYE. AND TO TELL YOU THAT YOU DIDN'T WIN. I DON'T KNOW HOW WE WILL MANAGE, BUT WE WILL.
WE'LL EARN AN HONEST LIVING AND WE'LL NEVER HAVE TO DEAL WITH YOUR KIND AGAIN.
MY KIND?
YES. YOU'LL BE GONE SOON, NO OFFENSE, AND NOW I HAVE FRIENDS. I HAVEN'T BEEN VERY GOOD TO THEM, BUT STILL--
IT WON'T BE ENOUGH.
WHAT?
YOU AND YOUR FRIENDS. IT WON'T BE ENOUGH.
WHAT DO YOU MEAN?
YOUR PLAN IS VERY CLEVER. AND I APPROVE. BUT--
I DON'T NEED YOUR APPROVAL.
I KNOW. YOU SEE, I LIKE YOUR PLAN.

ART GALLERY

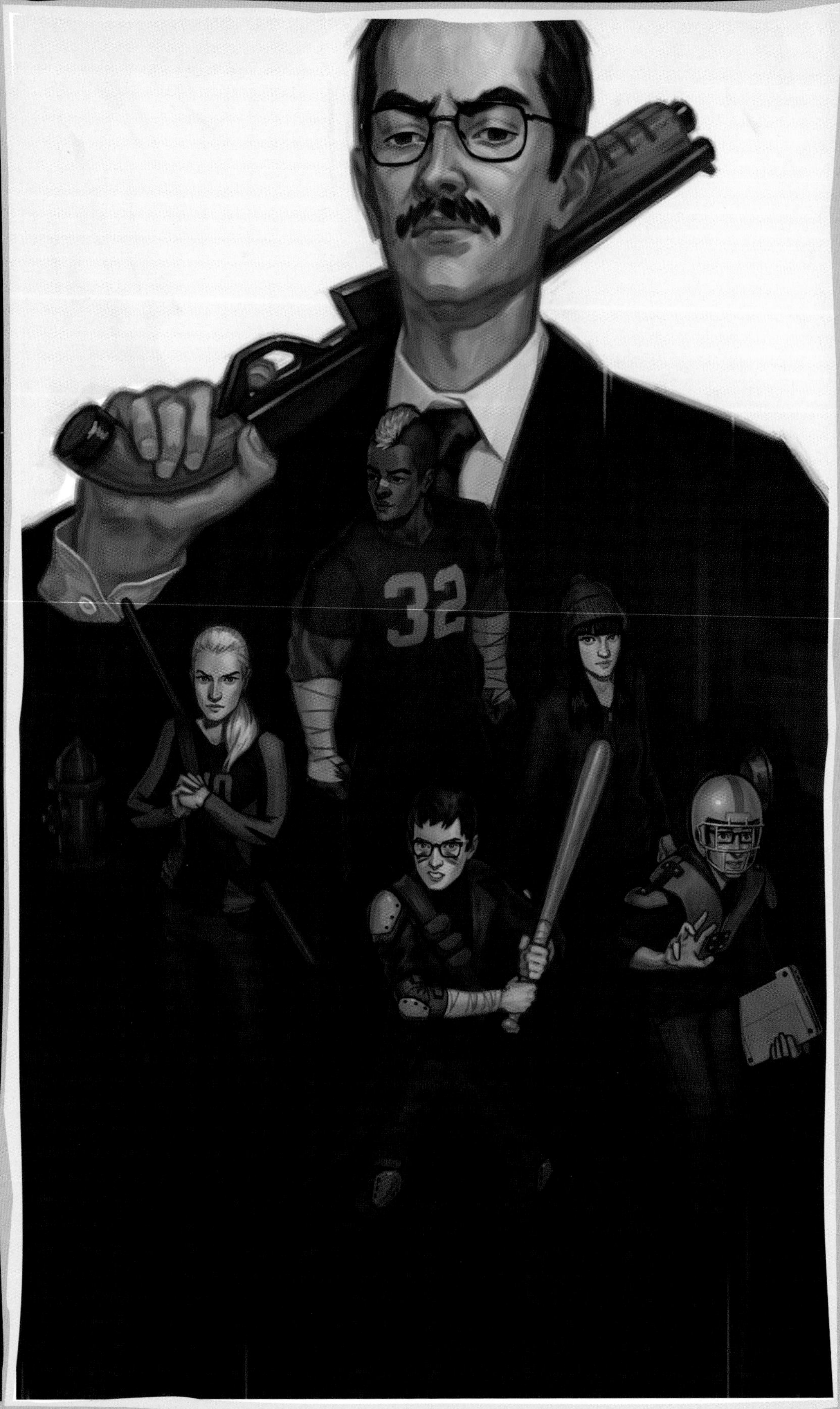
32

ART BY PIUS BAK

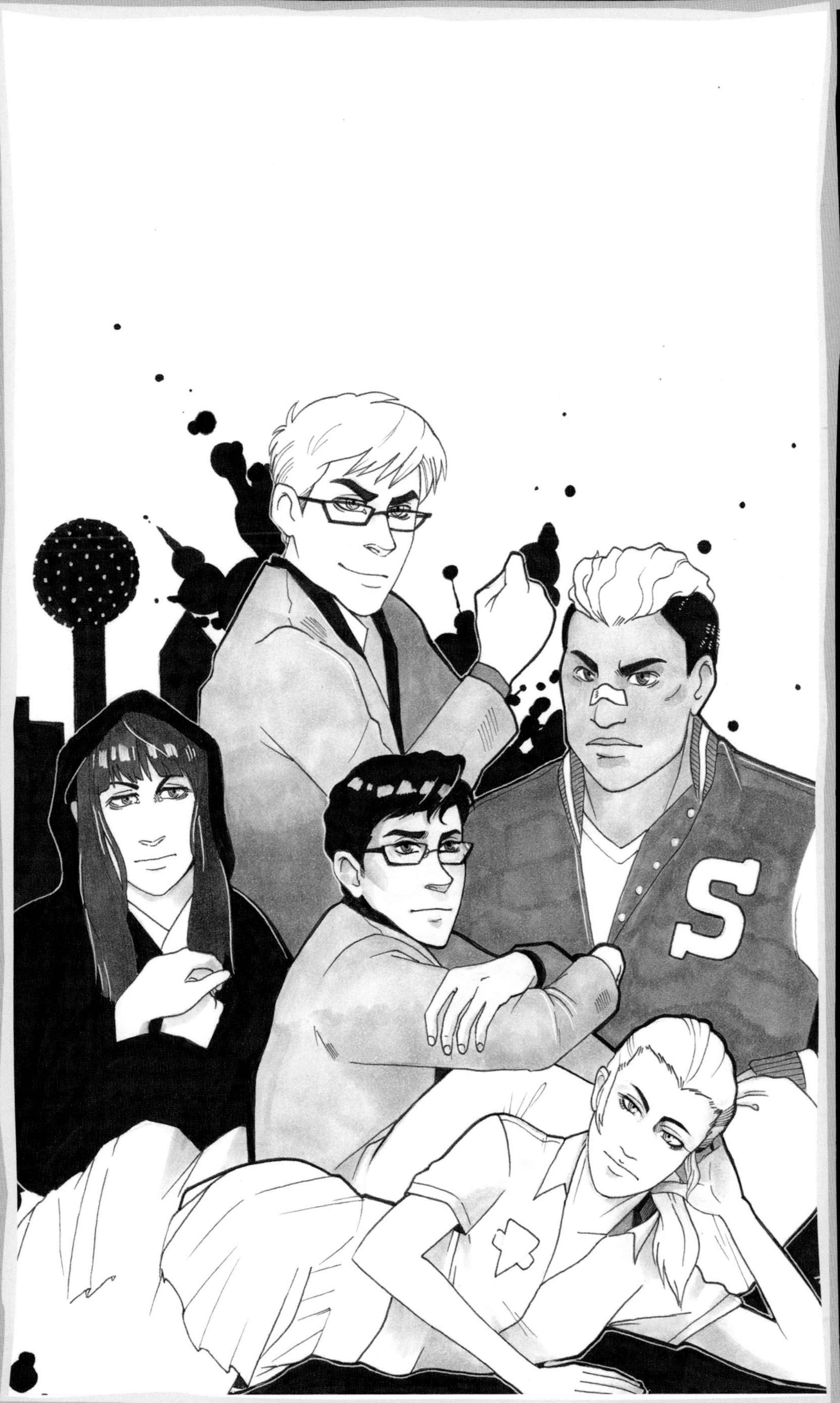
S
ART BY TOBIAS MORROW

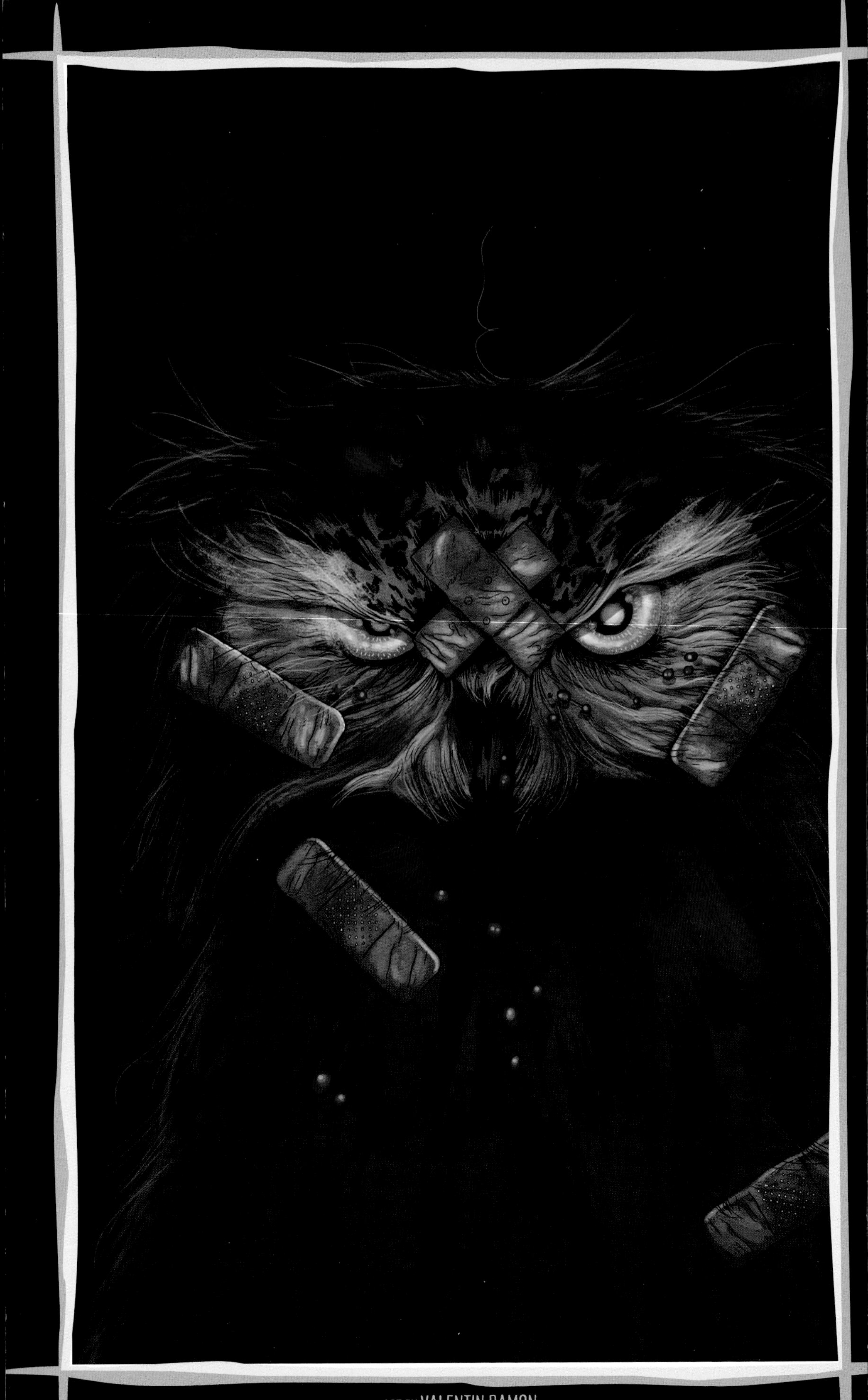

ART BY VALENTIN RAMON

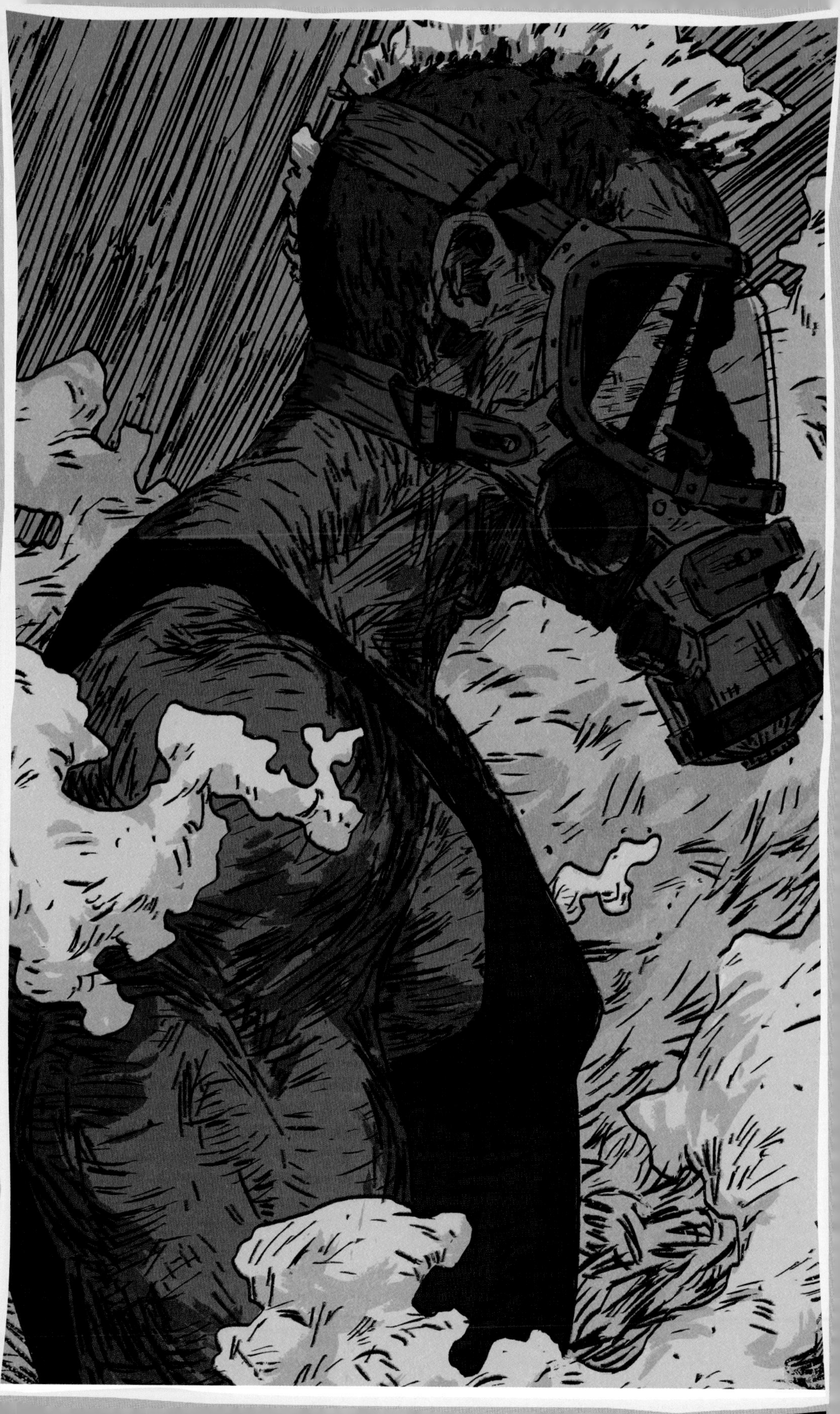

A.J.

The first person David recruits into the Night Owl Society is A.J. He is a football player with a big goofy grin and even bigger muscles. A.J. holds the distinction of being the only guy on the team who hasn't shoved David into a locker. He loves football because it allows him to hit people and not get into trouble. A.J. is a big, lovable guy who attends St. Cuthbert's on a scholarship. He doesn't fit into the mostly white, mostly rich school. He's smart, but he's not going to Harvard. He knows he's only here to play football, and his classmates love to remind him of how much he doesn't belong. But, he likes David. They are both outsiders.

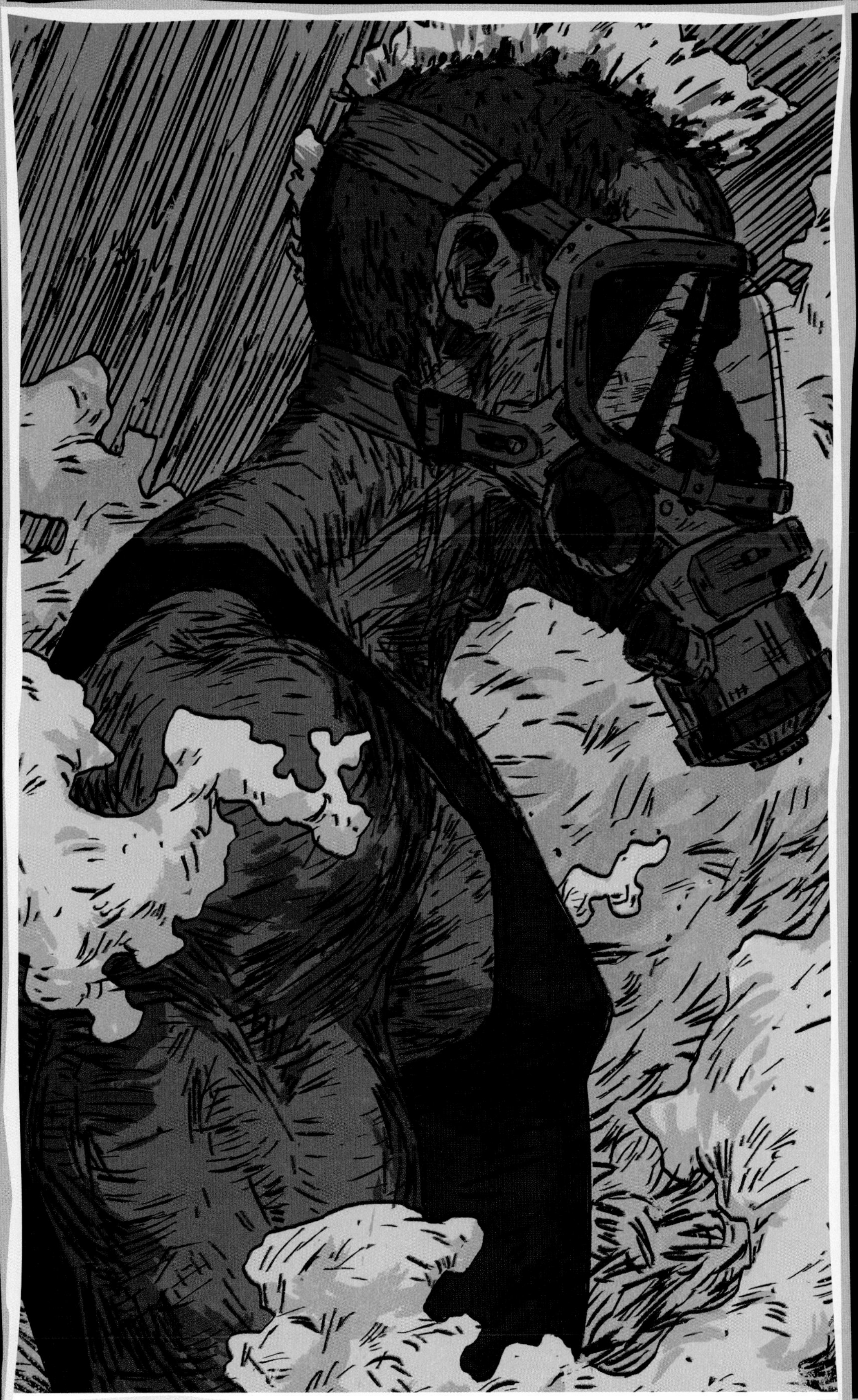

ART BY PIUS BAK

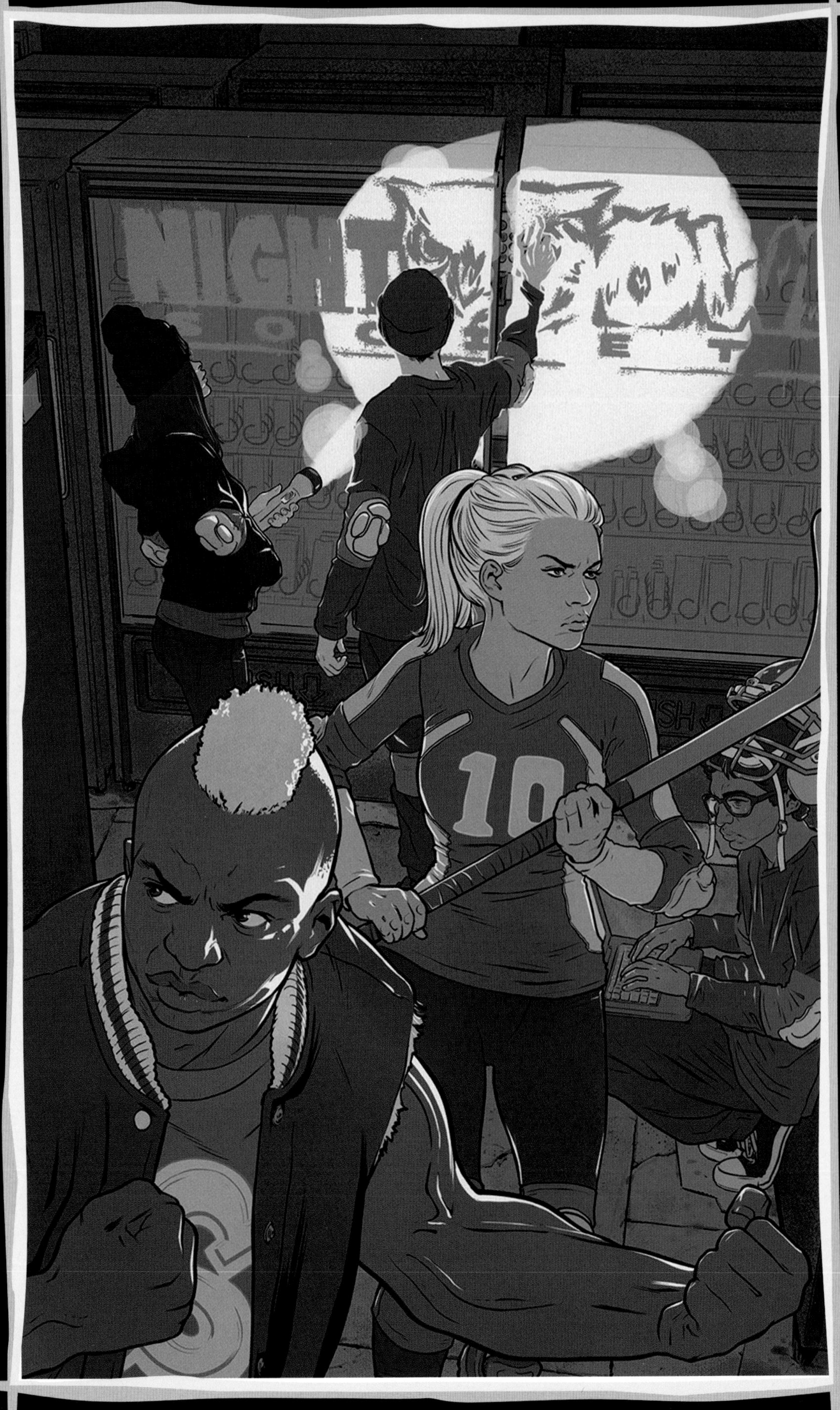
NIGHT
10

ART BY HUGO PETRUS

NIGHT OWL SOCIETY

DAVID

David Foxworth isn't the most popular kid at St. Cuthbert's School. In fact, since transferring from a large public school when he was little he mainly fades into the woodwork, ignored by the snooty rich kids. He's small, and not very athletic, which in a Texas high school means you are nobody. Not even the drama kids like him, and they like everybody. But, his Dad and his Dad's new, impossibly young trophy wife think this is the best place for him. Something about big public schools no longer being safe. Whatever.

NIGHT OWL SOCIETY

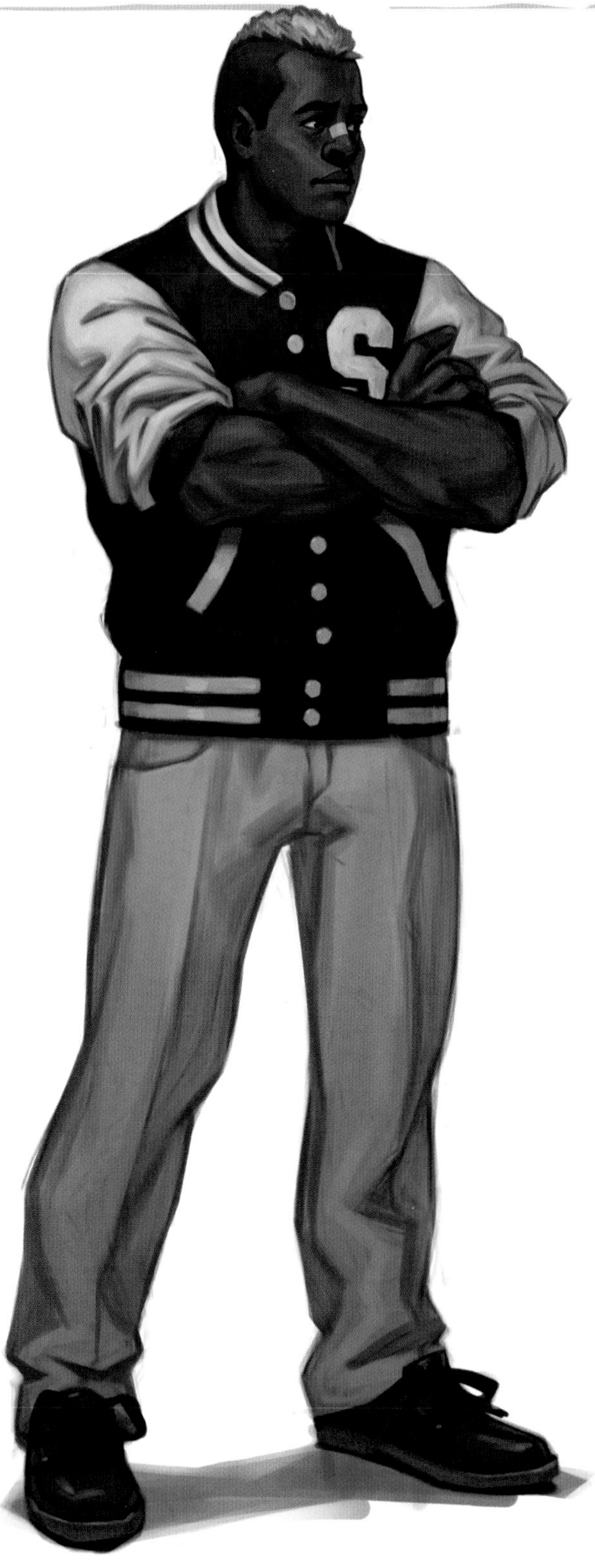

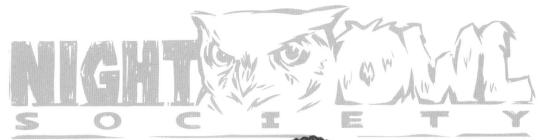

A.J.

The first person David recruits into the Night Owl Society is A.J. He is a football player with a big goofy grin and even bigger muscles. A.J. holds the distinction of being the only guy on the team who hasn't shoved David into a locker. He loves football because it allows him to hit people and not get into trouble. A.J. is a big, lovable guy who attends St. Cuthbert's on a scholarship. He doesn't fit into the mostly white, mostly rich school. He's smart, but he's not going to Harvard. He knows he's only here to play football, and his classmates love to remind him of how much he doesn't belong. But, he likes David. They are both outsiders.

DARSH

The next member of the team is Darsh, a student who is the leader of the computer science club. Until being recruited by David and A.J., Darsh had a strict policy of never using his computer skills to hack or do anything unethical. David and A.J. convince him that hacking is okay if it is being done for a noble cause. It's the first time Darsh has been invited to do anything with anyone at school, so he agrees.

LAURA

Next, they recruit Laura, a quiet girl who is always in trouble. David knows that she has been in trouble for stealing and possibly something worse. He feels that her skill set would be useful. Not only can she pick locks and break into things, she provides a connection to the underworld that no one else in the team has. In fact, Laura has a secret that could lead to the downfall of the group.

SARAH

The final member of the team is Sarah, the captain of the volleyball team and A.J.'s girlfriend. Because A.J. is very bad at keeping secrets, he tells her about the group and she insists on joining. She is focused, aggressive, and has a huge chip on her shoulder. Female athletes are second class citizens at this school, and she has a lot to prove.

NIGHT OWL SOCIETY

THE VICEROY

The Viceroy is a vicious mob boss. Despite his tough exterior, and terrifying reputation, he is conflicted about the work he does and the family he is trying to protect. Of course, the Night Owl Society becomes a big thorn in his side.